MURDER
IN THE
CHOIR

BOOKS BY ALICE CASTLE

SARAH VANE MYSTERIES
Murder at an English Pub
A Seaside Murder
Murder at the Tea Shop

A BETH HALDANE MYSTERY
The Murder Mystery
The Murder Museum
The Murder Question
The Murder Plot
The Murder Walk
The Murder Club
The Murder Hour
The Murder Garden
The Murder Affair

MURDER IN THE CHOIR

ALICE CASTLE

bookouture

Published by Bookouture in 2025

An imprint of Storyfire Ltd.
Carmelite House
50 Victoria Embankment
London EC4Y 0DZ

www.bookouture.com

The authorised representative in the EEA is Hachette Ireland
8 Castlecourt Centre
Dublin 15 D15 XTP3
Ireland
(email: info@hbgi.ie)

Copyright © Alice Castle, 2025

Alice Castle has asserted her right to be identified as the author of this work.

All rights reserved. No part of this publication may be reproduced, stored in any retrieval system, or transmitted, in any form or by any means, electronic, mechanical, photocopying, recording or otherwise, without the prior written permission of the publishers.

ISBN: 978-1-80550-210-4
eBook ISBN: 978-1-80550-209-8

This book is a work of fiction. Names, characters, businesses, organizations, places and events other than those clearly in the public domain, are either the product of the author's imagination or are used fictitiously. Any resemblance to actual persons, living or dead, events or locales is entirely coincidental.

To Ella and Connie, with love

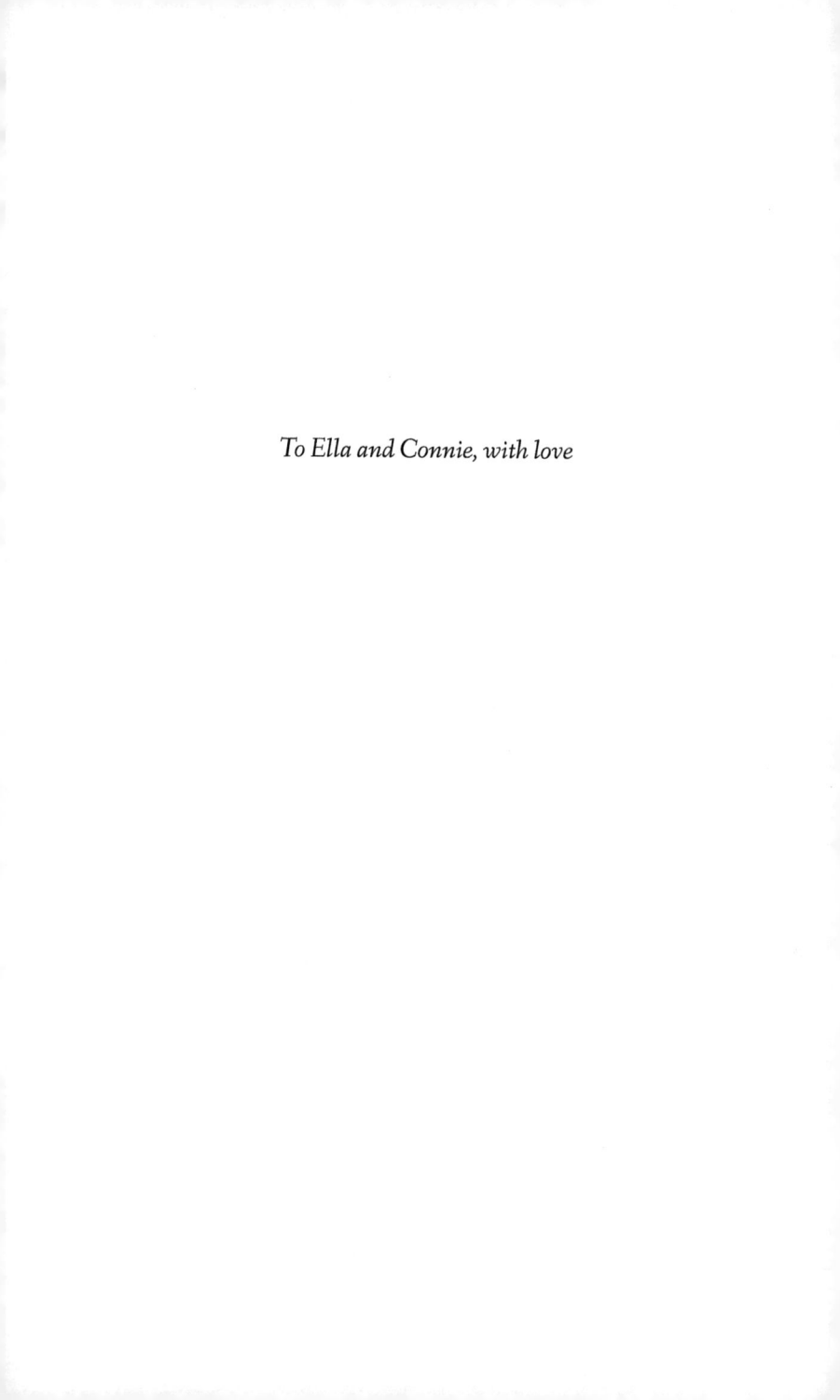

ONE

Sarah Vane leant forward and put another log on the fire crackling merrily in the grate. The retired GP and her Scottie dog, Hamish, had just come back from a bracing wintry walk along the seafront and, while the Christmas lights already up along the esplanade had looked magical, there was a decided nip in the air. It was lovely to be inside again, curled up on the sofa with a cup of tea and a novel.

Sarah turned another page, but something outside the window caught her attention. To her amazement, what looked like a flake of snow came drifting down. 'Do you see that, boy?' she said, then realised that the little dog was fast asleep on the rug, legs twitching as he chased phantom seagulls through his dreams. Just then the letterbox rattled. Curious. It was much too late for the postman. Sarah got up, careful to avoid disturbing the snoozing pooch, and padded out into the hall in her slippers.

Sure enough, there was something on the mat. She bent down, feeling her sixty-something years, and picked up a leaflet. On the front was a mock-up of the famous Kitchener poster, but instead of the moustachioed general there was a round-cheeked middle-aged man in the centre, wearing a Santa hat and pointing his finger. A speech bubble over his head said *The Merstairs Muses needs You this Christmas: Join our Jingle Belles tomorrow!* There was something familiar about that chubby face.

Hmm, the Merstairs Muses. Sarah had heard of them. They'd won various awards over the years, and according to this flyer they were in the running to bag the Kent Coastal Choirs Cup this season. Remarkably, it was the one organisation that her bubbly next-door neighbour and best friend, Daphne Roux, never seemed to have joined.

Sarah took the leaflet back to her comfy seat and laid it aside, taking a sip of tea and then opening her book again. But it was no good, she was now too intrigued to concentrate. There were lots of great things to be said for singing, from the warming feeling of being part of a community enterprise, to real physical benefits like stress reduction and heart rate regulation. She'd often suggested choir membership to patients at her busy London health practice. Belting out a carol was always lovely.

It would be great for Daphne, too. She'd been a bit quiet of late. Tarot and Tealeaves, her mystical shop on the seafront, was dustier than ever, with much lower tourist footfall now winter was setting in. She hadn't even mentioned the Beyond for ages. Perhaps that was because Sarah had seen a little less of her recently, since Charles Diggory, the handsome owner of the antiques shop on the seafront, had finally freed himself from his troublesome ex-wife Francesca, the mayor of Merstairs. As a result, he and Sarah had enjoyed quite a few candlelit dinners and hand-in-hand strolls – not to mention some delicious canoodling too. Sarah couldn't quite remember the last time she'd had a proper chat with Daphne – but this choir appeal would be the perfect excuse to put that right.

Sarah put the leaflet down, resolving to tell her friend all about it in the morning. She found her place in her book, and finally settled down to read. Immediately the peace was shattered by a peal from the doorbell. 'Who could that be at this time of night?' she said to Hamish, as he raised his head groggily from the hearth rug and peered around, as if wondering where all the seagulls had got to.

It was very late for visitors – but there was a chance it might be Charles, popping round for a nightcap. She smiled at the thought, and wondered if there was any of his favourite malt whisky left in her cut-glass decanter.

But when she flung open the door in welcome, it was Daphne on the threshold, not Charles. Resplendent in a tight leopard print leisure suit, she burst into the cottage, clutching a leaflet that looked very familiar. 'Have you seen this?' she said, brandishing it so close to Sarah's face that, if she hadn't already read it, she'd have had no chance of understanding a word.

'It's the Merstairs Muses, begging for new members. The choirmaster is always sacking people. He got rid of a couple of soloists last week and chucked out half the rest too. Well, he must have gone too far this time. This is our moment,' Daphne went on.

'What do you mean?' Sarah asked, a little baffled.

'Usually they audition people, but it looks like they'll take anyone now. So you can come along with me and sing with the chorus. I'll get a soloist role, obviously. I've wanted to give it a go for a while, but I didn't want to leave you out. You see what it says here, though,' she said, waving the leaflet again. 'They need me. I do have a *voice*, you know that better than anyone,' she said in reverent tones. 'I owe it to Merstairs to sign up.'

'OK,' said Sarah, somewhat doubtfully. While she'd thought it would be great for Daphne to be part of the massed ranks of a large choir, the thought of her singing solos was somewhat alarming. Her friend's singing was most definitely loud, but was it as tuneful as Daphne seemed to believe? Hamish certainly wasn't a fan. The cottage walls were surprisingly thin in places, and he often started to howl when Daphne belted out a song in her shower.

Oh well, Sarah would go along and keep an eye on things. She'd hate Daphne to get rejected from a choir that wasn't even doing auditions. Fingers crossed that wouldn't happen tomorrow.

TWO

The next evening, Sarah swapped the peace of her sofa for the hurly burly of the All Saints village hall. It was one of those big spaces used for everything from harvest festivals to yoga displays, with scratched parquet flooring and rows of uncomfortable-looking metal chairs facing a raised stage. The walls were painted a faint municipal green, and unforgiving metal-shaded lights dangled high overhead. There was a vague but not unpleasant smell of old plimsolls and hymn books in the air. If there hadn't been so many people, it would have felt quite chilly. But a large group of men and women had already gathered by the time Sarah and Daphne arrived. Everyone was chatting furiously and no one, so far, seemed to have sung a single note.

She'd rung Charles beforehand to see if he wanted to come too, but he was busy. 'I'm not sure choirs are really my thing anyway, my dear,' he'd said gently. It was probably for the best, Sarah decided. After all, the whole idea was to give her time with Daphne, not Charles, though he would no doubt have made a fabulous baritone.

They had been there for ten minutes already and the atmosphere was certainly lively. If the choir put the same energy into its performances as it did into socialising, Sarah was sure they could beat all comers in the Kent Choirs Cup or whatever it was. After what Daphne had said about a mass exodus, she was keeping a beady eye out for problems, but everything seemed lovely so far. Perhaps her friend had been exaggerating – not for the first time.

'Are you sure you're right about there being trouble in the choir?' she hissed to Daphne as they moved from one group of members to another, with her friend doing the introductions. 'The atmosphere is great and everyone seems to get on.'

'Of course I'm right. It's all fine at the moment,' Daphne answered out of the side of her mouth. 'That's because *he's* not here. You wait. He'll soon show his true colours.'

'Really?' said Sarah. But then a bell rang loudly and the hubbub died down. A small woman in her fifties in a brown woolly dress made her way to the front of the room. Pinned to the shapeless dress was a large, rather ugly diamanté brooch, stones glittering in the bright lights. It was getting tangled in a curious bag she was wearing around her neck on a thin string. She had a geometric bobbed haircut, and Sarah realised with a jolt of amusement that the brutal cut looked familiar – it was the same as the one sported by her granddaughter Amelia's favourite Playmobil model.

Then a great big bear of a man strode onto the stage, overshadowing the woman. He was dark and stocky, in his late fifties. She only just recognised him from the leaflet, which had to be a very flattering portrait from years ago. He certainly didn't look anything like a jolly Santa now, as he glared at the choir. Everyone fell deathly silent. The woman stepped forward and started speaking in a voice so quiet that Sarah had to strain to hear. Indeed, the whole choir seemed to shuffle forward so they could make out what she was saying.

'...and I'm sure he needs no introduction from me, but for all our new members tonight, here is the one and only, the world-famous, award-winning singer, Daffyd Jones, my husband!'

As the woman got to this slightly more audible conclusion, the burly choirmaster moved forward until he was right in front of her, blocking her from view. Then he flung out his arms as she tried to dodge round him and started to speak in a thunderous voice.

'Well, thank you, Deirdre, for that, and if anyone wants to know what she actually said, your guess is as good as mine,' he said shaking his head. 'Seriously, Deirdre, I've told you enough times about projecting from the diaphragm, but I might as well be talking to myself. Women, honestly.' He gazed at the men in the audience, shrugged his shoulders and laughed conspiratorially. 'Can't live with 'em, can't live without 'em, am I right?' There was an embarrassed murmur and a shuffling of feet. Behind him, Deirdre said something but no one could hear what it was. Then a slight man in his thirties stepped forward, wearing grey trousers and a fawn sweater. His right arm was in a sling and he was a little clumsy as he held out a cup of coffee, almost with a little bow. Daffyd Jones grabbed it, drank it in two gulps, said tersely, 'More sugar next time, boy,' and shoved the empty cup back in his direction.

'That's Daffyd's son, Matthew,' whispered Daphne. 'Poor thing.' Somehow he looked like a weedy cub in comparison with his bear-like father.

Sarah looked at Daphne. They'd only just got here, and already she was pretty sure she didn't like Daffyd Jones one bit. Daphne gave her a nod, as if to say, *I told you so.*

'Well then, troops, we need to get down to work. Good to see so many new faces. My leaflet obviously worked a treat. We've had to get rid of quite a lot of our dead wood... well, the least said about that bunch of idiots the better. So we now have some vacancies for blinding soloists.'

Daphne was now almost jumping up and down with excitement. Sarah hoped she wasn't going to be horribly disappointed. But Daffyd was speaking again.

'I will be listening out for brilliance as we rehearse. Now, as I always said when I was performing my great hit, "Dying to Be by the Sea this Christmas", make sure your voice is A sharp and nothing else will B flat.' He looked around, seeming surprised no one was laughing. 'Suit yourselves,' he said, shaking his head. 'Right. Let's do our warm-up exercises. Deirdre, get to the piano. Where is that woman?' Jones tutted, finally looking behind him. His wife jumped as though she'd been caught out in a terrible wrongdoing and scuttled over to the instrument in the corner of the room. Soon she was playing the opening bars of a voice exercise.

The choir started tuning up, the more established members happily running through their paces while Daphne belted out her own version and Sarah tried to follow along. Sarah kept looking over at Daffyd Jones. As soon as he'd mentioned 'Dying to Be by the Sea this Christmas', everything had slotted into place. She remembered the dulcet tones of the little choirboy, in a white ruff and red cassock, his perfect voice warbling the ethereal Christmas anthem that was still played all over the country from the first day of November onwards. So this was what that innocent-looking lad had turned into. She noted his bloated body, and his discontented, angry-looking face, his colour rising as the warm-up went off pitch in places, and tried to trace the sweet young child he'd seemed to be. Maybe he had always been horrible, even when he'd been twelve.

'You didn't say the choirmaster was *that* Daffyd Jones,' she hissed to Daphne.

'Shhh,' said Daphne. 'He'll kill us. He can't bear talking in the ranks.'

Sarah was astonished. Daphne had gone through school

chatting incessantly in assemblies, classrooms and services and not even the scariest of their teachers, or indeed the headmistress, had ever succeeded in getting her to shut up. She looked at Daffyd Jones with grudging respect. He certainly maintained discipline.

Just then, the man seemed to reach a new pitch of exasperation. 'No, no, *no*,' he thundered. 'You're all over the place, tenors. God, it's been a week since we last practised. What have you all been doing? Drink and drugs rotted your minds, has it?'

Sarah watched as the tenors looked mortified. The group of meek middle-aged men included the vicar of All Saints, the town optician who wore milkbottle glasses and Dave Cartwright of the Men of Merstairs, and Sarah was pretty sure none of them would recognise a rock 'n' roll lifestyle if they tripped over it on the esplanade. But Daffyd Jones had moved on. Now he turned to the sopranos.

She could see Marlene from Marlene's Plaice fish and chip shop smiling at Daffyd, fidgeting with her form-fitting lavender wrapover cardigan. 'No point asking what's wrong with you lot. Sand between your ears, the whole bunch of you,' Daffyd thundered. He turned away from the group of women and Sarah saw their crushed faces and Marlene's downturned mouth. 'Get your husbands to try and explain the notes to you when you get home. We've wasted too much time already. Let's get on. Now, everybody should be familiar with the programme for the contest – except the newbies. If you haven't sung with us before, just keep your ears open and those flapping mouths shut for the present, and try not to mess everything up.'

Sarah was now seriously regretting setting foot in the hall. She wasn't sure she could spend a second longer listening to this dreadful man insulting all the nice volunteers who'd given up their time to try and help him regain some of his past glory by winning this Kent Choirs trophy. Honestly, in her view, the man didn't deserve to succeed. 'Daphne, let's go,' she said, touching her friend's arm.

'Shhh! Not yet,' said Daphne. 'I haven't had a chance to try out for a solo. And look, we'll miss all the drama if we leave,' she said, pointing over to the hall entrance where, with an almighty crash, someone had just burst through the doors.

THREE

A tall, very blonde woman in her forties was standing in the rehearsal hall, wearing an outfit even Daphne might have considered a tad outrageous. A floor-length blue fun-fur coat swirled round her ankles, in an incredibly glamorous pop star kind of way. While Sarah watched, one of the sopranos darted forward to take it from her and laid it reverently on a chair. Under the coat, her dress was just as attention-grabbing. The long blue velvet frock had a high halter neck, the daring slit up the front revealing a perfect pair of legs teetering on exceptionally high heels at every elegant step. She had a matching satin clutch bag in her hand.

'Do forgive me for being late,' the woman said. She didn't seem to speak that loudly, but somehow every word rang out in a way that Daffyd Jones's wife surely could have used as a model. Sarah looked over, but the tiny woman was still bent over the piano and didn't seem to have noticed the new arrival – or else she was studiously ignoring her. Daffyd Jones, however, had certainly clocked her.

'Matilda. Nice of you to grace us with your presence.'

'I did explain to Deirdre,' Matilda said, jerking her head in the direction of his wife. 'Perhaps she didn't pass the message on? Little drinkies at the mayor's house earlier. I simply couldn't get out of it.'

Sarah stored this information away, wondering if it was the reason that Charles had said he was busy tonight when they'd spoken earlier. But she dismissed the thought quickly. She and Charles didn't live in each other's pockets. It was none of her business if he chose to spend time with his ex. She was perfectly fine about it, she decided, trying to smooth out her song sheet which had unaccountably become crumpled.

At that moment, Daphne nudged her. 'Matilda Webster is one of the soloists. Wait until you hear her voice, she's wonderful.'

Sarah wasn't kept in suspense long. 'Well since you've wasted so much of our time, let's run through your piece now and get it out of the way,' said Daffyd Jones, yawning rudely. With that he harrumphed over to the piano with a sheet of music and shoved it at his wife.

Deirdre Jones played a couple of notes and then Matilda, who hadn't been given time to go and stand with the rest of the sopranos, burst into song right where she stood, with a rendition of 'Silent Night' that was so beautiful it gave Sarah goosebumps. She had a wonderfully pure voice, quite at odds with the glitziness of her outfit, and the old-fashioned tune, simple and unadorned, sounded so heartfelt that Sarah could almost imagine herself back at that lowly stable, two thousand years ago. Apart from a slight stumble on the very highest note, it was utterly perfect.

As soon as the last notes died away, the choir burst into thunderous applause. But Daffyd Jones ran from the piano to confront them, waving his hands in the air like a demented windmill. 'No, no, no no! I've told you a thousand times, Matilda. Imagine you're an innocent soul singing from the heart, not some dreadful old slapper in a tarty dress,' he screamed, his face scarlet. 'And as for the way you messed up the top G, honestly, what is this? Amateur hour?'

Matilda looked at him, open-mouthed, colour mounting in her pretty cheeks. 'Well, now you've gone too far,' she said with dignity, picking up her velvet skirts and swirling out of the hall, stopping only to pick up the blue fun fur as she passed. The doors banged shut on her retreating form and the hall was left in silence.

'Right. Since we've got shot of that no-hoper, who's going to step up and sing the solo?' shouted Daffyd, rubbing his hands and glaring aggressively at the choir.

Sarah felt sick. She really hoped Daphne wasn't going to offer herself up. She clutched her arm just in case.

'I see, we're all too lily-livered to have a go, are we? What a shower. What have I done to get saddled with a bunch like you lot?' Daffyd griped loudly.

'Honestly, I'm not sure we should stay,' Sarah whispered to Daphne who, thank goodness, seemed to be in two minds now about volunteering.

'What's that? Got something you want to share with the group?' Daffyd said, pointing right at Sarah with a vicious look in his eye. 'Speak up, then, we all want to hear it.'

Sarah looked at her feet. Then, from somewhere, she gathered her courage. She wasn't a gawky schoolgirl any more, she was a grown woman with agency, and this man was nothing but a bully. And what had she always counselled her daughters to do with people like this? Stand up to them, that's what.

'I really think that solo was magnificent. I certainly couldn't hope to do any better. And I think the choir would be well served if we asked that lady to come back,' Sarah said, hoping the tremor of nerves engulfing her was not too noticeable in her voice. There was a tiny smattering of applause from the group around her, and she started feeling a little less uncomfortable.

'That's what you think, is it? And who the hell are you to

tell me what to do with my choir?' Daffyd thundered. Just when it looked to Sarah's professional eye as though his blood pressure might boil over, his wife left the piano and tugged at his sleeve.

'What do you want now?' he said impatiently, then he looked in the direction she was pointing. There was a man standing in the aisle; a man pulsating with anger.

'Who on earth is that?' Sarah hissed to Daphne, taking in the impressive biceps bulking out the rather garish choice of a festive jumper featuring Rudolph the reindeer with a light-up red nose. Mind you, with his looks he could be forgiven – his tousled blond curls and smouldering brown eyes under dark eyebrows were pretty unforgettable, even when competing with the awful sweater.

Daphne was fluffing up her headscarf and pouting her lips, as were half the other ladies in the choir. 'That? Oh, that's Ewan Smith,' she said, aiming for a casual tone. 'Haven't you seen him around?'

'I have not,' said Sarah, and she really couldn't help it if there was a pang of regret in her voice. She was silent for a moment, just gazing, then she went on. 'What's he so cross about, anyway?'

'Shh, listen,' said Daphne, and sure enough, a heated discussion kicked off.

'How dare you say those things to my fiancée?' Smith snarled at Daffyd Jones, in a strong Yorkshire accent. He had a messenger bag slung over his shoulder and he hit it at each word, giving Sarah the distinct impression he'd rather be thumping Daffyd. 'She's weeping out in the street. Sobbing, I tell you.'

'Deirdre, get Matilda a tissue,' said Daffyd in an off-hand way. 'Now if you'll excuse me, Ewan, we have a rehearsal to get on with. I'm tired and I want to get through this so we can all go home.'

'That's not good enough. I insist on having this out with you. Right in front of the choir, if you like.' Ewan Smith's mouth was set in an uncompromising straight line and now he clenched his fists – which made his arms look all the more sculpted in the absurd jumper.

Both men were now squaring up to each other and Sarah had the uneasy feeling that a full-on fight was going to break out. She could hardly bear to watch what happened next.

FOUR

Daffyd Jones looked every bit as though he was going to swing first, staring contemptuously at Ewan, but then Deirdre piped up. 'I've just had a call,' she said, showing him a mobile phone. 'I really think you ought to take this. In the office,' she said insistently.

Much to Sarah's relief, Daffyd's aggression seemed to melt and he turned away. 'I'll deal with you later,' he said over his shoulder, narrowing his eyes at Sarah. 'Honestly, these uppity old dears who think they know everything. Matthew, put the Hallelujah Chorus on. Show this lot how it's really done. Nice and loud, mind you. I want them to feel the music, even the tone-deaf ones. Come with me, you,' he snapped his fingers at Ewan, who glared and stomped after him. As Daffyd went, he seemed to trip over his own feet, then righted himself by putting a heavy hand on his wife's back as he passed, almost pushing her face into the piano.

Matthew started fiddling with the sound system on top of the piano. Somehow he looked even slighter in comparison with the brawny Ewan Smith, now disappearing to the office with Daffyd Jones.

'Now I have seen him around in Merstairs,' said Sarah, squinting over at the thin figure, bent over the complicated-looking equipment. 'But I just can't remember where.'

'Have you?' Daphne said in surprise. 'I wouldn't say he gets out all that much.' She thought for a second. 'Oh, hang on. It's coming to me,' she said through half-closed eyes.

Sarah looked at her in alarm. She hoped her friend wasn't getting a message from the Beyond, here of all places. But mercifully it just seemed to be a feat of memory at stake.

'He's one of those merry men, you know, Dave Cartwright's lot,' Daphne said, opening her eyes and smiling widely. 'That'll be where you've seen him.'

'Oh, the Men of Merstairs? That makes sense,' said Sarah. The group was a consciousness-raising collective comprised of various slightly unhappy chaps from the area. She could see how this Matthew would fit right in. 'I wonder what he's done to his arm.'

'No idea.' Daphne shrugged.

There was a blare of music as Matthew finally got the sound system to work and the babble of conversation died down as the choir dutifully listened to another, far more professional, group singing Handel's roof-raising classic at top volume.

'I'm not sure about all this,' Sarah said to Daphne. 'I could have stayed at home and listened to it in my nice warm sitting room. If I'd wanted to have my ears bashed, that is.'

'I don't know why Matthew's playing it so loudly,' Daphne agreed, trying to settle her scarf over her ears to block out the sound. 'Where is he, anyway?'

Sarah looked over at the stage, but Matthew was no longer standing by the sound system. 'I suppose he's gone to the loo or something.'

'Oh, look over there, it's my friend Flo. Coo-ee,' Daphne shouted, waving her arms. A tall brunette in a warm woollen coat spotted her and waved discreetly back, then put one finger over her mouth in a 'shh' gesture. Sarah wondered what that was about.

Meanwhile, all around the choir, there were tetchy exchanges as the members got increasingly restive. Fair enough, Daffyd Jones wanted to give them some idea of the standard they were aiming for. But he didn't have to leave them deaf in the process, did he?

Sarah sighed. For someone who didn't really like to make a fuss, she was certainly having to step up tonight. She edged out from her position in the choir and found herself marching up the stairs to the stage. Matthew was back, and now had his gaze fixed on one of the blank walls of the room. Sarah tapped him on the shoulder. He jumped, but once he'd recovered he seemed a little incredulous that a choir member had dared to deviate from the occupation laid down by his father.

'Yes? W-what is it?' he said timidly.

'It's just that the volume is so loud. I'm worried it might damage our eardrums. Could you possibly turn it down? Or off entirely? I'm sure your father has made his point by now.'

Matthew looked hesitant for a moment, then adjusted the sound slightly.

'Thank you. Anyway, shouldn't Mr Jones be back? Does this usually happen, are we all kept waiting for ages?'

'He's a b-busy man,' said Matthew automatically, then he seemed to reflect a little more deeply. 'But now that you come to mention it, it's a little odd. Where's Mum?'

He and Sarah both turned round, to look at the piano. Deirdre Jones wasn't there. Nor did she seem to be anywhere in the ranks of the choir. There was no sign of her. Just as Sarah was starting to wonder where she'd got to, she came in through the double doors that led out onto the street, fiddling with the pouch round her neck.

'Oh, she must have popped outside,' Sarah said.

'Huh. Having a sneaky cigarette, I expect. My father will go crazy if he catches her. Smoke p-plays havoc with the voice, you know,' he said.

'Your father doesn't sing professionally any more, does he?' Sarah asked. She was no apologist for smoking, which caused myriad health issues, but she did feel a sneaking sympathy for little Mrs Jones. Marriage to someone like that might well drive a woman to nicotine, if not worse. 'What's happened to your arm?' she asked Matthew. 'Do you want me to have a look at it?'

'What? No, it's fine,' he said, backing away.

'Don't worry, I'm a doctor,' Sarah said. 'Well, retired.'

'My GP says it's a sprain,' Matthew said diffidently. 'I fell awkwardly. I just need to rest it. Ah, there's Mum.'

Sarah smiled as Mrs Jones came towards them. 'I asked your son to turn down the volume a little, I hope that's all right. It was blasting out for quite a while and the choir was getting a bit fed up,' she said lightly.

Mrs Jones looked startled. 'You turned Daffyd's music down? Oh dear. Oh, goodness me,' she said, wringing her hands. 'Oh, that's quite serious. Matthew, why did you do that?'

'To be fair, Mum, it's been going for ages now. What's Dad doing back there?'

At once, Mrs Jones looked vague. 'An important phone call. Sponsors. He needed complete privacy so of course Ewan and I left him to it. Ewan went home. I think he got it all off his chest. Then, um, I went out for a breath of air,' she said, fishing in her pouch. 'Peppermint, anyone?' she asked, proffering a crumpled bag.

You didn't need to be Merstairs's foremost detective to guess Mrs Jones was covering up the cigarette fumes with those sweets. Sarah hoped it fooled Daffyd Jones. She would hate this inoffensive little woman to be on the receiving end of another of his tirades.

'Surely his conversation must be over by now? And if not, is it fair to keep the choir hanging around? Maybe we should go home. Or practise one of the songs. You or Matthew could lead us, I'm sure,' said Sarah.

Both recoiled at the very idea. 'Oh, Daffyd wouldn't like that,' said Mrs Jones, shaking her head rapidly.

Matthew agreed. 'Dad's very fussy about the way the choir is trained. He really doesn't appreciate anyone else interfering.'

'But if it's one of you… oh well, it was only an idea. I don't really want to twiddle my thumbs all evening, and I don't suppose anyone else does either. We won't get the benefits of communal singing if we don't manage a single note, will we?'

Both Mrs Jones and her son looked a little blank at this, and Sarah realised it was probably because they were unused to looking at things from the choir's point of view. As far as Daffyd Jones and his family were concerned, the choir was there to help the great man win prizes and relive his glorious past, and that was that.

'And, um, we won't win the Kent Cup like this either,' Sarah tagged on. Immediately she got a response.

'You're right, it's been a while,' said Matthew, looking at the large clock on the wall uncertainly. 'I suppose I'd better just stick my head round the door, see how long Dad's going to be.'

Immediately, Mrs Jones looked relieved. 'You do that, son. I'll stay with the choir,' she said, with a 'rather you than me' look in her eye. She sidled back over to the piano and seemed to be taking a lot of interest in the sheet music that had been left on top of it. Sarah went back to her place beside Daphne.

'What on earth's going on?' Daphne asked, breaking off her chat with her neighbour to the other side.

'Some terribly important call, apparently, but Matthew's going to see how much longer Daffyd will be. I must say, I hope we can all just go home. This choir isn't exactly turning out the way I thought it would.'

Someone tapped her on the shoulder. To her surprise, it was Matilda, the wonderful soloist. 'Sorry, I couldn't help overhearing. I know exactly how you feel, but it's worth sticking around. Once Daffyd gets going – and stops attacking everyone – he really is gifted as a choirmaster. You'll see.'

Sarah didn't want to contradict the woman. If Matilda could forgive his incredible rudeness, she ought to too, she supposed. 'I thought you'd gone home,' she said.

'I did get halfway down the high street,' Matilda admitted. 'Then I thought better of it. Daffyd's bark is worse than his bite.'

'Is it?' said Sarah doubtfully. Both seemed to warrant a hefty rabies injection, from what she'd seen. 'Oh, and Ewan Smith was here earlier, after you left.'

'Yes, I bumped into him outside and he saw I was in a state. He's such a staunch defender,' Matilda said. 'Of course, the fact that there's a prize on offer for the best soloist at the Kent Coastal Choirs Cup does come into it, as far as I'm concerned,' Matilda said with a twinkle in her eye. 'I'd like to win that, just to spite Daffyd. And there's the carolling competition coming up even before that,' she went on.

'Oh, what's that?' Sarah asked.

'Oh, it's great,' said Daphne enthusiastically. 'Every year Daffyd's choir and Gwendoline Randall's group of singers go head-to-head to see who'll sing when the clock tower lights go on. Francesca organises it. It's really fun.'

'I don't know why we didn't go to this Gwendoline person's carols, Daph. It sounds better than being shouted at by Daffyd Jones,' Sarah said.

'Oh, Daffyd's not all bad,' said Matilda. 'He's just a perfectionist. In fact, if he gets back out here soon then I suppose I'm willing to give it another go.'

'That's the spirit,' said Daphne. 'I've, er, slightly gone off being a soloist anyway, so that lets me off the hook. And after the start we've had, what else could possibly go wrong?'

Sarah was beginning to wonder. Surely Daffyd had been away much too long? And where on earth had Matthew disappeared to now? 'Listen, I'm going to pop round the back and see what's happening,' she said to Daphne and Matilda. 'I really can't abide hanging around like this.'

'Oh, do you think you should?' Daphne turned to remonstrate, but Sarah had already slipped away.

A few moments later, when the door to the backstage room creaked open, she really, really wished she'd stayed put.

FIVE

Sarah found herself staring down at the dead body of Daffyd Jones, sprawled on the floor of the small office. She'd kept an eye out for Matthew as she'd gone through the double doors to the backstage area but hadn't seen him. Then she'd tried a couple of doors that had been locked, before coming to this one. If only it had been bolted, too.

The enormity of death was perhaps even more shocking when a giant of a man like Daffyd Jones was snuffed out. She had only just met him, but she had felt the full force of his abrasive personality, his harsh words to the choir still echoing around her head. And yet he had been silenced forever, by what looked like a bullet wound to the temple. Sarah looked around, but there was no sign of a gun anywhere – and when on earth had anyone come across such a thing in sleepy Merstairs? On the floor, by his lifeless splayed feet, was a cushion, spewing its stuffing of feathers through a rough hole with burnt black edges. It looked as though it had been used as a rudimentary silencer.

Would that have been enough to deaden the sound of a gunshot? Sarah rather thought not. But then, Handel's Messiah had been blaring out in the hall throughout Daffyd's absence.

This no longer seemed like a passive-aggressive attempt to put the choir in its place. Had it been Daffyd's cunning way of making sure no one knew he was about to kill himself? But if this was a suicide, then where was the weapon? After firing it, he would have been in no state to do anything with the gun, except let it drop to the floor. Yet it was nowhere to be seen. There was no note either, though she knew that only around a third of suicides actually left one.

Sarah looked around the small, rather bleak room. It was a sort of office-cum-green room, used for admin and as a waiting room for people about to go on stage. There was a small upright piano in the corner, worn beige carpeting on the floor and a row of full-length metal lockers taking up a lot of space. A battered corkboard held a few notices about keyholders and fire exits. It was a grim place to breathe your last in.

There was no point in feeling for Daffyd's pulse. Instead, Sarah got out her phone, her hand trembling, and dialled Mariella Roux. Daphne's daughter was Merstairs's newest – and best – detective and it would be a huge relief to leave this room and its macabre contents to the clever young woman, her forensics team and the pathologist. The sight of Daffyd Jones was doing nothing for Sarah's equilibrium, despite her years of medical training.

'Mariella? Look, it's Sarah. No, no, I'm afraid it's not a social call. Well, yes, yes, I know, but it's really not my... Here we are, anyway. Who is it this time? Erm, the choirmaster, Daffyd Jones. It's murder, by the looks of things... Of course, yes, I'll leave that bit to you. We're in the All Saints village hall – yes, the whole choir – and I'm with the, er, body, in the back office. I've left Daphne keeping everyone under control... Well, exactly. The quicker you can come the better. Thanks, Mari.'

Sarah slid the phone back into her bag, thanking her lucky stars that Merstairs had such a bright, talented detective to call on. Mariella had been incredibly helpful in their previous investigations. Or should that be the other way round? Oh, Sarah was feeling too overwhelmed at the moment to work that out. She needed to concentrate on the matter in hand.

She took as deep a breath as she could, trying to steady herself and make the most of these moments alone in the murder room. As soon as the scene of crime team got here, she would be back on the sidelines, despite the increasing closeness of her working relationship with Mariella. Was there anything here that could cast more light on what exactly had happened to this man in the moments leading up to his death?

Sarah scanned the little room again. There wasn't a lot to go on. It was obviously used by all the groups who rented out the village hall – everything from aerobics to Zumba was held here, and there were notices affecting this group or that on the tatty noticeboard. The lockers presumably contained equipment for the various sessions, none of which was needed for the choir. One was slightly ajar. It was empty, but surprisingly roomy inside.

What had the choirmaster brought into the room himself, though? That was what Sarah needed to concentrate on. There was a briefcase open on the desk, with some sheets of paper peeking out. She moved a little closer, careful not to get too near the man's body. They looked like drafts of something, full of dimensions... was Daffyd buying new sound equipment for the hall, perhaps? But each of the papers had been roughly ripped up in two, she could see now she was closer. He obviously hadn't been happy about something. With the papers was a pen. It looked like one of those cheap biros given away to advertise businesses. Sarah squinted at it. Yes, there was a logo. Merstairs Mortar, it said. And underneath all that was something shiny, glittery, that was just catching the light. That was odd. What could it be? Just as Sarah was bending over it, the door was flung open.

'What on earth is going on, Sarah?' Unfortunately it was

Daphne, never great at a crime scene, and even worse, she had Deirdre Jones in tow. Both women saw Daffyd, and immediately began screaming. Daphne was a lot louder than Deirdre.

Sarah stepped forward to prevent them from touching anything – and also to try and block the dead man from sight as best she could. 'I'm so sorry, you really shouldn't be here,' she said as soon as she could make herself heard.

'How dare you?' hissed the little woman. 'Why should you be in here and not me? I'm his wife!'

'I have every sympathy, I'm sure it seems desperately unfair. But I am a medical professional, you see, and I have some experience with, um, situations like this,' Sarah said gently but firmly, refusing to budge from her spot. 'We want to catch whoever did this to your husband, and that means we have to be very careful not to contaminate the evidence... There will have to be a thorough police investigation.'

From somewhere behind Daphne, there came a harrumph. 'Thorough, the cops round here! You must be kidding. Look at the state of the investigation they made against my nephew.'

'Dave Cartwright, is that?' Sarah said, trying to see who was in the corridor. 'You know Albie committed a terrible crime. And that's got nothing to do with what happened here. Now, none of you should be back here. If you could just all follow Daphne back into the hall? Daph, if you wouldn't mind?'

'That's right, everyone,' Daphne said. Her tone was as brave as a lioness, but Sarah, who knew her so well, could tell she was badly affected by the horrible scene in the small room and probably wanted to do a lot more screaming, her usual outlet when she came up against calamities like this. But she rose to the occasion tonight. There was only the tiniest tremor in her voice as she spoke out again. 'My Mariella will be here in a moment and woe betide anyone cross-referencing the clues, like Sarah said.'

'Erm, absolutely,' said Sarah. 'It really won't be long before the police get here.'

'I'm going home, I'm not waiting for that lot,' grumbled Dave Cartwright.

'Oh no,' said Sarah quickly. 'No one must leave. They'll want to speak to all of us, I'm afraid. One of us might well have seen something vital.' Or might actually be the killer, she continued silently.

'That's right, everybody back into the hall,' said Daphne as brightly as she could, with a shooing motion. 'I tell you what, why don't we sing something lovely to keep our spirits up? Come with me, Deirdre dear, we need you to play the piano, we really can't manage without you.' Daphne put an arm around the little woman, who was shaking like a leaf, and steered her gently out of the room.

Sarah was left alone, her back against the closed door. The distant strains of 'Silent Night' were soon echoing out again, Matilda's glorious voice soaring above the rest of the choir. She was glad Daphne hadn't chosen anything too jarring. A man lay dead, after all. She got out her phone again to see what the time was – it felt like an age since she'd made her distress call – and suddenly she wondered why she couldn't see Daffyd's mobile anywhere. He had gone into the office in the first place to take a call, so he must have had it on him then. So where on earth was it now?

SIX

Sarah immediately started to search. Her own phones had a habit of wandering off, so she was well-schooled in looking in all the obvious places – without touching anything, of course. Frowning, she drew a blank. She couldn't risk delving into the briefcase. There'd be hell to pay if her fingerprints were found on it. But from what she could see, it wasn't in there either.

At the point where Sarah was contemplating poking Daffyd's pockets with one of the pencils from the pot on the table, just to establish whether there was a phone tucked in them, the door finally opened, and Mariella's beautiful but concerned face appeared, haloed by tumbling red curls.

'I was just getting ready for an early night when you rang. Both kids have got the flu and I'm shattered,' the young woman said, advancing carefully into the room after slipping on shoe covers. She fished a pair of thin latex gloves out of her handbag and snapped them over her fingers, before stepping over to the man lying on the ground.

'Hmm, not a pretty sight,' she said succinctly. 'Time of death?'

'It was between 8.30 p.m. and 8.45 p.m.,' said Sarah.

Mariella looked up from her inspection of the dreadful wound. 'Weren't you all in the hall? Didn't anyone hear the shot? That would have pinned things down exactly, surely.'

'That's the trouble. Daffyd got his son to put on Handel's Messiah, the Hallelujah Chorus part, before he left us. It was deafening. You wouldn't have heard the final trump over that, let alone a single gunshot. And as you can see, that cushion's been used as a silencer.'

'Hmm. What was he doing in here anyway? Wasn't he meant to be conducting you, or whatever a choir leader does?'

'Shouting at us and belittling the soloists was more the norm, from the little I saw of his leadership technique,' Sarah said quietly. 'He went off with Ewan Smith, do you know him?'

Mariella raised her eyebrows. 'The whole of Merstairs knows him. The best plasterer in the place – and not exactly a hardship to look at, either. The finest thing to come out of Yorkshire since, well, Yorkshire puddings, people say. What did he want with Daffyd?'

'Daffyd had been awful to Matilda, the soloist. I think Ewan was defending her honour.'

'OK, that makes sense,' said Mariella. 'They're an item. We'll have to chase him up.'

'Daffyd was also taking a phone call. Deirdre handed the mobile to him. The whole of the choir must have heard him say he was coming here to talk to whoever it was.'

Mariella straightened up. 'He was having a pretty busy time of it, then. Did anyone else follow him?'

Sarah sighed. 'The awful thing is that I just didn't notice. If I'd known he was going to get shot, of course I'd have been watching like a hawk. But as it was, I was just rather glad we were going to get a break from all the shouting and bullying. He and Ewan went off and that was that.'

'Sounds like you weren't enjoying the choir much. How long had you been a member?'

'This was my first session. I came with your mum. I feel awful landing her in this. A murder... And if I'd known what Daffyd Jones was like I would never have set foot in the place.'

'We don't know it's murder yet,' said Mariella cautiously. 'Though admittedly everything is pointing that way. I'm really surprised Mum was willing to give the choir a go,' she added, staring down at the blood-spattered carpet. 'Daffyd Jones once came in to my school to help the music teacher with the Christmas carol concert. They had to tell him to leave, he was so mean to the children.'

'Really?' Sarah stared at Mariella. 'Daphne didn't mention that. She was keen to come along and try out, um, as a soloist.'

'I see,' said Mariella, raising her eyebrows.

'I don't know why she'd risk it,' Sarah said. 'Daffyd was absolutely horrible to Matilda. In fact, she flounced out after what he said to her.' Mariella seemed to prick up her ears at this and Sarah immediately felt guilty. 'That's not to say she, or even Ewan, had anything to do with this,' she added quickly. 'In fact, Matilda came back just now and is singing with them all out there in the hall.'

'You did the right thing mentioning it,' Mariella said. 'You know how it is in an investigation like this. All the secrets come out, whether people want them to or not.'

Sarah nodded. 'I just wish I'd realised Daffyd was such an unpleasant man. I would never have come along. But I wanted to get your mum out of the house. You know how she's been since Pat...'

Both women were silent for a beat, remembering the raucous, lively old lady who'd been one of Daphne's closest friends, and had died recently after eating a slice of poisoned red velvet cake.

'Well, be that as it may, we need to focus,' said Mariella. 'What can you tell me about what you see right now?'

Sarah silently blessed Mariella. There had been a time when the young policewoman had been wary of involving Sarah, as a civilian. But nowadays she seemed a lot more relaxed about making use of her skills, which was very good news as far as Sarah was concerned. Although, in this case, it did mean she had to keep looking at Daffyd Jones.

'There are some papers and a pen on the desk that look as though they might be important, but the most obvious thing is what I *can't* see,' Sarah said after a moment.

A puzzled look came over Mariella's face. 'What do you mean, Aunty Sarah?'

'Well, Daffyd came in here to make a phone call. But where's his mobile?' Sarah said. 'I had a look around – without touching anything, of course – and I couldn't see any sign of it. Did the killer take it with them? And if so, why did they need to make off with it?'

Mariella wheeled around. 'And he definitely had it when he left the hall?'

'Yes. He and Deirdre were making a big deal about it. He was waving it around. But it's vanished.'

'Hmm. Something incriminating on it, maybe. OK, we'll have a look. But it's really not so difficult to get rid of a phone. They aren't huge, and once you've taken out the sim card and stamped on them a few times, they're just mangled plastic.'

'Well, that's true,' said Sarah. 'But at this point, no one should have left the hall. If you got everyone to turn out their pockets, and someone had two phones, well, that might be useful, mightn't it?'

'Yep, and it's a sudden death investigation so people can't really complain. Twee— I mean, Dumbarton and Deeside are securing the exits so we should be covered there.'

Sarah raised an eyebrow but didn't say anything. Mariella's

colleagues, widely known as Tweedledum and Tweedledee, were notorious in Merstairs. It was amazing the local force had the clear-up rate it did with those two bumbling around causing chaos.

'There's something even more obvious that's missing from this room, of course,' Mariella said, staring hard at Sarah.

SEVEN

'I suppose you mean the gun,' said Sarah, shaking her head. 'I can't believe someone's been shot – in Merstairs, of all places. Who on earth would have a weapon like that around here?'

'Search me,' said Mariella. 'I don't suppose you know what type it might have been?'

'I'm no expert,' Sarah admitted. 'Even in London, shootings are pretty rare, thank goodness. But I'd say this wasn't the sort of double-barrelled shotgun you might get on a local farm. To my mind it's more a revolver-style wound,' she said, glancing again in Daffyd Jones's direction. 'Used at point-blank range. Hopefully the pathologist will have some expertise in the area,' she added.

'Let's hope so. Fingers crossed it'll be Dr Strutton, she's the best,' said Mariella.

'Also, it might be nothing, but that cupboard on the end is open. It's big enough for someone to hide inside.' Sarah pointed to the metal lockers.

Mariella strode over, opened the door and looked inside. 'Interesting. For now, I'll get Deeside to secure this room and then we'll see what our hall full of potential witnesses has to say.'

'I should think talking to Ewan Smith would be a priority,' Sarah offered helpfully. 'And maybe chasing up that freebie pen? It has a company name on it—'

'Thanks, Aunty Sarah,' Mariella said, kindly but very firmly. 'Great ideas, but you'd better let me get on with it now. Come on, let's go.'

* * *

Sarah wasn't quite prepared for the pandemonium that greeted them when they walked back into the hall. The small office had been quiet and, while it wasn't exactly peaceful being in there with the recently deceased Daffyd, it had felt like a space where she could at least get some thinking done. Not so out here. Daphne's attempts at keeping the sing-song going were in the process of breaking down. Half the choir was over by the doors, arguing with Tweedledum and Tweedledee and trying to leave. Meanwhile, small knots of singers had formed here and there. Some were crying, others seemed angry, and some were just looking very frightened.

Thank goodness, Mariella instantly took charge of the situation and Sarah thought again how well the woman had grown into her role. Not so long ago, she had been a nervous constable undermined by some very unappreciative colleagues. Now she was a poised young detective, and even though Sarah feared she still faced a lot of challenges within the force, hopefully those would die away as her true merit shone through. Mariella clapped her hands loudly, getting everyone's attention. 'Deeside, secure the office please. Dumbarton, stay by those doors. The rest of you, do take a seat,' she said, gesturing to the rows of chairs facing the stage where they'd been rehearsing. 'Just to be clear, no one is to leave for the moment.'

After a lot of shuffling, everyone found a place to sit. Sarah stayed on the stage at Mariella's side, looking at a sea of faces turned expectantly towards them. Mariella was standing pretty much where Daffyd had held forth such a short time ago. Deirdre sat at the piano, as before, but now her head was in her hands and she was wailing, quietly but persistently. Mariella looked towards her and gestured to Sarah to go and sort her out.

Sarah went over obediently and put a comforting hand on the widow's back. 'Take a deep breath, now. You've had a terrible shock,' she murmured, patting Deirdre very gently. She handed the poor woman a couple of tissues and waited as she blew her nose and began to calm down. Then Sarah nodded over to Mariella. The worst of the poor woman's hysterics seemed to be over. In the slight pause, however, the choir had started chatting amongst themselves again.

Mariella cleared her throat but before she could speak, Daphne stood up and addressed the singers. 'Come on, you lot. You heard my Mariella. Hush up now, she's got something to say to you all.'

Mariella gave Daphne an affectionate but exasperated look. 'Um, thanks, Mum, but you need to sit down too. Now look, everyone. As you'll know by this stage, Daffyd Jones has been found dead. I'm afraid that means you will need to give my constables your contact details, plus any insights you might have on people who left the hall while you were all listening to the Hallelujah Chorus, or any strangers you might have seen around the entrance as you came in. Anything unusual.'

A shaky hand went up in the audience. 'Yes, you,' said Mariella encouragingly to a sandy-haired woman in her fifties.

'It's just that... it's just...' the woman hesitated and seemed to blush.

'What is it? Don't be afraid to speak.' Mariella leant forward.

'It's just that I need the loo,' the woman said, covering her face with her hand as titters burst out from the rest of the choir.

'Right,' said Mariella, leaning back. 'Sarah, if you wouldn't mind?'

Sarah stepped forward quickly, happy to help. 'Come with me,' she said kindly. 'Anyone else?'

A few other ladies got up and soon Sarah was leading a small band off to the chilly toilets which were, unfortunately, a stone's throw from the office. Deeside stood outside it, playing a rather loud game on his phone, the tinny signature tune at odds with the grim scene behind the closed door. Sarah coughed pointedly and the man had the grace to put his mobile away. 'You can't come in here, it's a crime scene,' he said gruffly, fixing Sarah with a malevolent stare.

'We're going to the ladies' loos,' Sarah said, managing to stop herself from rolling her eyes. Did he really think a bunch of meek-looking women wanted to burst in on all that horror?

The first few in line shuffled into the cubicles and Sarah and the rest settled down to wait, their backs turned on Deeside. At one point, Sarah heard the chirrup of his phone again but when she turned round, he'd switched it back off.

The queue seemed interminable and Sarah found herself wondering, not for the first time, why architects didn't cater better for their female users. Then there was a bustle in the corridor and Dr Strutton arrived, carrying her black bag. She was accompanied by Detective Inspector Brice. Well, wonders would never cease. In Sarah's view, Brice usually kept an unreasonably low profile in investigations, considering the number of serious incidents occurring on his patch. The tall, thickset, dark-haired man, with the high colour that came from a deskbound job and a grumpy mindset, cast an eye over the group of mainly middle-aged ladies queuing and seemed to dismiss them out of hand. Then he did a double-take as he spotted Sarah.

'Mrs Vane, isn't it?'

'Doctor,' Sarah said brightly, putting out her hand to shake his.

'Right,' Brice said, ignoring her gesture. 'Well, just to say, if you could stay out of the way on this, it would be appreciated.' His hard dark eyes didn't quite meet hers. 'Murder enquiries are not for civilians. Especially... elderly ones.'

Sarah gasped. A burning desire to get to the truth and see justice served, plus a talent for solving puzzles, seemed to cut no ice with a man like him. Not when he could see a few grey hairs and a wrinkle or two. She felt chastened.

Dr Strutton stepped forward. 'Actually, Dr Vane, if you could hold my bag while I take a look at this it would be appreciated. Come along in,' she said. Then she nodded briefly to Brice. 'You might want to stay outside.' She whispered something to him, evidently giving him an idea of the injuries the corpse was likely to have suffered. Luckily the ladies still waiting for the loo were too far away to hear anything although, this being Merstairs, their ears were out on stalks. 'Bit of a nasty one, I imagine,' she said more audibly in conclusion.

It was enough to turn Brice a pale shade of green. 'Right, ladies, can we all get back into the hall as fast as possible?' he said, turning to the queue and trying to chivvy the women as they waited their turn. Some looked at him in surprise. There was not much that could be done to hurry this process. But Brice's brusque intervention was just a tactic to cover his retreat. 'Well, quick as you can,' he snarled at them, then beetled off back down the corridor. They could soon hear him bursting into the hall and shouting at the choir about this and that.

Sarah and Dr Strutton, once they were inside the office with the door closed, looked at each other briefly, but both forbore to say anything. It wasn't Sarah's place, and Dr Strutton was far too professional. They turned, instead, to the corpse.

'What can you tell us?' Dr Strutton asked the ruin of a man gravely, as she approached his body.

Sarah, meanwhile, was wondering more about those few sheets of paper on the desk and that small, glittery stone, not to mention the branded pen. They had to be clues of a sort. But how on earth did they fit into what had happened here?

EIGHT

'I thought we'd be in there forever,' grumbled Daphne as they made their way up the path to Sarah's door a while later.

'I know. It took ages for everyone to give their details, didn't it? At least we're back now. And we'll soon be having a nice hot drink,' Sarah said, her mind whirring as she spoke gently to her friend, getting out her key. But before she could put it in the lock, the door swung open – and Daphne jumped a mile.

Sarah put a calming hand on her arm. 'Nothing to worry about, Daph. I texted Charles earlier to explain things and asked him to come and sit with Hamish.'

'Yes, it's only me,' said Charles Diggory, with an appealing shy grin on his handsome face. Sarah couldn't help an answering smile lighting up her face.

'Oh, you two. If you're going to make goo-goo eyes at each other all night, I'm off back to my place,' Daphne said crossly, rather destroying the force of her words by pushing past Charles into Sarah's sitting room. 'Thank goodness you've kept the fire going at least,' she sniffed as she flung herself down on the sofa. Hamish, who'd rushed into the hall to greet his mistress, padded over to Daphne and gave her hand a little lick to cheer her up. 'A hot chocolate would be great,' she said, grabbing Sarah's book club novel. The bookmark fell to the floor and Daphne flicked through the pages to find her own place.

Out in the hall, away from prying eyes, Sarah and Charles exchanged a lingering kiss. He followed her into the kitchen, where she was soon looking out her favourite milk saucepan and measuring enough for three mugs. 'I was going to make that,' he protested.

'Oh, thank you, but it's better if I keep myself busy,' Sarah explained as she bustled about. 'That wasn't quite the fun evening I had in mind. It's lucky I got a couple of pints of milk this morning down at Seastore. You never quite know what's going to happen around here, do you?' she said, reaching down the cannister of luxurious chocolate flakes to fold in.

'You really don't,' said Charles, his tone serious now.

Sarah shut the cupboard door and turned round. 'Look, Charles, I know you feel all this investigation work is dangerous, and OK, you have a point,' she said. 'I'm not looking for trouble, I promise.'

'But it does seem to keep finding you,' he said, head on one side as he met her gaze. 'You can't blame me for being concerned. You nearly got thrown off a cliff not so long ago, for heaven's sake. And those wounds that dreadful woman Hannah Betts inflicted have only just healed.' He reached out and touched her forearm, where the sleeve covered up a snaking pink scar.

Sarah put down her spoon and shivered, remembering the terrible scene in the dark amusement arcade which could have been so much worse – for her and for brave little Hamish. 'I know. Believe me, I don't want to put myself in danger. Not at my age. Or any age, come to that,' she said, frowning deeply.

'Look, let's not worry about all that now,' said Charles,

relenting and taking her in his arms. 'Hopefully this is one case Mariella can wrap up without any help from you.'

Sarah had her doubts. What she had seen in that room had been perplexing, to say the least. But she lost herself in the embrace, until she heard the whooshing sound of the milk boiling over. Thankfully, there was still enough left in the pan to make three cups. She shooed Charles into the sitting room while she topped the mugs up with a good swoosh of squirty cream, bought for her granddaughters' last visit, and put everything on a tray with some chocolate chip cookies.

When she got into the sitting room, Daphne was wearing a 'what took you so long' expression. 'I can't believe all that just happened,' she said, taking her mug gratefully. 'We'll never really know why, though. Oooh, this is lovely, Sarah. You always did make the best hot choc.'

'When you say we'll never know,' Sarah began, a little carefully given the conversation she'd just had with Charles in the kitchen, 'does that mean you're not interested in, erm, looking into the whole thing?'

'Looking into what? He killed himself, didn't he?' Daphne said with a wince. 'You saw how vile he was to Matilda. Ewan must have had a go at him, he saw the error of his ways, and, well, there we are. Awful thing to do. Poor Deirdre. And I dread to think what it'll do to that wet son of theirs.'

'That's a little harsh on Matthew Jones, Daph,' said Sarah, realising Daphne had missed out on some vitally important details – she'd been in the hall with the choir when Sarah had realised Daffyd's phone and the gun were both missing. 'And I'm afraid it wasn't suicide.'

Daphne looked up from her mug, a lavish moustache of cream on her upper lip. Sarah gestured to her own mouth, but Daphne didn't seem to notice. 'Are you kidding me?' she said, the foam 'tache wobbling. 'You mean... someone shot him?'

'Why do you think the constable was stopping people from leaving, and searching people's pockets?' Sarah asked mildly, making a mental note to try and check with Mariella if they'd turned up anything interesting – like the murder weapon or that phone, or even the way either could have left that godforsaken room. Deirdre had that funny pouch she wore round her neck – she could have popped them both in there. Ewan had a messenger bag, and even Matilda's dainty powder blue clutch would have been big enough. And that was without considering the rest of the choir.

'Well, I don't know, do I? Honestly, Sarah, you have a nerve getting me involved in another of these fandangos,' Daphne said, taking an outraged swig of her drink.

Sarah decided not to remind Daphne how keen she'd been to go along and prove herself as a soloist. Her friend's anger was coming from shock and was completely understandable.

The little trio were silent for a moment or two as they sipped. Sarah busied herself stroking Hamish's ears. She realised she hadn't drawn the curtains when her attention was grabbed by a few white flakes floating past the window again. 'It's a shame the snow doesn't seem to settle,' she said wistfully.

'There's too much salt in the air here, from the sea. It just doesn't last,' said Daphne, biting into one of the cookies. Hamish instantly started wagging his tail and abandoned Sarah, sitting to attention by Daphne's side instead, but he was doomed to disappointment. She nibbled her biscuit as daintily as a dowager duchess and not a morsel fell to the ground. Sarah was starting to get worried about her, until she began to slurp up the last of her drink. 'You could have given us spoons, Sarah. There's lots of nice stuff at the bottom of my mug I just can't reach,' she said.

'Hmm, sorry,' said Sarah. 'Now, if we're feeling a bit better, perhaps we should go back to this choir business.'

'Right before bedtime? It'll give me nightmares, Sarah.' Daphne shuddered. 'I honestly can't bear it.'

'Fair enough,' said Sarah, realising she'd probably been pushing it. Daphne was reluctant to think about the more challenging aspects of life at the best of times. Eleven p.m. after a grisly death was asking too much.

'I'll see you home, then, shall I, dear lady?' Charles said, rising hopefully. Sarah caught his eye and shook her head.

'You'd better stay here tonight, Daph.'

'Yes... the path to my cottage is probably icy,' Daphne said weakly.

That wasn't the problem, and they all knew it. Charles couldn't help suppressing a sigh. The cottage was definitely too small for all of them to be milling around in it. 'I'd better be getting back, Sarah,' he said reluctantly, unfolding himself from his chair. 'Let's have a chat in the morning.'

Sarah, hovering between making Daphne feel like an unwanted guest or leaving Charles as a rejected suitor, gave him a sympathetic smile and made as if to see him out.

Daphne leapt to her feet, dropping her reading glasses in the process. 'Don't get up, Sarah, I need the loo anyway so I'll make sure the door is locked behind Charles.'

Sarah watched them troop out of the sitting room, and then turned back to the fire, which was dying down now, only the embers glowing brightly in the hearth. Nothing about the evening had turned out as she'd expected, and she could have done with Charles's arms round her. She felt shivery even at the thought of that dreary little room back at the village hall, and the ghastliness it contained. Well, the sooner they got this solved, the sooner Daphne would be back in her own house. It wasn't that she wanted to get rid of her oldest friend, she knew she needed support, but she also had to give her fledgling relationship with Charles every chance to thrive. This choir business was already casting a pall over things. She didn't want

Daffyd Jones's death to freeze everything it touched, like the snowflakes whispering against the window outside.

She had a feeling she'd have to think very hard to solve this one. The police were working on the gun and the phone. What did that leave her? Perhaps the ripped-up paperwork spilling from the briefcase? Ah, that little bit of diamanté, too. Now that reminded her of something. But what on earth was it?

NINE

The next morning, Sarah woke later than usual, having spent what seemed like forever thinking obsessively about that grim crime scene. She stretched her legs, trying to motivate herself to get up and get going, when her toes struck a firm little lump down at the bottom of the bed. She lifted herself on her elbows and stared – into two unrepentant black button eyes. Hamish must have sneaked onto the duvet at some point in the early hours and made himself a cosy little nest. It was the latest chapter in a long story of tussles about who slept where. If the dog had his way, she suspected she'd be consigned to his tartan basket and he'd be tucked up under the covers.

As she got up and approached the window, she realised the light coming through the curtains was brighter than usual, and of a different quality. In fact, now that she came to think of it, she couldn't hear any of the usual Merstairs morning sounds – the squawking of the seagulls and the lulling continuous background noise of the waves crashing on the Kent coast so close to her little cottage.

It couldn't be, could it? But when she drew back the pink

sprigged curtains with their merry clatter of brass hoops, she could hardly believe the scene before her eyes.

The outside world was a wilderness of still whiteness, leading almost down to the sea, which was as flat and calm as she'd ever seen it. So much for the salt in the air stopping the snow from settling. It was everywhere, and as neatly laid as a new fitted carpet: crisp, pristine and white.

'It's so beautiful, Hamish, look,' she said, hefting the dog up in her arms so he could inspect the scene. He barked suspiciously, then froze as he discerned a trail of small but suspiciously deep paw prints in the snow, wending their way up *his* garden path. Just as he'd always thought, Mephisto, the thuggish marmalade cat next door who owned Daphne, had clearly spent the whole night defying him by prancing around on his property. Well, he wasn't going to have such flagrant breaches of his boundaries going unavenged.

'All right, all right, give me a chance to get my dressing gown on. Then you can go out. Hush now, Hamish, we don't want to wake Daphne up, do we?' Sarah said, tiptoeing onto the landing.

'Too late,' said Daphne, appearing around the spare bedroom door, her hair in wild disarray. 'Any chance of a spot of breakfast?'

Sarah blessed yesterday's trip to Seastore even more as she cracked eggs into a frying pan and popped slices of granary bread into the toaster. On a day like this, a proper breakfast would help fortify them for what was to come.

She poured boiling water onto the coffee in her biggest cafetiere and, as she'd thought, the wonderful aroma brought Daphne downstairs to take her place at the table, having almost won the battle to get her hair under control. 'I'm glad you decided to leave a few essentials here, Daph,' she said, passing her friend a loaded plate.

'Mmm,' Daphne said, focussing on the task in hand as she

dug into her eggs. 'You should do the same, leave some bits at my place.'

Sarah turned back to the stove, wondering how bad the crisis would have to be before Daphne's house was the answer. She loved her friend dearly, but she wasn't sure she could do even one night there. Hamish, under the table, confirmed her view, giving her a yap as though to say, 'over my dead body.' It was impossible to imagine him sleeping under the same roof as Mephisto.

'Well, we've got a busy day ahead of us, when we've finished up here,' said Sarah, putting a couple of rashers of bacon on Daphne's plate.

Daphne gave a little snuffle of pleasure, echoed by the ever-hopeful Hamish under the table. Once she'd chewed her first mouthful, she said, 'What do you mean? Have you got a lot on? We don't need to finish the book club novel until a week on Wednesday.'

'Well, true, but there is the little matter of the choir investigation.'

Daphne winced. 'I suppose so. But Mari's on the case. And you know how she hates us getting under her feet.'

'Well, yes. But I also know how useful we can be to her. Come on, Daph. She wouldn't have done nearly as well, or got so far, if we hadn't been, um, supporting her all the way.'

'There's certainly nothing like a mother's backing,' said Daphne. 'But it's dangerous... And you know how Charles gets cross about it, too. He won't like you showing an interest, my girl,' she added.

Sarah snorted. 'Oh come on, now, Daph. You're just saying that to make me go ahead, surely? Charles doesn't own me.'

Daphne gave a tiny giggle. 'That's the spirit! Well... I'm a bit torn. You know me, I'm a stickler for respecting other people's boundaries,' she said, shoving Sarah's fruit bowl almost off the table so she could heave her bag onto it. 'I hate the whole idea of murd— *the M-word*, as you know. But there's been something odd going on in the choir for a while, not just Matilda being bullied by dreadful Daffyd. Oh goodness, I shouldn't speak ill of the departed before his soul has found refuge, but he was horrible, Sarah.'

'He really was.' Sarah nodded her agreement. 'But what's been happening?'

Daphne hesitated for a moment. 'I have this client, you see… I don't want to break the confidentiality of the parlour,' she continued, suddenly looking pious. 'It's every bit as serious as the seal of the confessional, you know. I would be drummed out of the Tarot community if I gave her identity away. She came to me for a reading about her late mother but I said to her, "Flo, if you need to get anything else off your chest while you're at it, now's your opportunity." And what she said really made my hair stand on end.'

Sarah nodded as seriously as she could, given that Daphne had just let slip the name of her client, and had even briefly introduced her to the lady last night at the choir meeting. She remembered the tall brunette in the woolly coat. The way she'd put a finger to her lips made sense, now. 'So, what did your, um, mystery client say? And was it connected with the choir issue you wanted to look into?'

Daphne drank her coffee thoughtfully, and then seemed to make a decision. 'As you saw last night, Daffyd Jones wasn't a nice man,' she said, pursing her lips. 'But you'd have thought he'd have made enough money out of that song of his. Honestly, "Dying at Christmas" isn't even a very festive sentiment, I can't imagine why people buy it.'

'It's "Dying to Be by the Sea", Daph, which is a little bit different,' Sarah put in. 'I agree, though, he must have sold millions over the years. Perhaps that's tailed off over time? After all, it's probably forty years since it first came out.'

'I couldn't stand it from the moment I heard it. Oh well, I

thought then, Christmas will soon be over and I'll never hear it again. But no. Every single year, out it comes, like the mouldy old decoration on the tree you can't quite throw away.'

Sarah nodded, though all her own decorations were in tip-top condition, and put away promptly each year on 6th January. 'But it wasn't only that Daffyd was horrible, was it? You could have just said that to me and we wouldn't have trooped along to the rehearsal. What did your, er, client mention?'

Daphne put down her fork with a clatter and pushed her plate away. 'I really couldn't eat another thing,' she said tremulously. It would have all seemed terribly dainty – except that she'd already munched her way through a very hearty breakfast. 'Well, it was to do with the very worst thing.'

'Sex? Betrayal? Drugs?' said Sarah, running the frying pan under the tap and leaving it to soak.

'No, no,' said Daphne. 'Your imagination! Honestly, Sarah. No, it was to do with something much more horrible,' she added with a shudder.

'What on earth could be worse?' Sarah asked, agog.

TEN

'It was always money, with Daffyd,' Daphne said with a shrug. 'The root of all evil.'

'Well, I'm really surprised,' said Sarah. 'We were on a taster session and no one mentioned payment... do the other choir members pay? I thought it was all free and organised by the council or something.'

'No, not at all. It is – or was – Daffyd's private choir. He charged a pretty penny. And even more if he decided you needed special coaching. Take Matilda. She was his golden girl for ages, he really took her under his wing.'

'She has an exceptional voice, though,' Sarah said, sitting down and topping up their coffee mugs again.

'Yes, very much in the same register as mine,' Daphne said modestly. 'Even she'd admit Daffyd gave her loads of pointers about breathing and all that technical stuff. But then she said she couldn't afford the private lessons any more. She owns the Red House wine bar in the high street, but I don't think it makes a lot.'

'What about Ewan Smith? Doesn't he help out?'

Daphne shrugged. 'Maybe he doesn't make enough to bail

the bar out. Or she was just using the money as an excuse to drop the sessions with Daffyd.'

'So Matilda kept up with the choir but stopped the special sessions,' Sarah said.

'That's right,' Daphne agreed. 'And ever since then, Daffyd has gone for her every single rehearsal. That's what Flo, er, oops, my Tarot client, said.'

'That's so vindictive,' said Sarah, shaking her head. 'But would one person's contribution really make that much of a difference to his finances?'

'Well, it wasn't only her. I mean, would you like to spend extra time with a man like him?' Daphne, forgetting she'd lost her appetite, was now picking at a bunch of grapes in the fruit bowl.

'Absolutely not. Do you mean lots of people cancelled lessons? I'm surprised anyone signed up in the first place.'

'You underestimate how much people want to get on, in a small place like this. Being a choir soloist is considered something to really swank about,' Daphne said, munching away.

'But not if you're just buying entry via these private lessons, surely?' Sarah sipped her coffee. It was good and strong, just the way she liked it.

'Oh, Daffyd wasn't silly. I've heard he only offered tuition to the people who had some talent. That way they could enrich the choir – and him.'

'I still don't see how that could really have brought in enough money to get excited about,' Sarah said absently.

'Well, there were the entry fees, as well,' Daphne said, patting Hamish who was now leaning against her knee. He'd given up all hope of a supplementary breakfast but was very fond of Daphne.

'Fees for what?' Sarah asked, pricking up her ears. This sounded more promising.

'When he entered something like the Kent Choral Cup, he

charged everyone in the choir. He said it was only fair. He was having to pay the organisers himself, and so all the singers had to chip in to reimburse him.'

'Hmm,' said Sarah thoughtfully. 'I don't like the sound of that. What's the prize for winning the Kent Choral Cup, anyway?'

'Well, it's a large silver cup, isn't it?' said Daphne, rolling her eyes. '... And also £10,000,' she added.

'So if the choir wins that, what happens to the money?'

'Exactly!' Daphne leant forward excitedly, snaffling the last of the grapes in the process. 'Apparently, according to my source, the choir never saw a penny of any of the winnings, even though they'd all contributed towards the entrance fees.'

'Well, that does sound quite unfair,' said Sarah. 'And £10,000 is probably enough money for someone to want to kill over.'

'Of course it is! If someone's in need, then a fiver is enough. But you could do a lot with £10,000, or even that amount shared by all the people in the choir. Say there are forty people in the choir, give or take. That would still make, ooh, quite a tidy sum each.'

'Two hundred and fifty pounds.' Sarah was quiet for a moment, thinking. It didn't seem like a life-changing amount of money, but a lot of people in Merstairs were retired, and on tight budgets. And, if they were having to line Daffyd Jones's pockets, week after week, they might well feel they deserved a share of the bounty if the choir managed to win. 'This is very interesting, Daph. You could be onto something.'

Daphne brightened up a little, then slumped back in her seat. 'It's all very well being the clever-clogs for a change, and I must say I do like it, but I'd much prefer it if we weren't thinking about death at all.'

Sarah looked at her sympathetically. 'I know, Daph. It's terrible. But look on the bright side. Mariella will be thrilled that we've got this great information to tell her, it could really help.'

Daphne's face darkened. 'Didn't you hear what I said about the sanctity of Tarot and Tealeaves?'

'Well, of course I did, Daph, and I take it, ahem, very seriously,' said Sarah quickly. 'But if we don't use any names, perhaps don't even say how you came by your information, I think we can pass the gist of it on without compromising your integrity.'

Daphne sighed. 'All right, then. I suppose you want me to ring her and set up a meeting.'

'I couldn't have put it better myself, Daph,' said Sarah, collecting the dirty plates.

Hamish, shooting up from under the table, wagged his tail furiously. He might not have had any luck in the crumbs department today, but he knew the next thing on the agenda was his top favourite – walkies.

'Well, look at you, Hamish,' said Daphne, giving him a cuddle. 'You think I've had a good idea too, don't you,' she crooned.

Hamish wasn't too sure about that, but he knew humans needed an awful lot of encouragement to leave the house on wintry days and he was willing to do whatever it took.

'No need for barks, Hamish,' said Sarah reprovingly. 'I suppose we'd better take him for a you-know-what. But before we do, how about putting in that call to Mariella?'

'Well, all right,' said Daphne unenthusiastically. 'But she'll only tell us off about something. Besides, do we have to go out? It's nice and toasty in here,' she added, looking thoughtfully at the drained cafetiere and even more longingly at the cupboard containing Sarah's jams and spreads.

'We also need to talk to Ewan Smith, do you have his number?' Sarah asked, deciding not to cave in and make yet more toast.

'Ewan? OK then,' said Daphne, suddenly much perkier about the idea of making a call. 'Oh, but why?' she added. 'You don't think he could have had anything to do with this, do you?'

Sarah put her head on one side. 'Well, he was visibly furious with Daffyd in front of the entire choir, then he went into a small room with him, and only one of them came out alive. So I'd say it's definitely worthwhile us having a chat, wouldn't you?'

ELEVEN

Daphne surprised Sarah by roaring with laughter. 'Oh, honestly! Ewan's not like that. But I'm always happy to look at him, I mean look him up. I've got his number from when he replastered the hall after Mephisto ate the skirting board that time.'

She dialled quickly and a few moments later, a slightly groggy-sounding Ewan was on the other end of the line.

'Cat wrecked something else, has it?' he said on speaker, his voice with its tinge of a northern accent sounding even deeper than usual.

'No, no,' said Daphne hurriedly. 'Sarah just wanted to ask if you killed Daffyd Jones last night.'

Sarah frowned ferociously at Daphne, and Ewan spluttered. 'What? No! I tried to talk to him about picking on Matilda, but he told me I'd have to wait until after his important phone call. Then he threw me out onto the street.'

'Oh, OK, I think that covers it,' said Daphne. 'Thanks, Ewan.' With that, she unceremoniously cut the call. 'You see, I told you he'd had nothing to do with it,' she said to Sarah.

'Honestly, Daph,' said Sarah. 'I'm not sure that counts as a thorough investigation. No one is going to admit to murder over the phone. Can you ring Mariella now?'

'All right. What did your last slave die of? I thought we were going out,' Daphne grumbled.

'We will after this, don't worry,' Sarah said. 'Just make the call, it won't take a second.'

Daphne dialled and a few moments later, Mariella answered. 'What is it, Mum?'

'You're on speaker, love,' Daphne trilled. 'Sarah wants to give you some helpful pointers.'

'Does she, now?' said Mariella, and it didn't take much to imagine her grinding her teeth.

'It's just that Ewan's told us he's not involved...' Sarah said tentatively.

'But he would say that, wouldn't he?' Mariella chipped in. 'All right. He's on our list of people to speak to anyway.'

'And I was wondering...' Sarah said carefully. 'Did you happen to find the gun? Or the phone?'

'I'm really not going to give out details about a live investigation,' Mariella said. 'But let's just say enquiries are ongoing.'

'That's a no, then?' Sarah persisted.

Mariella drew in an audible breath. 'There are a lot of people to check, but no arrests have been made so far. Do you have any other brilliant ideas to pass on or is that it?'

'Well, there were a few things – that paperwork, the pen and that diamanté—' Sarah said.

'No need to be sarky, young lady,' Daphne cut in, speaking right over her friend. 'I'm on hand if you need any babysitting this week.'

'Thanks, Mum. All leave's been cancelled until we sort this out. Listen, I'll catch up with you soon. Got to go now.'

'Love you,' trilled Daphne as the call went dead. 'She's run ragged, poor thing. I'm not sure it's the career for her.'

'She's doing so well at it, though,' Sarah said, but she wished she'd got her tuppence-worth in about the crime scene. 'Come on, then, let's get out and about. Hamish wants to see the snow before it melts,' said Sarah. 'And there's nothing like some good sea air to fire up those neurons.'

'I don't think I've got neurons,' said Daphne, zipping up her furry boots. 'Besides, don't you need to take beta blockers for that?'

Sarah shook her head and went to find her thickest coat, somewhat impeded by Hamish's enthusiastic help. 'We'd get out quicker if you just sat quietly by the door,' she told him, but at last they were ready, Daphne muffled up to the eyeballs in an assortment of Sarah's scarves which she'd decreed it was strictly necessary for her to borrow before she'd consider poking her nose round the door.

Initially, Sarah feared Daphne's caution was justified, as the wind whipped off the sea and seemed to sail right through her very bones. The morning's snow had almost entirely vanished and instead the sky looked grey and angry. But, as soon as they'd crossed the road and got down onto the beach, the gusts changed direction and instead of hitting them head-on, the strong breezes played around them, rather like Hamish, who darted hither and thither, bringing them a variety of sticks to admire.

'There's nothing like this, is there?' said Daphne, taking Sarah's arm and completely forgetting how reluctant she'd been only a few minutes before. 'Out here you'd almost swear nothing bad could happen, wouldn't you? Oh dear, that's brought the whole Daffyd thing right back again,' she said with a downward pull to her mouth.

'Try not to dwell on it too much,' Sarah said, patting the hand resting on her arm. 'Or if you do, see it as a puzzle rather than, I don't know...'

'A terrible human tragedy?' said Daphne with a shiver that

had little to do with the cold. 'Look, who's that over by the shoreline? It can't be, can it?'

Sarah peered over. Her eyes weren't as good as Daphne's and she was at the point now where she really needed to acknowledge that fact and get an eye test. A thin, rather drab-looking chap, wearing an ordinary beige coat... it could have been any of a thousand Merstairs men. But there was something about his very unremarkableness that brought Sarah forcibly back to the rehearsal hall and the ill-fated choir meeting last night. Was it, could it be, Daffyd Jones's son, Matthew? But what could he be doing?

After a moment's thought, she realised he had as much right as anyone to be out here this bracing morning, watching the seagulls being flung across the sky, and maybe finding some kind of solace in the huge grey-green unchanging vastness of the sea. There was no particular reason why people suffering from extreme shock and grief had to stay tidily indoors. It was just that they usually did.

To Daphne's evident horror, Sarah rapidly changed direction and started marching towards the man. 'Sarah, no. We have to leave him be, poor soul. He's trying to come to terms with his father's passing. I told you, Daffyd's essence is still all around us.'

'I hope not, he really wasn't a very nice man,' said Sarah. 'Listen, if Matthew's feeling up to a walk, then the least we can do is offer our condolences.'

'Except that's not what you want to do at all, is it?' Daphne hissed, now pulling on Sarah's sleeve. 'You want to try and make some headway, since Mariella's hardly going to let you sit on any interviews with him. Honestly, Sarah, you can't take advantage of the man's distracted state like that.'

Sarah paused for a second. She hated to admit it, but Daphne had a point. Perhaps this was unseemly. Matthew Jones had just lost his father, in horrible circumstances. The poor inoffensive chap could probably do with a bit of solitude. She shook her head, slowed down and was about to change direction, when Hamish took matters into his own paws, and bounded forward.

'Hamish! Hamish, no, come here,' Sarah said, but her words were whipped away by the wind.

The little dog, who'd been doing so well in remembering not to leap up at people, seemed to throw every lesson he'd ever learnt out of the window as he jumped around Matthew Jones like a pogo stick gone haywire. Matthew, with his bad arm, was having trouble avoiding him.

'Oh dear,' Sarah said, darting forward.

'Don't pretend you're not secretly glad Hamish's doing your dirty work for you, you're dying to question Matthew,' said Daphne darkly, as she too broke into a lumbering run.

TWELVE

When Sarah finally got a hand on the dog's collar, Matthew was looking quite pink in the face and Hamish was completely overexcited.

'Hamish! Down boy,' Sarah said. 'I'm so sorry, Matthew, he never usually behaves like this. Please accept my apologies,' she said, her cheeks red as she put Hamish back on the lead and got him to heel. 'He's normally a very well-behaved boy.'

Daphne finally puffed up to them. 'Matthew, so sorry, hope you're OK,' she said, grabbing his arm, as much to steady herself as to apologise.

'That's... that's fine, I suppose. I'm not really a dog person. And on a day like today...'

'Of course,' said Sarah quickly. 'I can only apologise again. I think he just got carried away. The beach is his favourite place.'

Matthew Jones nodded. 'Mine too. Usually. I mean... well, as it is, I'm not really taking much in. It's been a lot.'

'Of course it has,' said Sarah understandingly. 'It must be simply dreadful for you. And your mother. How is she coping?'

'Oh. It's hard to tell. I think p-people usually say they're bearing up, don't they? Except I'm not sure she is. I don't think it's sunk in yet.'

'It could take some time,' said Sarah sympathetically.

'I can always do a reading for her, smooth your father's path to the Beyond,' said Daphne, swinging one of Sarah's scarves around her neck. 'That often does the power of good.'

Sarah frowned a little, not sure it was exactly the moment for her friend to be touting her services, but luckily Matthew seemed to have disappeared into a reverie. Sarah noticed how pale and drawn he looked.

'How about a cup of tea at the café, and a bit of a sit-down? You look, well, pretty done in,' she said sympathetically.

Matthew neither agreed nor disagreed, but instead just kept pace with the women as they turned and walked towards the Beach Café. To Sarah's relief it looked as though it was open. It had changed hands recently and had become quite erratic in its hours, though that was perhaps to be expected in the low season, when parts of Merstairs seemed to go into hibernation. Today, however, there were a couple of hardy souls sitting at the little tables which faced out to sea, gripping their hot drinks for warmth and watching the majestic sea pounding the Kent coast.

'Here we are,' said Sarah encouragingly as they reached the café. 'Coming in?'

'Oh, why not?' said Matthew bleakly. 'I don't have anything important to do. Not any more.'

Daphne and Sarah exchanged a glance as they shepherded him to a table. He sat down like a sleepwalker, eyes wide open and fixed on the tide.

'I'll fetch some teas,' said Daphne kindly.

'Make them good and strong. And ask for extra sugar,' said Sarah in an aside. It looked as if Matthew was still in shock. With good reason. Who would ever expect to lose a parent to a gunshot, in Merstairs of all places?

'How are you feeling, Matthew?' Sarah asked gently as

Daphne strode off to the counter. There was no reply, so she tried again. 'Matthew?'

After a beat, he turned to her. 'Oh, were you talking to me? Sorry, I was miles away.'

'Thinking about your dad?' Sarah was sympathetic.

'Not really,' Matthew said, his voice jerky. 'It's just that... Oh, I don't know.'

'What's bothering you?' Sarah asked quietly.

At this, Matthew looked surprised. 'M-my father died last night... isn't that enough?'

'Of course, please forgive me,' Sarah said quickly.

Just then, Daphne got back to the table with a laden tray. As well as the tea, she'd got an array of cakes. 'I thought Matthew might need something to keep his strength up,' she said carefully as she slid a large éclair onto her plate and tucked in.

Sarah set about pushing a cup in front of Matthew and offering him the tempting bakes. He shook his head, reaching out with his left hand to pick up his tea.

'Would you like sugar?' Sarah gestured to the bowl on the tray.

'I don't think that's going to magically make everything all right.' He shook his head glumly.

Sarah, who remembered how often she'd pepped up a poorly patient with a well-sweetened cuppa in the past, merely smiled supportively. 'Whatever you prefer. You were saying your mum is not too good this morning?'

'She's crying a lot,' said Matthew. 'It's been the most awful time, it goes without saying. My father shot himself, after all.'

Daphne nodded. Sarah was surprised, though. Surely Matthew didn't still think Daffyd had committed suicide?

'Sorry to even mention this, but any idea where the gun came from?' Sarah asked as gently as she could. 'I don't know anyone in Merstairs with a gun.'

'You mean he hasn't shown you his collection yet?' Matthew

said, his mood seeming to lighten for the first time. 'I don't believe that.'

'Who? I'm not with you,' Sarah said, puzzled.

'Oh, perhaps you're keeping it all a secret because of the mayor? Got you,' said Matthew with a lopsided grin.

Sarah shook her head – then the penny dropped. He must be talking about Charles Diggory, her only connection to Francesca. Since when was their romance the talk of Merstairs? Oh, who was she kidding, of course it was. Gossip made the wheels of the town go round. Daphne started to giggle and Sarah gave her a reproachful glance.

'Why would Charles know anything about guns? If it's really him you mean,' Sarah said.

'Don't you know?' Matthew looked from one woman to the other.

'Know what?' Sarah asked briskly, taking a sip of her tea.

'About his gun collection, of course,' Matthew said.

Sarah spat out her tea everywhere. 'What? What on earth do you mean? Why would Charles, of all people, have guns?'

Matthew just sat there and shrugged after delivering his little bombshell. 'You'd better ask him that, hadn't you?'

THIRTEEN

'Didn't you think it might be a great idea to mention this famous gun collection of yours, when we told you someone had been shot last night?' Sarah said to Charles, her voice trembling with barely expressed frustration.

'Dear lady,' said Charles spreading his hands in a pleading gesture.

'I don't know how you can *dear lady* me,' Sarah snapped. 'How do you think I felt, being told by the murder victim's son that my, erm, partner, or whatever this is, was certain to be the prime suspect?'

'Well for goodness' sake,' said Charles, brows shooting skywards as he stood behind the till in his antiques shop on the esplanade. Behind him was a rather motley selection of 'vintage' Christmas decorations, which to Sarah's jaundiced eye looked eminently bin-worthy. Unluckily for him, it was a very short stomp away from the Beach Café, where Sarah had just heard the jaw-dropping news from Matthew Jones about the Diggory gun collection. On the plus side, for Charles, there was a good foot of solid mahogany between him and his lady-love, thanks to the hefty craftsmanship of the Victorian counter (price on application). 'And did Matthew Jones also tell you that all my guns are antiques?'

Sarah looked at him for a few moments in silence. Then, accompanied by a snort from Daphne, she said quietly, 'No, he did not tell me that.'

'Ah. Well, it's true,' said Charles, with a returning twinkle in his blue eyes as he surveyed Sarah's small, cross form. 'If you two, er, three,' he added, at a bark from Hamish, 'would like to sit, then I'll get the collection out of the gun cupboard. Everything's kept under lock and key, naturally.'

'Naturally,' said Sarah faintly, as she found a seat on one of a set of rosewood dining chairs with tatty upholstered backs, ranged against one of the walls of the claustrophobic shop. She had never been a fan of Charles's place of work, always finding it looming with the kind of ancient bric-a-brac that she loathed, which he displayed lovingly and did his level best to sell to tourists. 'I feel like a total idiot now,' Sarah confided to Daphne, who'd sat on a matching chair and plonked her purple velvet handbag on a third.

'I did try and stop you rushing round here,' Daphne said, with an I-told-you-so look about her.

'Only because you didn't want to leave any of those cakes,' Sarah muttered.

'Don't remind me,' Daphne said, looking pained at the memory. 'I suppose if we go back soon... no, it's no good, someone will have cleared them away. Or eaten them!' She shook her head at the folly and waste.

'Sorry, Daph. I don't know what got into me,' Sarah said, feeling very small. Hamish leant against her comfortingly and gave her a steadying look with his dark eyes. She patted him fondly. He was always there for her, even when she made a twit of herself.

Just then, Charles re-emerged from the back of the shop with a large wooden box. He set it down on the counter and got out a duster, giving the already glowing wood a loving buff-up before producing a key from his pocket and slowly unlocking it. Sarah pursed her lips during this performance, but decided she'd better not say anything. Daphne, however, had no such scruples.

'Honestly, Charles, do get on with it. You've got our full attention, you know.'

Charles shifted his feet behind the counter but centuries of breeding meant that he showed little sign of disgruntlement – and nor did he hurry himself, either. With a leisurely movement, and fixing both Sarah and Daphne with his gaze, he finally flipped up the lid of the box.

Both women shot to their feet and craned over the counter, eager to see what was within. Both stepped back, seconds later, and exchanged a glance. 'Well, really,' said Sarah.

'What?' said Charles innocently, now looking down at his guns with unquestionable pride.

'It's just that, if you'd said they were four-hundred-year-old blunderbusses, or whatever these are, then we could have cleared all this up in a moment,' said Sarah, resisting the temptation to tut. The guns nestling in the moth-eaten blue silk lining of the box in front of them would have been perfect for Dick Turpin to use in one of his highway robberies. They were not, however, anything that could remotely have injured Daffyd Jones at the choir rehearsal, unless he'd dropped one on his foot. And anyway, they were both present and correct in their case.

'I do have other guns,' said Charles, who now sounded a bit disappointed that he hadn't produced the weapon that had done away with the choirmaster.

'Are they all still in their locked cupboard, or wherever you keep them? Because if they are, it's very unlikely they're what we're searching for,' Sarah said patiently.

'I haven't checked every single one. I just got these out to show you because, well, they're my favourites,' said Charles, a little bashfully. He was now polishing the handles of the blunderbusses, which were inlaid with pearl. They were beautiful objects, Sarah conceded – if you could forget their violent purpose and the fact that they were totally irrelevant to her investigation.

'They're very nice, Charles,' she said kindly. Daphne, behind her, snorted again but turned it into a cough. Hamish whimpered to be let out. He was as amenable as the next dog, but this shop was an impediment to his quest to conquer the world of smells out on the beach. 'Perhaps you could have a quick look at the others? Are they all as old as this pair?'

'Sadly, no,' said Charles. 'But I do have a nice collection I snapped up when *Broomstick Battalion* folded.'

'*Broomstick Battalion*? What was that, a homewares shop?' Sarah asked.

'Of course not,' Daphne said. 'Don't tell me you never saw it? It was such a great TV show, years ago now. All about a troop of Home Guard volunteers in the Second World War. People used to tease them because they didn't have proper guns, that's where the name comes from. It was filmed along the seafront here. People were always trying to get into the shots as extras.'

'Oh, it sounds fun. What happened to it?' Sarah asked.

'No idea,' said Daphne. 'One minute they were doing an episode about a fortune teller, and I was just helping them out with a few really useful tips, and then we were told it was going over budget due to interruptions on set, and that was the end of that.'

'Ahem, yes,' said Charles drily. 'But the silver lining was that this TV battalion did have a few guns. So when the plug got pulled I snapped up some of the props they didn't want to reuse, including a couple of lovely Second World War revolvers.'

'Wait a minute, those sound much more like it,' Sarah said. 'Surely one of them could be our weapon?'

Charles smiled. 'There's just one problem with that idea, dear... er, Sarah.'

'What's that?'

'They were decommissioned long before the TV company bought them. So they don't work.'

'Well, I know how they feel after all this,' said Daphne. 'I really need something to perk me up. I think we've established that none of these guns are the right one. How about just popping back to the café to check to see whether...'

'Those cakes won't still be there, Daphne,' said Sarah quickly. 'Charles, could anyone mend the guns, as it were? Somehow fix whatever has been decommissioned, to make them function after all?'

'Well, I'm not entirely sure. They were altered a long time before the current legislation, which is much stricter,' conceded Charles. 'I've never actually tested them with ammunition. But I'm pretty sure they haven't been tampered with,' he said with a shrug.

'Are you sure about that? You've laid eyes on those guns this morning?' Sarah persisted.

Charles sighed. 'Well, I can go and have a look, if you insist,' he said, somewhat unwillingly. 'But they're not really very interesting pieces, not like these blunderbusses.'

'We know that, Charles. The blunderbusses are obviously, um, very special. But nevertheless. It could be important.' Sarah smiled winningly, hoping Charles would forgive her earlier exasperation.

Charles pottered off and Daphne took the opportunity to give her views on people who wasted cakes. Sarah was about to respond when Charles came back, his face ashen.

'You won't believe this,' he said, in a faltering voice.

'No, Charles! You can't be serious?' said Sarah, folding her arms across her chest.

Charles, looking shamefaced, nodded sadly. 'Yes. One of my guns is missing.'

FOURTEEN

A few minutes later, once it had been firmly established that one of the Second World War pistols had disappeared, and hadn't just mysteriously fallen into a display of chamber pots or got mixed up with the collection of ancient cricket bats Charles loved so much, he had bowed to the inevitable and agreed to call the police.

Sarah and Charles were now standing outside on the pavement with Hamish, while a brisk easterly wind nagged at them. Inside the shop, Mariella, Deeside and Dumbarton were looking serious while the SOCO team did important, hushed things with fingerprint powder and little evidence sachets. Daphne, completely unabashed, had her face pressed up against the window and was giving Sarah and Charles an unwanted running commentary on the situation.

'Dumbarton's just picking up that battered old wooden boat on your counter,' she said. 'You know, the rickety one with the rigging that looks like spaghetti... Oh, whoopsie,' she said with a smothered laugh.

Charles whipped round.

'Oh, don't worry, Charles, it's fine,' said Daphne airily. 'It didn't really need both sails, did it? It's not like it's going anywhere.'

Charles harrumphed, glaring through the window at the officers milling around inside. 'This is the last straw! I'm having to give up a morning's takings, and then those idiots ruin my stock on top of it all. And it's quite ridiculous. My gun can't possibly have been involved in the shooting. The whole thing is preposterous.'

Sarah and Daphne had exchanged a glance at the thought of lost sales, knowing these must be purely imaginary as Charles's shop was rarely troubled by customers. But the issue of the gun was more serious.

'If there's the least chance that someone's used it to commit a crime, they have to look into it. You know that, Charles,' said Sarah, putting a soothing hand on his arm. Charles looked a little mollified but his chin still jutted out in an angry way.

'It's absurd, I tell you,' he muttered.

'Well, while we're having to wait, perhaps we should do something practical,' Sarah reasoned.

'You mean, go back to the café?' Daphne said hopefully, and Hamish wagged his tail to signal his approval of this excellent idea.

'Not that, Daph. Maybe later,' Sarah said. 'Can we think about who has keys to your shop, Charles? If someone did steal your gun, how did they get access to it?'

'That's a good point,' Charles conceded, now unable to tear himself away from the window, where he'd replaced Daphne and was watching Dumbarton trying on a straw boater hat he kept in stock for the more discerning tourist – which he was quite partial to wearing himself. It perched on top of the policeman's huge head for a moment before crashing to the floor. Charles winced and turned his back. 'Let me just think. No one, really. I don't employ anyone else, I'm not at that stage. Yet. I soon will be, of course,' he said to Sarah. She nodded kindly.

'What about a cleaner? You must have someone, erm, dusting occasionally?'

'Not enough,' said Daphne under her breath.

That was a bit rich, thought Sarah. You could hardly see into Daphne's own shop further down the esplanade, the windows were so opaque. At least with Charles's place, you had a clear view of the goods on offer, and could therefore make an informed decision not to go in.

'Yes, Molly Ferguson. She comes in once a week.'

'Where did you get her from, an agency? Sometimes they keep a set of keys,' Sarah said.

'No, she works for Francesca, actually. It was all arranged, um, years ago,' Charles said, rather pink about the ears now. 'In fact, now I come to think of it, Francesca probably still has her own keys too. But she was never interested in the shop. I can't for the life of me think why.'

Charles always got rather anxious when discussing his ex-wife. Sarah had initially found this annoying, but now it was rather endearing. The news that Francesca had keys was intriguing. She couldn't imagine why on earth the woman would have taken a gun from the shop, let alone had it refitted to make it usable and then killed the choirmaster – but stranger things had happened. And she had to admit the idea of the frankly awful Francesca being in the frame for murder was not unappealing. Even if she didn't think for a moment the woman could have done it.

'We're going to have to mention that to Mariella, of course,' said Sarah, careful to sound as neutral as possible. 'Anyone else you can think of?'

Charles shrugged. 'No one's springing to mind. But I suppose I have a couple of sets of keys in my flat. I keep a close eye on them, but anyone going in or out *might* have noticed them.'

'Well, you don't have people drifting through your flat night and day, do you?' said Sarah lightly.

'Of course not,' said Charles heartily, but he didn't quite meet her eyes. Sarah suddenly remembered the early days of their relationship, when Charles had blown hot and cold, and half the ladies of Merstairs had seemed to be sharing secret smiles with him. Hmm, she thought.

'It never occurred to me that anyone would use one of my guns for criminal purposes,' Charles said miserably. 'I really hope they don't decide it was the weapon in question.'

At that moment, Mariella pushed open the shop door and emerged, followed by Dumbarton and Deeside. Deeside was carrying a plastic evidence bag containing several guns and had an insufferably smug look on his face.

'Ooh, bright out here when you've been inside for a while,' said Mariella, blinking in the weak sunshine which had replaced the wind. Sarah knew the feeling; she often wished she was wearing one of those miner's headlamps when she was in Charles's shop, though now she maintained a straight face and said nothing.

'The gun... my missing gun. It's not the one, is it?' Charles sounded distinctly nervous and Sarah pressed his arm comfortingly.

'Too early to say,' Mariella said, in her official voice, though she did seek out her mother's eyes and give her a bit of a look. The fact that the detective hadn't simply arrested Charles on the spot had to be a good sign, though.

'Can I get back into my shop at least? I don't want to disappoint my customers,' Charles said.

Sarah resisted the temptation to look up and down the esplanade in search of these elusive beings, yearning to get their hands on Charles's old boat, or even the moth-eaten moose head that always fascinated Hamish. Mariella let him know that the SOCOs were still finishing but would lock up after themselves.

'I'll give you a ring the moment things are clear,' she promised him. With that, Charles had to be content.

'Any thoughts on those ripped-up pages? Or the pen?' Sarah managed to get in.

'Bagged and tagged,' said Mariella with a rather stern look. 'Oh, but I will tell you one thing – someone had definitely hidden in that cupboard. No prints though. Right, I'll be off, then,' said Mariella.

'Just one thing, Mari,' Daphne said urgently.

'Yes, Mum?' The detective turned to her.

'Are you wearing a vest?' Daphne said, in one of her very loud whispers. 'It's just that this wind...'

'I'll see you later, Mum,' Daphne said, turning on her heel.

'What?' said Daphne, in response to Sarah's look. 'I don't want her to catch a chill, do I?'

'She's a big girl now,' Sarah said absently. The news that someone had concealed themselves in that room, waiting for their moment to shoot Daffyd, was chilling. 'Right, come on now then, everyone,' she said with a renewed sense of urgency. It was imperative they caught this person, and as quickly as possible. 'Let's get on with our first interview.'

Daphne and Charles turned to face her. 'Who are we talking to?' Daphne asked.

'Isn't it obvious?' Sarah said. 'Someone who has the keys to Charles's shop. And who – I have to say this, Charles – wouldn't mind causing you a bit of trouble.'

Daphne looked from Sarah to Charles and back again, none the wiser. But Charles's face fell.

A moment later, Daphne's expression cleared. 'Oh. You must mean Francesca. Do we really have to go and see her? She's only going to be mean to us. I thought you wanted to check up on Ewan.'

'Well, Mariella said she'd do that, so we'll leave it in her capable hands,' said Sarah evenly. 'And the news about the gun has made this more pressing than talking to him anyway.'

Charles remained silent, but he certainly wasn't rushing to disagree with Daphne about the meanness that might ensue. Sarah hadn't seen much of the mayor since the woman's divorce from Charles had become final, but she doubted it had improved her mood much.

'Sarah, shouldn't we wait until we know for certain that it's Charles's gun that was used? Otherwise we'll have a wasted journey,' Daphne wheedled.

'I'm not so sure we will, you know,' said Sarah, looking over both their heads towards the beach, where a dog walker strode into view, throwing a very big stick for a very, very small pooch. Instantly, Hamish's ears pricked up.

'Oh,' said Charles, gazing in the same direction as Sarah. 'I see what you mean. It's Tinkerbell. And Francesca, of course.' He was looking rather glum. Sarah could hardly blame him. Francesca was at her most toxic when confronted by Sarah and Charles together.

'Well, no time like the present, is there?' Sarah said as brightly as she could. 'And after we've had a little chat, well, we'll be in exactly the right spot to go and see if the Beach Café really did keep that plate of cakes for you, Daph. A restorative cuppa will be just the thing.'

'Why didn't you say so earlier?' said Daphne, plunging across the road, causing one car to swerve out of the way and another to slam on its brakes. 'Come on, you lot, don't lag behind.'

Charles looked at Sarah. 'Shall we, my dear?' he said with a brave smile.

'Why not?' said Sarah, looking up at him and linking her arm in his. It was nice that they could present a united front. Francesca had an uncanny way of getting under her defences.

Maybe this would be the one time when she could hold her own against the dratted woman.

They crunched across the sand in silence for a while. Now that the wind had died down and the very last patches of snow had melted, the beach was a wonderful place to be, its wide arc spreading out like a smile as far as the eye could see, the sea rushing to meet it then swooshing away again in a perpetual game of tag. The closer they got to Francesca, the tighter Sarah held Charles's arm, and the slower his own pace was.

In the end, though, when they got closer, Francesca seemed to be grinning almost as broadly as Hamish, who was sitting gazing adoringly into his beloved Tinkerbell's large round eyes. The reason soon became plain. She ignored Daphne, but hailed Charles, and even Sarah, very brightly. As usual, a silk scarf was knotted savagely at her throat and her camel coat and pristine wellies looked much too expensive to be worn on a wet and windy beach.

'You two! Just the people I wanted to see. I feel a little coy about this, but really, what better way could there be to spread the good news? I know Sarah has her finger in every pie in Merstairs and by teatime everyone will know… so… ta-dah!' she said, pulling off her rather chic leather gloves to reveal a left hand almost buckling under the weight of an enormous diamond engagement ring.

FIFTEEN

To say that Sarah felt Charles's recoil would be an understatement. He seemed to leap backward by about a yard, almost causing Sarah to lose her footing.

'Oh, er, whoops,' he said, with a clumsy attempt at a laugh. 'Must have tripped.'

Sarah righted herself and looked at him in astonishment, while an expression of smug fake sympathy spread over Francesca's face. 'I know it will come as a terrible shock, Charles. Perhaps I should have broken it to you more gently. Of course I suspected you still had feelings for me... even though you've been consorting with this floozy for months.' Francesca raked Sarah with a glance.

'Oh, er, not at all, not at all, loose bit of rock I think,' said Charles, looking pink about the gills.

'Talking of rocks... that's quite the sparkler,' Daphne said, breaking the awkward moment by stepping forward and seizing Francesca's hand, eyeing the stone like a master jeweller. 'Very nice. Cushion cut, is it?'

'Princess,' snapped Francesca. 'Anyway, now that I've shared my glad tidings, I'd better—'

'Just a minute, Francesca,' Sarah began, when Daphne cut in.

'Yes, you need to tell us who the lucky man is.'

Sarah tried not to look too sceptical – in her view, the poor chap was in for a world of pain – but Francesca stopped and sighed deeply. She clasped her left hand to her cheek in a romantic gesture, much enhanced by the weak sunlight playing on the diamond ring. It certainly was impressive. Sarah, despite wanting to get to the matter in question, couldn't help being arrested by the sight.

'Well, if you must know, if you have to drag it out of me... It's Rollo.'

Charles, having been pink before, now progressed to a deep puce. '*Rollo*? You mean Rollo Henderson?' he spluttered.

'The very same,' cooed Francesca. 'You always used to complain about him. You never told me what a gentleman he is. Yet you must have known, having been to school with him.'

Charles snorted. Sarah suddenly remembered an awful man they'd encountered a while ago in Whitstable. She had unfortunately backed her car into his showy Jaguar and he'd been incredibly patronising about women drivers. Not much sign of his gentlemanly side then. Charles had smoothed everything out. But Sarah remembered him saying Rollo had sold his family home – a gorgeous Elizabethan manor – to the Wittes hotel chain so perhaps it was the size of his wallet, not his heart, that was making Francesca go all gooey-eyed in this most uncharacteristic manner.

'Well,' said Charles, recovering himself now after what seemed to Sarah like much too long a pause. 'I'd like to wish you every happiness. When is the, er, wedding?'

'As soon as we can arrange everything. We want to have a lovely intimate do. Just five or six hundred of our closest friends. I'll send you an invite. Well, some of you.' Francesca narrowed her eyes at Sarah. 'Must be off now.'

'Francesca, just a second, before you go,' Sarah said, seeing her chance.

The mayor, who'd been about to march away with Tinkerbell tucked under her arm, turned back in a long-suffering fashion. 'What is it now?'

'Do you still have a key to Charles's shop?'

Francesca looked from Sarah to Charles and back again. 'And why on earth is that your business? Whether I have one or not is between me and Charles.'

'Of course,' said Sarah quickly. 'But it will soon be between you, Charles and the police. They'll want to question everyone who has access.'

'Don't tell me this is another one of your silly "investigations",' Francesca said crossly. 'Charles, I don't know why you can't get her under control. Oh, on second thoughts, I do,' she sneered. 'She's completely unmanageable.'

'Just answer, Frankie. I'd like to know, too. Probably about time I got the key back. After all, I don't want Rollo getting his hands on my warming pan collection, do I?' said Charles with an attempt at a cheery laugh.

'As if he's got time for such nonsense,' Francesca said with a sniff. 'He's got a real job, you know.'

'More fool him,' said Charles bravely. 'The shop is just the thing for me these days. So, I take it you do still have a key?'

Francesca was silent for a moment. 'Come to think of it, I probably do. It's in the garage, on the key rack. I don't remember seeing it, but then I've hardly been looking for it. I've been much too busy. Plenty of other things on my mind,' she said, with a twinkle in her eye.

This time, Charles didn't rise to the bait. 'I suppose the garage is kept unlocked, as usual?'

Francesca shrugged. 'No one's going to steal that old banger you gave me, are they? Rollo says he'll upgrade me to a Jag any day now, just like his,' she sighed.

'I'm sure he will.' Charles raised his eyebrows and looked significantly at Sarah.

Sarah was thinking hard. It seemed that the key to Charles's gun cupboard had been pretty much accessible to anyone. Anyone who could bear to spend a second of time with Francesca Diggory, that was.

SIXTEEN

It was a rather subdued little party that took their seats under the tinsel-trimmed awning at the Beach Café a few minutes later. Sarah tutted and went to get a tray of hot chocolates and toasted teacakes. Then she passed round some of the fleecy blankets the café left out for customers at this time of year, in a red rich enough to rival Santa's favourite outfit.

'Drink up now,' said Sarah, once everyone was snuggled under the throws and looking a lot happier. 'Let's all think. Who is likely to have been rummaging in Francesca's garage?'

Daphne looked up from her teacake with a bit of a snort. 'Is that code? Bet you don't like the sound of it, Charles.'

Charles tried to look dignified as he wrapped his hands around his cup of hot chocolate. 'I'm sure I don't care what my ex-wife gets up to these days. I'm amazed at Rollo, though. I always thought he didn't think much of Frankie.'

'Maybe he was just trying to cover up his true feelings?' Daphne chipped in.

'Anyway,' Sarah hurried on. 'Apart from Rollo, I suppose Francesca's gardeners, whoever the new lot are, and the housekeeper, Mrs Chivers is it, had access. They would surely be the only ones who'd know where the keys would be inside the garage.'

'You're forgetting,' said Charles. 'Francesca does love her lady of the manor status, I'm afraid. So the annual Women's Institute shindig is held there. And then there's the lifeboat association tea, the Scouts fundraiser, the meeting for the town carol singers... There's not much to stop people wandering around once they're there.'

Sarah shook her head. She didn't envy Francesca hosting all those meetings, but of course for the mayor it was an essential part of her eternal quest to broadcast her importance to the world. What on earth had Charles been thinking of, though, allowing the key to his gun cupboard to be so accessible?

Charles spoke up. 'Before you say anything, Sarah, in my day, the keys were always locked away in my desk in the study. Then the key to the study itself was kept in my pocket at all times. I had no idea she'd let things get so lax. It's extraordinary.'

'Well, as she said, she's had her mind on other matters,' Daphne said with a chortle, which she suppressed when Sarah gave her a look. 'What? I think romance in later life is a great thing,' she said with a pointed look at Sarah's hand, which was now lying reassuringly on Charles's jacket sleeve. Sarah removed it and sipped her chocolate before speaking again.

'All right, then. We'll just have to work with what we've got. Can you think of anyone from any of those organisations that Francesca patronises, erm, acts as patroness for, who'd have a grudge against Daffyd Jones? That's really the issue at hand.'

'I suppose the carol singers might have,' Charles said slowly. 'Daffyd was notoriously territorial, and I don't think he was that keen on Gwendoline Rendall.'

'Gwendoline runs the carols,' Daphne explained to Sarah. 'She's, well, what would you say, Charles? A force of nature just about sums it up I think.'

'Takes one to know one,' said Charles, saluting her with his tea. Daphne preened.

'Carols are only once a year, though. Would Daffyd be that bothered?' Sarah asked.

'Oh, come on, Sarah,' Daphne said. 'You saw him last night. Like Charles says, he didn't tolerate anyone on his turf. He was always desperate to win the choir sing-off against Gwendoline. That's probably why he was so mean to Matilda about 'Silent Night', trying to get it top notch. In fact, I wouldn't be surprised if Matilda goes straight over to Gwendoline's group, now the Merstairs Muses have had it.'

'Do you think the choir is finished, then? You don't reckon Matthew will try to keep things going, with Deirdre's help? It could be his moment to shine. He'll finally be out of his father's shadow at last.' Sarah popped a fragment of teacake into her mouth.

'I just don't think he's got what it takes to keep the choir together,' Daphne said. 'He's a follower, not a leader.'

Sarah considered what she'd seen of the man. Obviously they'd met under terrible circumstances, but it was true, he did seem a meek soul. 'Oh well, in that case, maybe we should see if we can get a word with this Gwendoline? We can leave the other groups who had access to the garage to Mariella's lot, they've got the resources, but we might be able to get somewhere with her,' Sarah said.

Then she looked at the others. Daphne was doing her best to suppress a jaw-breaking smirk, and Charles looked as though he wished he was currently on Mars. 'What? What did I just say?'

Daphne and Charles exchanged a loaded glance. Sarah was thoroughly fed up with being kept in the dark. 'Come on, you two, spill the beans. What is it that I ought to know about this Gwendoline character? And how come I haven't seen her around in Merstairs before?'

'Oh, Gwendoline's much too busy to be in Merstairs during the summer,' Daphne said. 'She runs a whole fleet of holiday lets in Whitstable and Tankerton. Rents them out for thousands to all the DFLs.'

'DFLs? I've heard that before, I'm sure...'

'It means "down from London",' Charles put in. 'But it doesn't apply to people like you,' he added a bit too quickly. 'People who've settled here permanently, buying houses and actually living in them, are absolutely fine. You're *quite* different from the weekenders.'

'Am I, indeed?' Sarah said. 'Well, anyway, I'd love to meet her.'

Charles and Daphne looked at each other again. 'I'm sure we can arrange that, at some point,' Charles said warily.

'Oh, it's no good, Charles, you're going to have to come clean,' said Daphne chirpily. Then, before he had a chance to do so, she leapt in herself. 'Charles was having a bit of a thing with Gwennie before you arrived on the scene.'

Sarah, who'd been taking a last sip of her rather cold hot chocolate, coughed rather inelegantly. Another woman who'd fallen victim to Charles's charms! He must have romanced half the population in between his marriage to Francesca ending and her own arrival at her seaside cottage.

Charles patted Sarah on the back with tender consideration, while throwing an outraged glance Daphne's way. 'I really don't know how all these rumours get about,' he said in perplexed tones.

'Well, be that as it may,' said Sarah, shaking off his assistance and dabbing her coat with a tissue. 'I still think I – we – need a word with Gwendoline. Where would we find her right now?'

'Now?' This time even Daphne seemed a little nervous and put out. 'But it's daylight. Surely we can't...? Charles, you tell her.'

'We are looking into a sudden death, you know,' Sarah said. 'And Gwendoline sounds like she might have some useful information. Come on, Daphne.'

Daphne rustled her scarves and rummaged in the large bag on her lap, then gave up and raised her gaze to Sarah's. 'Oh, it's no good, you always see through me. All right, then, she's probably going to be in... the Ship and Anchor,' she finished with a gulp.

Sarah looked from one to the other. 'You're kidding? The pub neither of you have let me set foot in since I arrived here? Is this Gwendoline actually the reason why we never go there? Even though it's so pretty from the outside, with the lovely window boxes and the gastro pub menu of delicious food?'

'It's not really because of her,' Daphne said miserably. 'It's also all the business with Gus Trubshaw, back when he was the landlord of the Jolly Roger. We were being loyal, as the Ship was his biggest competitor... and yes, now you mention it, Gwen does spend quite a lot of time there. Don't shoot me, Charles.'

The phrase could have been better chosen, given recent events. The three of them lapsed into silence, Sarah thinking furiously about all the nice lunches she could have had at the Ship, instead of making do with the very peculiar décor of the Jolly Roger, and its even stranger menu masterminded by the new landlady, Claire Scroggins. And that was without getting started on this new evidence of Charles's philandering past. She wondered whether he had been as active romantically during his marriage to Francesca. For the first time, it struck her that the mayor might have a point in all her anger and resentment towards her ex-husband.

She shook herself. This wasn't getting them any further forward. She gathered up her bag and Hamish's lead. 'Well, I don't know about you two, but I'm off to the Ship and Anchor.'

* * *

Twenty minutes later, a rather shamefaced Charles and Daphne were facing Sarah across a shining oak table in the warm and welcoming interior of the Ship and Anchor. The place was delightful, and the aromas wafting from the kitchen were mouth-watering. Sarah wondered for the umpteenth time why she had spent so many months dodging plastic lobsters in the shabby Jolly Roger next door.

And then she caught the eye of a woman sitting at one of the high stools by the bar. She was of a certain age, but all you noticed were yards of shapely leg ending in dainty little boots (not at all practical for a day like today, Sarah thought firmly), a figure-hugging cherry-red jersey and short matching corduroy skirt. The woman smiled and waved at her, as though they knew each other. Sarah did a double-take. This had to be Gwendoline.

Well, no time like the present for making her acquaintance. Both Charles and Daphne were sheltering behind the Ship and Anchor's large menus, with not even an eyebrow visible, so she told Hamish to stay, and sauntered over to the bar.

'Hi, we haven't met before. I'm Sarah Vane,' she said, fixing the woman with a friendly smile. 'And you must be...?'

'Gwendoline Rendall. I've heard a lot about you,' she said. 'Take a seat, why don't you?' She patted the next bar stool along, and Sarah eyed it rather suspiciously. It looked very high and she had no intention of making an idiot of herself, trying to hoist herself aboard.

'Why don't you come and join us instead?' she suggested, gesturing to the table where Charles and Daphne were now peering over the tops of their menus. As soon as they saw Sarah and Gwendoline glancing over, they raised them again and disappeared abruptly from sight.

'I'm not sure Charles would be that thrilled. And was that Daphne Roux I glimpsed for a moment? Not like her to be shy.' Gwendoline smiled, and a little dimple appeared in her cheek.

Sarah couldn't help an answering grin spreading across her face.

'Oh come on,' Sarah encouraged. 'We wanted to ask you some questions, but it'll be fun, too.'

'You know, I rather think it will,' said Gwendoline looking at Sarah approvingly.

For the first ten minutes, Charles acted as though he'd been unexpectedly called upon to defuse a bomb, blindfold, with a clock ticking, no instruction manual and oven gloves taped to his hands. But gradually he calmed down and even gathered the courage to entwine his fingers with Sarah's under the table.

By the time Sarah got round to tackling the issue at hand, they were all enjoying generous helpings of the Ship's excellent beef bourguignon, just the thing to warm you up on a blustery day.

'So... you will have heard about Daffyd Jones?' she started.

'Yes, poor blighter. Who'd have thought he'd feel so bad about all his bullying?' Gwendoline said, cutting her beef up into tiny pieces and putting a morsel in her mouth.

Sarah raised her eyebrows. 'You think it was suicide?'

'Of course.' Gwendoline shrugged. 'What else could it be?'

Daphne, across the table, leapt into the space left by Sarah's silence. 'You wouldn't know where he got the gun, would you, Gwen?'

'Me?' Gwen washed her stew down with a mouthful of Merlot. 'Why should I?'

'Well, it's just that you spend time over at Francesca's place for all the carol rehearsals... let's face it, you two have a lot in common,' Daphne said with a suspicion of a wink. 'Maybe you saw the keys in the garage?'

As Gwendoline stared at Daphne, Sarah leapt in. 'I think what Daphne means is—'

'I know what she means. And what the three of you are up to, coming in here after all this time,' said Gwendoline. All signs of her dimple had disappeared and she was working up quite a head of steam. 'For your information, Sarah Vane, I had no knowledge at all of Charles's gun cupboard so I can't possibly have had anything to do with what you're alleging.'

With that, Gwendoline picked up her drink, swigged back the remnants, and swept out of the pub, her little boots clicking on the shiny tiles as she departed in high dudgeon.

'Well, that's that, then,' said Daphne glumly, looking down at her cleaned plate. 'And now you've seen Gwennie's nasty temper, too, all for nothing. She didn't have a clue about the keys. I hope Claire Scroggins doesn't find out we've been consorting with the enemy.'

'If she does, maybe she'll up her game and the food at the Jolly Roger might improve,' said Sarah bracingly. 'As for Gwendoline, I really wouldn't be too sure she isn't involved. I'm certainly not letting her off the hook.'

Charles looked at her, astonished. 'What do you mean? She said quite categorically that she didn't know anything about the gun cupboard.'

'Yes, she did,' Sarah said crisply. 'That's exactly what I mean.'

Daphne threw down her scarf in frustration. 'It's obvious Gwen is in the clear. We need to find another suspect,' she said.

'Not yet,' Sarah said. 'Don't you see?'

'See what, dear lady?' Charles's blue eyes looked hazy with the effort of understanding her.

'Just this. Did you mention a gun cupboard to Gwendoline, Daph?' Daphne shook her head. 'Charles?' Charles did the same. 'Exactly,' said Sarah. 'So... how come she knew all about it?'

SEVENTEEN

Sarah, Charles and Daphne looked at each other, one with the clear-sighted gaze of someone who'd just pulled off something rather clever, the others with dawning comprehension.

'Oh my goodness, you're right,' Daphne said, delving into her bag and throwing a paperback book, a water bottle and a half-finished bag of crisps onto the table.

'What are you doing, Daph?' Sarah asked her, rather dreading what was going to be flung in front of them next.

'What do you think? I'm going to ring Mari and get her to arrest Gwen, that's what!'

'I say, come on,' said Charles, squirming in his seat.

Sarah looked at him with interest, then spoke up. 'That could be a little premature, Daph. Let's think about this.'

'Think? How can I possibly think when I'm almost dying of dehydration?' Daphne said in martyred tones, holding out her empty glass.

'All right. I'll get another round. Then we can have a proper ponder.'

'Let me, dear ladies,' Charles said, shooting up.

As he rushed over to the bar, Daphne looked over at him.

'Do you think he's trying to take your mind off the whole Gwen thing?'

'Which bit of the Gwen thing? The fact that he didn't mention her to me at all, or that she might be a murder suspect?' Sarah said drily.

'Well I must say, you're taking it pretty well,' Daphne said, settling her scarf more securely. 'I thought you'd go nuts at the idea of yet another notch on Charles's bedpost. But you don't seem that keen to have her taken into custody.'

Sarah looked at her friend in surprise. 'I don't have a right to control Charles's past. Anything that happened before I got here is between him and, er, that bedpost, I suppose. And I can't just get people arrested for having flings with Charles. The jails would be full.'

Daphne snorted. 'That's my girl.'

Sarah was silent for a moment. 'Still, it would have been nice to have had a heads-up,' she said. 'You didn't mention her at all. And, er, why did they split up, do you know?' she added, keeping her tone casual.

'I don't think it was because she was a homicidal maniac, if that's what you're thinking,' Daphne said. 'But then, you really can't tell in Merstairs these days.'

At this, Sarah met Daphne's eye and the two couldn't help giggling, despite the seriousness of the situation.

'I feel better after that,' said Sarah quietly to Daphne, dabbing her eyes as Charles finally came back with the drinks.

'Here we are, ladies,' he said, depositing the glasses with a flourish. 'This should see us right,' he said, taking his seat and holding his own pint aloft.

Sarah saluted him with her tonic, which was garnished not with the usual limp piece of lemon offered by the Jolly Roger, but with a mass of dainty twists of lime peel, and several large chunks of ice. When she took a sip, it tasted even better than it looked. But Charles was about to ruin all that.

'I've been thinking while getting the drinks in. I realise I may have... mentioned the gun cupboard to Gwennie, erm, Gwendoline.' He said, fiddling with the beer mat on the table in front of him. 'That will be how she knew about it.'

'Oh? Oh,' said Sarah, feeling curiously deflated. 'I see. Did you really?'

'Well, she was showing some interest in my collection,' he said, studying the table carefully. 'She thought it sounded very fine.'

'I bet she did,' said Daphne. Sarah glared at her, and Charles continued.

'So of course I got talking about the rest of the collection and I, well, I told her where they used to be kept at Francesca's, and at my shop and, um, where the keys were, too.'

Sarah tried not to sigh. 'Well, that doesn't quite get her off the suspect list yet, but it does make her seem less suspicious. Do you remember the context?'

Now Charles swivelled miserably in his seat. 'I may have... I think I probably showed her my blunderbusses.'

Daphne gave a gasp of laughter, which she turned into an unconvincing cough when both Sarah and Charles turned to look at her.

'I see,' said Sarah, a little tight-lipped. 'Well, I suppose that pretty much rules *Gwennie* out. Plus there was no sign of her anywhere near the rehearsal. I'm not sure I believe hijacking the Christmas carols at the lights ceremony is a good enough motive for murder anyway. So, who else could have done it? Was there anyone in the choir, Daphne, do you think? Someone who nipped out during that phase when we were all supposed to be listening to the dratted Hallelujah Chorus?'

'Gosh, it was so loud, wasn't it?' Daphne screwed her face up at the memory.

Charles, recovering from the embarrassment of his revelation about Gwendoline, sounded tentative. 'I say, Daffyd chose that music, didn't he? And it covered up the sound of the gunshot. So maybe it really was suicide after all...'

Sarah put her head on one side. 'The trouble is, the gun couldn't have walked out of the room on its own.'

Daphne, meanwhile, was having another go at disinterring her phone from her bag. 'I wonder if Deirdre snaffled it! She had that funny bag round her neck, remember? And she certainly had a motive to kill Daffyd, he was always horrid to her. This time I really am going to ring Mari,' she said, and before Sarah could get a word in, she had dialled and was striding outside to take the call.

'I hope Mariella isn't too cross, she doesn't usually love our input during an investigation,' Sarah said.

'I'd say Mari has more reason to be grateful lately than to complain,' Charles twinkled at her. 'After all, she'd still be in uniform being bossed around by that brace of idiots if it wasn't for some of your bright ideas.'

'*Our* bright ideas,' Sarah said modestly, while inwardly rather agreeing with Charles. 'But I bet she'd prefer it if we didn't go around questioning people.'

'Yes, like poor Gwennie, erm, Gwendoline. She took it rather well, I thought,' Charles said, sipping his pint.

Sarah, with a vivid mental image of Gwendoline storming out of the pub, decided she and Charles must have very different ideas about what a successful interrogation looked like. In Sarah's view, the suspect staying put was essential, for a start.

Just then, Daphne burst back into the pub, putting almost as much energy into her reappearance as Gwendoline had done with her exit. 'Well, honestly! You change their nappies for years, and that's all the thanks you get,' she said, taking a hefty swig of her Dubonnet. 'I don't want to say my own daughter is a monster of ingratitude, but she really takes the biscuit,' she added darkly.

Sarah couldn't help smiling. 'I take it Mariella didn't exactly thank you for your suggestion?'

'She did not! If I ever hear another word out of this ear it will be a miracle,' said Daphne. 'Mind you, Daffyd was such a tricksy man, I wouldn't put it past him to pretend to kill himself and then hide the weapon afterwards.'

'Well, I would,' said Sarah drily. 'He really wouldn't have been doing much of anything after that shot,' she added, patting Daphne's arm. Her friend made a moue of disgust. 'Sorry, Daph, I do wonder if someone forced Daffyd to shoot himself, though? That would leave the shot at the right angle.'

'In that case, why wouldn't they leave the gun and the phone?' Charles asked.

'It doesn't add up,' said Sarah, her spirits unaccountably rising. 'It's illogical. And there was one person at the scene who was acting in a particularly irrational manner. I think you might just have had a really brilliant idea, Daphne.'

'Have I? I mean, of course I have,' said Daphne, beaming. Then her face fell. 'But, erm, what was it again?'

'Just that there's one very obvious person we need to talk to next. Right, let's go,' said Sarah, getting to her feet.

EIGHTEEN

'I'm really not sure about this,' said Daphne as she and Sarah strode up the road.

'Come on, Daph, it was your clever notion,' Sarah said bracingly. 'You just suggested it to Mari, after all.'

'Yes... but I wanted the police to do the questioning, not us,' said Daphne.

'Look,' said Sarah. 'Like you said, Deirdre was the person who knew Daffyd Jones best, and one of the last people to see him alive. And she was acting oddly, and had a pouch round her neck that could have contained the murder weapon. If anyone has an insight on what happened, it's going to be her.'

'But please don't ask her anything too awful,' said Daphne. 'She's grieving, it wouldn't be right.'

'Murder's the thing that's not right,' Sarah said. 'Now, where does she live?'

'Oh, they've got a place on the esplanade. One of those wonderful houses with the bowed fronts that you're always gawping at on our walks,' Daphne said reluctantly.

'OK then.' Sarah hitched her bag onto her shoulder. 'No time like the present.'

'You let Charles off, though,' Daphne remonstrated.

'You heard what he said, He needed to reopen his shop,' Sarah said, raising her eyebrows.

'Oh honestly,' said Daphne. 'Well, all right. I suppose I can offer her some spiritual comfort. It's so awful, what that woman must be going through. And after Daffyd led her a merry dance for so long... She should have divorced him at the height of his fame, then she could have started again.'

'Surely he was at his most popular when he was about thirteen? As a chorister, with that lovely pure voice. They can't have got married until many years later,' Sarah said practically as they reached the esplanade.

'Oh well, you know what I mean,' Daphne said. 'She should have divorced him a long time before she killed him. Before things got to the grumpy stage. Ah, here we are. This is the place,' Daphne announced, pointing to a fine white stucco-covered building in a parade of houses with magnificent bow windows. They looked like a row of pigeons, puffing out their chests to impress the sea.

'The views must be amazing,' Sarah sighed, taking in the splendour of the house, then turning back to the waves currently pummelling the coast.

Daphne squared her shoulders. 'Let's get this done, then.'

'Only if you're totally sure, Daph. I can go solo,' Sarah said.

'No. I'll be fine. We need to do this as a team,' Daphne said, throwing her scarf over her shoulder. 'We've got Hamish with us, haven't we? He'll look after us.'

Hearing his name, Hamish wagged his little tail frantically. He wasn't exactly a guard dog, but surely not even a murderer could resist his charm. The little group trooped up the slight hill towards the white house. As they got closer, its windows sparkled in the faint sunshine. Flanking the front door were two stone urns, which probably looked splendid in summer when filled with a bright display of bedding plants. Now each boasted a solitary and rather sickly-looking stunted fir tree. Someone had attempted to jolly them up by putting brightly coloured baubles on them, but in the circumstances these struck rather a sorry note.

Daphne marched up the wide Georgian steps, grabbing hold of the dolphin-shaped door knocker and letting it fall. The noise was tremendous, and for a while all was silent inside the house. Then Sarah heard a shuffling sound. The door creaked open, and Deidre's pinched little face peered round it. 'Not today,' she started to say, and was about to swing the door shut again, when Sarah stepped over the threshold.

'We're so sorry to disturb you, Deirdre, I'm Sarah from the, er, choir, if you remember... and this is Daphne Roux of course. Oh, and my dog, Hamish.'

Deirdre stared at her, uncomprehending, and Sarah was sure she was about to try and shut the door again, right in her face, when Hamish padded towards her and sat down on the mat, extending a paw as though asking to shake hands. This was a trick Sarah had never seen him do before, and she was almost as startled as Deirdre.

'Well, you're a cutie and no mistake,' the woman almost whispered, seemingly snapped out of her misery for a moment by the antics of the dog. She bent down to shake his paw and stroke his head, then looked up again at Sarah and Daphne. 'What is this about? It's not a good time.'

Her voice, now that Sarah could hear it properly, was rather beautiful. It was very quiet, it was true, and when Daffyd had been around with all his bombast and histrionics, it had been hard to focus on what she was saying. But now, with her overbearing husband out of the way, Sarah was left thinking that Deirdre, too, must have had a lovely singing voice in her day. 'We just wanted to have a chat, really. To try and make sense of what went on last night. It must all be so terrible for you.'

'It is. It's awful, you can't imagine,' said Deirdre, dissolving into tears. 'I miss Daffyd so much. I can't think that talking to you two is going to make things any better.'

'It might shed light on how it all happened, though. Isn't that what you want? We thought it could be useful,' said Sarah, handing Deirdre a tissue from her bag, and hoping against hope she would let them in. 'It's really cold out here,' she added, with a bit of a theatrical shiver.

'Oh, come in if you must,' Deirdre said with a shrug. 'It's all the same to me. I suppose you'll be wanting tea?'

'I'll make it,' said Daphne brightly. 'Kitchen downstairs in the basement, is it? I'll only be a jiffy,' she said, taking off with a jangle of bracelets.

Sarah, now resigned to quite a wait before they got a cuppa, followed Deirdre into the sitting room. It was a magnificent space, with a high ceiling and those amazing floor-to-ceiling windows giving out onto the Kent coast. She couldn't help but feel the furniture in the room let it down. It consisted of a very standard, blocky three-piece leather suite of sofa and two chairs, with a long, low dark wooden coffee table in the middle, nothing wrong with any of it, except everything looked rather new and lumpy within the classical Georgian proportions of the room.

There were a couple of big fake plants, of the type you got in offices, positioned on either side of the chairs. Again, someone had tried to liven these up with a handful of baubles and a bit of tinsel, and there was a single card on the mantelpiece featuring robins and holly. Sarah couldn't help thinking it wasn't that festive, for a family which owed its income to a much-loved Christmas song. A large television was pushed up against the windows, slightly obscuring the view, and one of the chairs had an array of complicated-looking remote controls balancing on the arm rest, as well as a pair of men's glasses and a copy of the *Racing Post* folded on the seat.

Sarah looked towards what had evidently been Daffyd's usual chair, and said, 'I'm so sorry for your loss,' to Deirdre.

Deirdre sniffed a sob and gestured to the sofa. She was wearing another drab woolly dress today, with the same pouch dangling round her neck and yesterday's diamanté brooch. Sarah wondered about that. Somehow the sparkliness of it seemed out of character with the woman in front of her. And there was something else about it that was nagging at her... She sat down somewhat gingerly on the shiny leather sofa while the grieving widow took the second of the two armchairs.

Sarah was racking her brains for a way of opening up the ticklish subject she wanted to discuss – something along the lines of 'So, Mrs Jones, even if you didn't kill your husband, did you take his phone, and where is the murder weapon?' – when her musings were interrupted by a loud crash from downstairs.

Deirdre jumped a foot, as though someone had inadvertently plugged her into the mains, then put a hand to her chest, making an effort to calm her laboured breathing. Interesting, thought Sarah, while going over to pat her gently on the back. Granted, the noise had been pretty dramatic, but she'd done a training course a few years ago on the signs of domestic violence. Hypervigilance, or oversensitivity to sounds and gestures, was a common trait amongst abused women.

'Sounds like Daphne's having fun down there,' Sarah said lightly, hoping to raise a smile.

Deirdre turned a hunted glance to her. 'What do you mean?' she asked fearfully.

Sarah was searching for a reply when Daphne's voice fluted up to them. 'No need to panic! Just, um, a saucepan falling. Oops, there goes another,' she said as there was a further crash. 'I'll be up in two ticks.'

It did not have the desired effect. Deirdre shot to her feet. 'What is that woman doing down there?' she said distractedly as she made for the door.

This was pretty much the question Sarah was asking herself, but instead she adopted a cheery tone. 'Oh, you know

Daphne! She'll be along in no time with the tea, like she said. While we're waiting, we might as well get comfortable,' she said, sitting down on the large sofa and patting the seat next to her.

The fight seemed to go out of Deirdre immediately, like air escaping from a popped balloon, and she subsided back into her original chair, looking as though she'd just had a good telling off. This must be the result of years of mistreatment. The poor thing now always assumed she was in the wrong, and meekly did as she was told, even though Daphne running amok in the kitchen would have sent most people running to defend their property.

'Let's, erm, take our minds off the tea and have a chat,' said Sarah, bolder now that she'd realised Deirdre had very little capacity to resist a stronger will. It was awful, taking advantage of her at such a vulnerable time – but this could be a vital opportunity to close the case quickly. 'I'm sorry to raise this, when you must be feeling so awful, but I do need to ask you a few questions about what happened to poor Daffyd. Is that OK?' she asked.

Deirdre sat mutely with her head bowed, so Sarah decided to take this as permission of a sort. 'This is awful, but I wanted to try and understand how on earth there was a gun involved in what happened. Did Daffyd have an interest in weapons?'

Deirdre shrunk even further into herself. 'Weapons? I don't know what you're talking about,' she said quickly, averting her gaze from Sarah and staring fixedly at Daffyd's empty chair.

'Well, one did get into that room with him somehow.' Sarah's voice was gentle. 'Would you have any idea how that happened? Could Daffyd perhaps have kept any firearms in the house, for example?'

This time, Deirdre swivelled to look at Sarah as if she were mad. 'Of course not. Why would he do that? And where on earth would we get a gun from?'

'Well, that's what I was wondering. Did you know, for example, that Charles Diggory has one?'

'Charles? From the antique shop?' Deirdre passed a weary hand over her face. 'None of this is making any sense. Why would Charles have a gun?'

'And why would he give it to Dad, to kill himself?' came a voice from the doorway.

Now it was Sarah's moment to turn so fast she almost gave herself whiplash. 'Goodness me, Matthew! I had no idea you were in the house.'

Matthew Jones stood staring at her, still in his sling and the same fawn-coloured jumper. It looked more washed out and unflattering than ever, while she could have sworn his hair had receded since they had last seen him on the beach, the few curling strands clinging to his scalp like seaweed as the tide went out.

'Um, I don't think you have any right to come here and interrogate my mother, however well meaning you might be,' he said, not looking Sarah in the eye. 'The p-police are supposed to be sending an officer to sit with us. Hopefully they'll protect us from stuff like this.'

Thank goodness, Daphne arrived at this moment, heralded by the merry clatter from the loaded tea tray she was bearing in front of her. 'Matthew! How lovely. Just pop down and get an extra cup, would you?'

To Sarah's surprise, after wavering for a second, he did just that, turning away from Sarah and almost bobbing his head at Daphne as he passed her. The Joneses were a very odd bunch, she decided.

Daphne put the tray down on the coffee table with a hearty sigh. 'There! That weighed a ton. I found some nice china hiding at the back of a cupboard and look, there's biscuits,' she said, waving a plate at Deirdre, as proud as though she'd baked them herself.

'That's Daffyd's mother's tea set,' Deirdre said in horror, looking at the rather sombre sage green plates and cups. 'Oh, I don't know if we should...' But then she tailed off, and for the first time, a tiny glimmer of a smile peeped out on her careworn face. 'Well. I suppose we can. After all, no one's going to complain, are they?'

'I should think not,' said Daphne heartily, sloshing tea into a cup and passing it to Deirdre. 'It's all yours now, isn't it?'

The realisation seemed to sink in a bit, as Deirdre added sugar and stirred her cup slowly. 'I suppose so,' she said just as Matthew came back into the room.

'Matthew, there you are. Like a nice cup?' Daphne gestured to him with the teapot and he went over meekly. A few moments later they were all settled with their tea, Daphne chomping heavily on a Ginger Nut. 'These are a bit hard,' she said, putting a hand to her jaw. 'Watch your teeth, everyone. So, have you asked them, Sarah?'

'Asked them what?' said Matthew, looking from Sarah to Daphne and back again.

'Why, who hated your dad enough to kill him, of course,' said Daphne, looking astonished that this hadn't been the number one topic of conversation. 'Or maybe it was one of you two?' she asked, crunching her biscuit.

NINETEEN

To say the silence that followed Daphne's comment was chilly would have been an understatement. Matthew stood up. 'Right, I-I'm sorry, but that's it. It's time you two left,' he said, still not making eye contact.

Deirdre seemed to shrink into herself at his raised tone. Sarah felt fleetingly sorry for her, but realised if they were going to get anywhere in their enquiries, she had to make a case for them staying.

'We'll be very happy to go,' she prevaricated, silencing Daphne with a look. 'It's just that we need to make sure of a few things first. Of course, we don't really think either of you were involved in Daffyd's death,' she said, with a slightly insincere smile. 'But, you may not be aware but, um, Charles Diggory is in quite big trouble right now.'

'What's that got to do with us? Don't you think we've got enough on our plates right now without worrying about him?' said Matthew, flopping down again into his seat.

'Talking of plates, does anyone mind if I just...' said Daphne, her hand sneaking out to capture another Ginger Nut.

'Seriously, Mother, aren't you going to put your foot down?'

Matthew turned to Deirdre. 'Why did you let these two in anyway?' His usual downtrodden manner was now overlaid with peevishness.

Daphne almost choked on the biscuit she was loudly biting into, but Sarah held a hand up. 'Matthew, I quite understand your emotions are raw right now. You've just lost your father. But you must be as keen as we are to get to the bottom of all this. If it wasn't you who took the gun from Charles Diggory, then who was it?'

'Diggory?' said Matthew quickly. 'Why on earth would he give me a gun?'

'Oh, but Matthew—' Deirdre started, and then fell silent as all eyes converged on her. 'And you're in that group... That is, oh, I don't know what I'm saying, ignore me.'

'We definitely don't want to do that, Deirdre,' said Sarah. 'I have a feeling you've been overlooked all too often in the past. Time to change that. Your voice deserves to be heard, as much as anyone else's. Now, what was it that you were about to tell us?' she coaxed.

All eyes were on Deidre. She seemed to sink into her chair, desperate to merge with the buff-coloured cushions and avoid scrutiny. 'Oh— it's just that, well...'

Sarah reached over and patted her hand. Although she could feel the woman almost wincing at her touch, it seemed to give her strength. 'Go on,' Sarah said gently.

This time, Deirdre lifted her eyes to Matthew's. 'Well, Matt. You do know Charles Diggory. I don't know why you'd pretend. You used to work for him, for goodness' sake. There's no point trying to cover it up, it'll come out as soon as the police start to look into it all.'

This showed quite a healthy faith in the Merstairs police, Sarah thought. While it was certainly true that Mariella would get to the bottom of things, she wouldn't be surprised if anything delegated to the two PCs disappeared like the lost city of Atlantis.

Matthew, meanwhile, let out a gusty sigh. 'Oh, Mother. I used to work with him ages ago but that doesn't mean I know anything about his gun collection now, does it?'

'You did mention he had guns to us, Matthew,' Sarah reminded him. 'And you didn't say you'd worked with him. At the shop, do you mean?'

Matthew smirked. 'Ha! No.'

Sarah, who often thought of Charles's antiques emporium in quite dark terms, felt herself bristling. 'He does a good trade,' she said. Daphne arched her eyebrows at her, but Sarah remained firm.

Matthew ducked his head to avoid a confrontation. 'I'm talking about when he was still working in the City. As a stockbroker.'

Sarah remembered Charles mentioning this every now and then. It made sense of the fact that he was able to keep going with his shop despite the dearth of customers – and why he owned such a lovely flat further down the esplanade. 'I see. So you know Charles really well, then. Plenty of opportunity to discuss hobbies and so on.'

Matthew shrugged. 'Well, I suppose so. Yes, I knew Charles liked guns but I had no idea he had a cupboard full of them in his shop.'

At this, Daphne started so much her scarf started to unravel. Sarah gave her a stern warning glance, and she confined herself to trying to rearrange it with a tut. Deirdre watched them both, her face blank. Matthew, meanwhile, continued to describe the high-octane world of stockbroking. 'We scarcely had time for lunch most days. Working round the clock.'

'Sounds awful. You must have been glad to give it up,' Sarah observed mildly. Such a diffident man must have found the cut and thrust of the money market difficult.

'Oh no, you were quite upset, weren't you, when Charles had to let you go,' Deirdre chipped in.

'It wasn't like that, Mother,' Matthew said. 'Anyway, I can't help feeling we've taken up *far* too much of your time,' he said to Sarah and Daphne. 'And the police will be round again, as I said. I'm sure they wouldn't be at all pleased to find you here.'

'Actually, I need to have a word with Mari, so maybe we should stay?' Daphne said, appearing to relax into her seat again.

Sarah shook her head briefly. 'I think it's probably time we were going, Daphne. Well, thank you so much, Deirdre. And so sorry again for your terrible loss,' she said to them both.

Hamish, who'd been curled up very politely at her feet throughout, paused to give Deirdre's hand a quick lick on the way out. What a good boy he was, thought Sarah.

As soon as they were outside, and back down on the esplanade again, Daphne turned to Sarah. 'Well! Did you hear that? About Charles's gun collection? How did Matthew know it was in a cupboard in the shop? He gave himself away, just like Gwendoline Randall. Do you think he did it? Should I ring Mari and get her to pick him up?'

Sarah put a hand on Daphne's arm. 'Hold your horses. The trouble is, I'm beginning to feel that an awful lot of people know about Charles's gun collection. Maybe he hasn't been that discreet about it. Did you know he had guns, for instance?'

'Well of course I'd heard about it over the years, but I didn't really think anything of it,' Daphne said. 'But I'm one of the inner circle, of course. You'd expect him to tell me.'

Sarah pondered this. 'But Matthew? I mean, if Charles sacked him quite a while ago, would he have told him something like that?'

'I wouldn't tell that boy where I put my butter knives, but that's me, the soul of discretion, you know,' said Daphne with a sniff. 'Like I was telling Flo, I take my secrets to the grave. But from what Matthew was saying, it sounds like Charles gets a bit of a kick out of boasting about this collection of his.'

'Hmm.' Sarah was thoughtful. Boastfulness wasn't a character trait she admired particularly. Her late husband, Peter, hadn't had a boastful bone in his body. It would be a terrible shame if Charles turned out to be the sort of person who couldn't resist showing off. She hadn't noticed this about him so far – but then, how well did she really know him?

That was a question she was beginning to ask herself more and more as this investigation went on.

TWENTY

Sarah was still preoccupied as they strolled home. Probably the best thing to do would simply be to have it out with Charles. But could their fledgling relationship stand the strain of such a direct confrontation? She hesitated to use the phrase 'honeymoon period' when there was no question of marriage on the horizon – as far as she knew – but they hadn't been together long. Things had been pretty lovey-dovey, and real life hadn't impinged much on their time together. If she accused Charles of talking to all and sundry about his guns, how would he react? Would he be furious, or would he brush it off elegantly? She was hoping for the latter – but was worried she might get the former.

It took Daphne jogging her arm to bring her out of her reverie, just as they approached the paths up to both their cottages. There was someone waiting on her doorstep.

The few golden gleams of light they'd enjoyed earlier were fading fast, and the wintry afternoon was getting quite dark. 'Who on earth is that?' whispered Sarah to Daphne, suddenly feeling a frisson of fear. The figure was tall, shapeless, quite large – it was impossible to tell if it was male or female. Hamish, at Sarah's side, let out a very low growl – one of the type he usually reserved for Mephisto. Sarah dropped a soothing hand on his head as Daphne peered forward into the gathering twilight.

Then she stood back and laughed loudly. 'Oh, come on, Sarah! You had me going then. It's only Matilda!'

'Who?' Sarah said warily.

'From the choir, you know,' Daphne said, then added in her loudest whisper, 'the one who got sacked last night as our soloist, just before Daffyd got shot.'

On Sarah's doorstep, the tall figure laughed too, and moved forward a little. The streetlight shone on her fluffy fun fur, and Sarah realised why she'd looked such a threatening shape – and possibly why Hamish had growled. The coat really was enormous, and the blue looked very dark now night was falling. 'Daphne, I'd recognise that voice a mile away. Any chance of a cuppa? I just wanted to talk to you, well, about everything that went on last night.'

'Actually, this is my house, not Daphne's,' Sarah said, making her way up to the door and getting out the keys. 'But yes, absolutely, we'd love to hear what you've got to say. And I think tea is what we all need.'

* * *

A few minutes later, everyone was settled at Sarah's scrubbed kitchen table. Hamish was in his basket by the cooker, and a large pot of tea was centre stage, swaddled in an immense rainbow-hued cosy crocheted by Daphne.

Daphne peered forward at the tray. 'Oh, you've forgotten something, Sarah. I'll just get it,' she said, shooting up and rummaging in a few cupboards. Finally, like a conjuror pulling a rabbit out of a hat, she produced the packet of extra-special chocolate biscuits Sarah had tucked away for her granddaughters' next visit. 'There we go,' she said, tearing open the package, taking one and then somewhat belatedly offering them round.

'Thanks, Daphne,' said Sarah drily. 'Now, Matilda, what is it we can do for you?'

The atmosphere in the room became sombre. 'It's about last night,' Matilda said, refusing a biscuit with a shudder.

'As the actress said to the bishop,' snorted Daphne, munching away and most definitely unaffected by the change of mood.

Sarah gave Daphne a look and turned again to Matilda. 'It must have been a very uncomfortable evening for you, even before the tragedy. Can I just say, I thought your solo was wonderful.'

'Oh, thank you,' said Matilda, clasping her hands. Her large mouth turned up in a smile, but it was tremulous, and it wasn't long before she was looking downcast again. 'But I can't believe what's happened to Daffyd. Who knew he was feeling that depressed?'

'Hmm,' Sarah said quietly.

'I mean, one moment he was full of all that rage, having such a go at me. Then the next minute... Well, maybe it was remorse.' Matilda shook her head sadly.

'Did he ever strike you as the kind of person who'd, well, kill themselves?' Sarah asked.

'No, not at all. He always seemed so full of energy, so dynamic. If it had been his wife, it's awful to say it, but Deirdre's such a mouse really. It's as though she's had the life sucked out of her. If she'd decided she'd had enough, well, no one would have been very surprised.'

'So you think the wrong person died?' Sarah was thoughtful.

'Oh, I wouldn't say that.' Matilda seemed startled at the idea. 'It's just that it was such a shock. I can't pretend I really liked the man – well, you saw what he was like to me. But his passing does leave a void,' Matilda said, clasping her hands round her mug of tea.

'What if it wasn't suicide, would that seem more plausible?' Sarah said carefully. 'From the sounds of it, there were a few people Daffyd had picked on in the past. Perhaps one of them got fed up? Deirdre, for example. Sometimes the worm turns – um, not that I want to compare her with a creepy crawly,' Sarah added.

Matilda looked startled. 'What are you talking about? What's the point in thinking about different ways it could have happened? He killed himself, and that's that.'

'I'm not sure it is, though,' Sarah said gently. 'You might want to consider that.'

Matilda turned first to Daphne, then back to Sarah again, as though to get some sort of confirmation that didn't materialise. 'You are joking, aren't you? This isn't a laughing matter. If Daffyd didn't kill himself, that would mean...'

'Well yes, exactly,' said Sarah when Matilda's voice had entirely tailed off. 'Someone else did it.'

'But how? He was alone in there, with a gun, and now he's dead. It's obvious, isn't it?' Matilda looked from Sarah to Daphne and back again.

'It's not quite that clear cut. Someone could have, erm, helped him to do it – or forced him,' Sarah said.

There was a pause, while Matilda digested the implications of what had been said. Then Sarah spoke again. 'You didn't like Daffyd much, did you?'

Matilda reared up like a scalded cat. 'Me? *Me?* What are you saying? You can't possibly think I had anything to do with this.'

Sarah shrugged. 'We saw the way he treated you last night. You had every right to be very angry with him. You stormed off, after all.'

Matilda seemed to seize on Sarah's words. 'Yes, I left. I went off in a huff. I admit it. I turned my back on him and waltzed out of the hall and I had no intention of ever going back. So there you have it. I wasn't even on the premises when he... when whatever happened, happened.'

Sarah shrugged. 'Except that you could easily have nipped back inside. And in fact you did, didn't you? There was no one on the door at that point, checking who was coming and going. You could have sneaked round to the green room where Daffyd was killed, and no one would have been any the wiser.'

'Steady on, Sarah,' Daphne said. 'This is Matilda we're talking about. She's not very likely to have done that, is she?'

'Why not?' Sarah said. 'Someone did. And Matilda was the only one Daffyd humiliated in public that night.'

'What about Deirdre?' Matilda said quickly. 'Everything Daffyd did was designed to show how much contempt he had for her. The way he stood in front of her all the time... the endless snarky comments... she had just as good a motive as me, you have to admit that.'

Sarah couldn't ignore the justice of this. Then Daphne chipped in.

'He was also vile about the sopranos that night. Not to mention the tenors. Honestly, Sarah, the more you think about it, the longer the list is. No one really liked Daffyd. He was such a meanie.'

'That's the irony,' said Matilda sadly. 'I did really like him, for a long while.' She lowered her eyes. 'I even thought, at one point,' she said with a little sob, 'that he might leave Deirdre.'

'Goodness,' said Daphne. 'You mean you were having, um...'

'An affair? Yes. We were,' said Matilda.

TWENTY-ONE

'I don't want you to get the idea that there was anything sordid between Daffyd and me. We were in love,' Matilda said with a reminiscent look on her face. 'But Deirdre, wet blanket that she is, still had a hold on him. I don't understand why or how, but she wouldn't let go. That woman had a death grip. Oh, I shouldn't have said that.' She bowed her head and tears trickled down her face.

Sarah and Daphne looked at each other in consternation. They were getting valuable nuggets of information for the investigation, it was true – but neither had bargained for turning up an illicit affair, nor having such an overwrought soprano on their hands. Luckily, Daphne rose to the occasion.

'Now then, Matilda, you just let it all out,' she said, scooting her chair over to the other woman's side and clamping an arm around her. 'Sarah will get you some tissues – and a fresh cup of tea, oh, and why not another biscuit while you're at it, Sarah – and you just tell us all about it.'

Sarah put the kettle on. This really wasn't how she'd expected to be spending her evening. But then, it was probably a whole lot better than confronting Charles about why half of Merstairs knew about his gun collection.

* * *

Sarah and Daphne soon started to get the full picture about Matilda's relationship with Daffyd Jones. In many ways, it was the old story – a man in a position of some power, overpromising and underdelivering. He'd sworn blind his marriage was finished... until he'd had enough of his new love, that was. Then he'd taken refuge in his tattered vows to Deirdre. She was 'too frail' to leave; she depended on him. Who knew what she would do if Matilda forced Daffyd to live up to his promises? And did Matilda want that on her conscience?

Matilda, who despite her towering stature and forthright manner, turned out to be a very sensitive soul, had not taken Daffyd's betrayal well. 'I didn't think for a moment he'd ever go back to his wife. Not after he'd kept on telling me how awful their relationship was,' she sniffed to Daphne and Sarah, a tissue clamped to her brimming eyes. 'He was poisonous about her, about how she couldn't live up to his image, about how she didn't enjoy, you know, *that* side of things,' she said delicately. 'He told me that his musical genius could only flourish with me, that I was his muse,' she said, lifting eyes glittering with tears to the two women. 'Then, from one day to the next, it was all over and he never wanted to see me again,' she wailed. 'Apart from at choir, of course. And only then because he knew I could help him win all the trophies he coveted.'

Sarah murmured comforting words and Daphne hugged her, but they exchanged a glance while she was deep in yet another tissue. The poor woman. Things had turned out very much the way they usually did, with broken promises and a man running back to his wife, who might not have had any idea an affair was going on. That had to be a point worth checking up on.

'Do you think, um, Deirdre realised... that Daffyd might be straying?' Sarah asked gently.

It was the wrong tack to take. Matilda was outraged. 'He wasn't just *straying*, as you put it. We were actually engaged,' she said with dignity.

'But he was still with Deirdre, wasn't he?' Daphne wrinkled her nose. 'Can you get engaged while you're married?'

'I think Henry VIII did it a couple of times,' said Sarah.

Not surprisingly, this didn't go down well with Matilda. 'I know how it looks,' she wailed. 'But this wasn't just some fling. He gave me a ring.' She brandished her hand, upon which gleamed a large green stone.

'Goodness, is that an emerald?' Daphne asked, squinting at the stone. 'It's massive.'

'I think it's a type of onyx, actually,' Matilda said with quiet dignity.

'And it's not on your left hand, I can't help noticing,' Sarah added.

'Well, we couldn't go public,' Matilda said. 'So I wore it on my right... but that doesn't alter the fact that what we had was special. Really special,' she said solemnly.

Sarah raised her eyebrows. People had been murdering their 'special' partners for millennia – mostly men, it was true, but women rose to the occasion and killed their lovers every now and then. 'I wonder why Daffyd was being so mean to you at the choir practice. In view of everything we now know about your, um, great relationship?'

Matilda started to cry again. 'Well, it wasn't nearly so good once he went back to Deirdre, of course. I was angry. Very angry. I took every opportunity I could to make my feelings plain. I'd often go out of tune during solos just to annoy him –

only during rehearsals. I missed that note last night, just to wind him up. But I never did it during performances. That would have been too much. And I took up with Ewan as well.'

'Yes, lovely Ewan.' Daphne clapped her hands together. 'Surely he took your mind off Daffyd? You can't possibly have preferred Daffyd to him?'

Matilda had the grace to look a little shamefaced. 'The heart wants what it wants.'

The thought of Ewan had given Sarah an idea, though. 'By the way, as Ewan is a plasterer, has he ever done any work for a company called Merstairs Mortar?' she asked Matilda.

'Not that I know of. But I don't keep track.' Matilda was dismissive.

'And you've not had any dealings with them?' Sarah sipped her tea.

'Why would I? Ewan does everything round the house. He's great at DIY, even if he doesn't have Daffyd's charisma.'

Sarah and Daphne looked at each other for a second. It was indeed proof that love was an unfathomable mystery. On the face of it the handsome plasterer was so much more of a catch than a nasty, middle-aged bully. But there you were.

'So you were still pretty furious with Daffyd, even though it looked as though you'd moved on. Were you angry enough to, um, do something drastic?' Sarah asked gently.

'What, you mean like keying his car that time?' Matilda said, a blush rising to her cheeks. 'I didn't know anyone realised that was me. He'd told me he was going to a hotel on his own for a break, to get over us – then I saw him check in with *her*. I couldn't believe he'd told me yet another lie.'

It was interesting that Matilda had been angry enough to resort to criminal damage – and that she'd been more or less stalking Daffyd Jones.

'Oh, I bet that got it all out of your system,' Daphne said

encouragingly, as though it was the healthiest thing in the world to wreck your lover's paintwork.

'Yes, it was quite satisfying, but I think letting his tyres down on the morning of the carols sing-off last year was even better,' Matilda continued, seeming rather pleased with the memory.

They were discussing these acts of sabotage as though they were normal and proportionate, Sarah thought, but Mariella would no doubt have a different view. Might someone who considered this sort of vandalism perfectly acceptable move on to physical attacks? She couldn't help but wonder.

Matilda, meanwhile, seemed to realise what she'd said. 'Of course all that has been over for ages. I'd accepted the position. I'm happy with Ewan. I'm fine with Deirdre. Daffyd and I were on perfectly cordial terms.'

'Well... we were at the rehearsal, Matilda,' Daphne said.

'Yes, I'm not sure "cordial" is the word I'd use,' said Sarah.

'Fine. All right,' Matilda snapped, with one of her mercurial changes of mood. 'But I can tell you that I was completely done with him. Yes, he was still rude to me and yes, I did flounce out. But that was all, I tell you! There's no one less likely to have murdered him than me.'

With that, she shot to her feet, shedding all the tissues that had accumulated in her lap since she'd arrived. Then she struggled into her coat, shouldered her bag, and before Sarah or Daphne could really react, she'd sidestepped Hamish, rushed up the corridor and left, slamming the front door behind her.

'My goodness,' said Daphne. 'Another dramatic exit! She really doesn't do anything by halves, does she?'

'No,' said Sarah thoughtfully. 'I don't believe she was over Daffyd for a second, do you?'

Daphne looked surprised. 'Well, she certainly *said* she was,' she said with a shrug.

'People say all sorts of things, Daph. But do they mean

them? We have to look at their actions, not their words. At the rehearsal, Matilda became so angry her flight-or-fight response kicked in, and she flounced out. We have to ask ourselves whether all that adrenaline in her system led to her returning not long afterwards, with a weapon. With Charles's gun. That's what we need to look into next.'

TWENTY-TWO

As it was already so late, Daphne ended up staying another night at Sarah's place, much to the delight of Hamish. Sarah, though, was a little worried by this development. Much as she loved her friend's company, it could prove awkward if Daphne got too used to the spare bedroom. There was an unspoken agreement that Charles didn't come round when Daphne was in residence. Would it end up with Daphne as a permanent fixture at Sarah's place, with Sarah forced to tiptoe out to Charles's flat further down the esplanade?

Sarah shook such thoughts from her head as she stood in the kitchen the next morning, laying the table for a breakfast of creamy scrambled eggs and toast and spooning coffee grounds into the cafetiere. She was formulating a plan of action for the day when Daphne clambered downstairs, with Hamish running excitedly up to greet her.

'There's my big boy,' Daphne said, giving the Scottie a cuddle. 'He's such a gorgeous lad. If anyone could turn me from cats to dogs, it would be him. Ah toast, lovely,' she added, swiping both slices from the toast rack and sitting down in Sarah's place.

'How would you feel about driving out to see Francesca?' said Sarah, cutting more bread.

Daphne shuddered. 'Really? We had that chat with her when she was going on about her engagement... and, actually, I should get on top of the paperwork at Tarot and Tealeaves,' she said, adding milk to her coffee.

'Hmm. I understand your lack of enthusiasm. But I don't think we've got everything out of her. Francesca knows better than anyone who would have had access to Charles's keys, plus Matilda is a friend of hers.'

'Is she?' said Daphne, absent-mindedly crunching into her toast.

'Yes. Don't you remember, when Matilda arrived at the rehearsal, she made a big thing of saying she'd been at Francesca's drinks, wearing that incredible outfit.'

'You know what,' Daphne said, putting her eggy toast down. 'If I was Matilda, and my lover had gone back to his wife, I'd turn up to rehearsals in a glamorous gown and swank in looking like I'd just had the time of my life. Even if I'd been sitting at home crying all evening.'

'You've got a point, and that makes it all the more important to check with Francesca. We can't trust much that Matilda says.'

'How do you work that out?' said Daphne. 'I like her.'

'I do too, but she doesn't exactly keep her story straight, does she? First she said she hated Daffyd, then she said she loved him, then she claimed to be over him, then she admitted more or less stalking him. Which one was it? If it was the stalking, then I'd say she's definitely in the frame.'

'But it's all been over for a while,' said Daphne, finishing her slice and looking longingly at the loaf. Sarah obligingly got up and stuck two more slices in the toaster. 'She said she's happy with Ewan.'

'You would say that, wouldn't you? Particularly if you hadn't got over it at all, and had actually killed your ex.'

'When you look at it like that, I don't know why Mari hasn't arrested her already,' Daphne said, levering herself into position at the exact moment the toast popped up.

'Nevertheless,' said Sarah firmly. 'I still think that a visit to Francesca is going to be in order. You don't have to come, Daph. You could stay here and do the dishes,' she said, a smile peeping out as Daphne's face fell. 'Oh come on, don't fight it. You know you'll be dying to know what rude things Francesca said to me. You might as well witness it all first hand.'

'Go on, then. You've talked me into it,' said Daphne, stooping to pet the little Scottie, who was wagging his tail in joy at the realisation that they were finally on the move. Breakfast was all very well, he enjoyed it every bit as much as the next dog, but going on an adventure was better by far.

He wasn't so enthusiastic when he realised the trip meant car travel, not a lovely long beach walk, but he made the best of it, settling down in his harness to chew painstakingly through the blanket Sarah had just bought to protect the seats of her once-pristine Volvo.

By the time they had swished onto the long gravel drive leading to Francesca's perfect Georgian mansion outside Merstairs, Sarah had got her thoughts in order. She'd been rather glib about the woman being horrible to her earlier, but in truth it wasn't easy being belittled constantly in such a toxic way. Normally, she would have responded briskly, but as Francesca was Charles's ex, it was a little complicated. No matter how dead their marriage was, the mayor was still the mother of Charles's beloved daughter, Arabella, and his two adored grandchildren. Those were ties she could never loosen, even if she'd wanted to.

There was a huge Christmas tree outside the house festooned with glowing fairy lights, and an enormous wreath tied with scarlet ribbons took pride of place on the shiny front door. It was ironic that Francesca's decorations were so lavish, as there surely couldn't be anyone more lacking the warmth of true Christmas spirit.

Sarah braced herself as best she could as she turned off the ignition. Then, just as she was about to open the car door, Daphne turned to her and put a warm hand on her arm. 'Don't worry. We'll protect you,' she said earnestly, and Hamish woofed from the back seat to second that.

'Thanks, you two,' she said, and felt a lot more cheery as they got out and crunched across the drive to the imposing entrance – though she did notice both Daphne and the dog were hanging back somewhat. This allowed her to take the full brunt of Francesca's displeasure when the door swung open.

'Good grief, it's Susan, isn't it? And Daffy. Please don't tell me you want to come in, I'm about to run to a council meeting,' Francesca said, standing in the hall, also thoroughly decorated with Christmas lanterns, swags of holly and ivy and, the pièce de résistance, a huge bunch of mistletoe hanging from the central light. The glitziness of the display rivalled even the massive engagement ring on the mayor's left hand.

'If you're after donations to the Women's Institute jumble sale, and from your outfits I'd say you must be, then you can get them from the garage. Chivers will show you.' Francesca gestured dismissively to her housekeeper.

With that, she made to dart around the women and into her waiting car. But Sarah, emboldened by mention of the garage, held out a hand.

'If you could wait one moment, please. It's the garage situation we've come about, Francesca. This is important. I think the council might have to wait.'

For a moment, Francesca looked astounded at Sarah's cheek. Then a cunning look came over her face. 'All right, then,' she said. 'If you're so interested in my garage, I suppose I'll have to show you it, won't I?'

'Thank you,' said Sarah, trying not to sound too eager. 'That would be great.'

Francesca picked up her handbag and her keys and strode out of the house, with Sarah and Daphne following meekly behind, Hamish trailing slightly on his lead. The garage turned out to be behind the main house, in a courtyard that once upon a time would have been home to the stables, the sculleries and other outbuildings the owners wanted to hide from sight. Now there was only a smart redbrick building big enough for a family of four.

Francesca strode over to the double doors and swung up the iron bar that held them closed. It was well oiled and didn't take any strength to move. They obediently trooped in behind her. It was quite gloomy inside, and Sarah found her eyes were taking a while to accustom themselves to the dark. Just as she was turning round to ask Francesca where Charles's keys were usually kept, she realised the woman was outside, pulling the door to, and by the sound of it replacing the bar that kept the garage shut.

'Oops,' Francesca said, calling through the door. 'That slipped right out of my hand. And I don't have time to hang around and open it for you, as I'm already late. I did explain. I really can't be expected to interrupt my busy schedule for the likes of you. Bye.'

Sarah and Daphne rushed over to the doors and pushed against them. They gave slightly, but didn't budge, the iron bar made sure of that. The two women looked at each other dimly in the shadowy, silent darkness of the garage.

'What on earth do we do now?' Daphne shrieked.

TWENTY-THREE

'I'll look around for a light switch, you see if you can find the torch on your phone,' said Sarah calmly. She started feeling her way slowly over to the side of the double garage, narrowly avoiding colliding with what felt like a ride-on lawnmower and a leaf blower. She was trying to stay composed, but inside she was fuming at Francesca's high-handed treatment. Daphne dropped her phone with a clatter and Hamish barked. 'I can't believe there isn't any electricity in here, it's such a large garage. Ah, here,' Sarah said, fumbling near the door and then flicking a switch.

A neon light stuttered on, blinding at first, but gradually they saw the neatly laid out interior of the garage, with tools arrayed along one wall, as well as the shiny, brand-new convertible Jaguar that Francesca had mentioned her fiancé was buying, plus a row of hooks near the door with keys dangling from them. There was a space with the letter 'C' beneath it, and the hook there was bare.

'What do you bet that's where Charles's keys were?' Sarah said thoughtfully. Then she stepped forward. Even in the dim light, something was shining out at her from a crack in the floor.

She bent down and picked up a piece of diamanté, which glittered in the harsh light. Now where had she seen something like this before?

'What are you doing? Why aren't you trying to find the way out? That dreadful woman has locked us in here. We may never get out alive!' Daphne shrieked.

'Calm down, Daph. You'll upset Hamish,' Sarah said, reaching to pat the little dog, who was so far looking surprised rather than anxious. 'We can ring Mariella and she'll have us out in a trice. Or we could just call for Mrs Chivers,' she said.

'Did I hear my name?' said a voice outside the garage, and a moment or two later, natural daylight flooded in as the doors swung open.

'Oh! Thank goodness! I thought I'd never get out,' said Daphne, running past Mrs Chivers and waving her arms in the air as she hurtled round the courtyard. 'Light! Air! Freedom,' she yelled.

'I don't think Daphne enjoyed that little prank,' Sarah said to Mrs Chivers. 'It's a good job you happened to be passing.'

'Isn't it?' said the housekeeper, with just the hint of a blush. Not for the first time, Sarah wondered what sort of employer Francesca made. She must pay handsomely, she supposed, or who on earth would put up with her?

'We're very grateful,' Sarah said with a smile. 'We'll get out of your hair, now,' she added, picking up Hamish who she felt could do with a cuddle.

Mrs Chivers patted him on the head as they passed. 'I've always loved a Scottie. My old granny had one in the Highlands,' she confided with the smallest of winks.

Buckling themselves back into the car, Sarah said, 'I think we owe our liberation to Hamish. Turns out Mrs Chivers has a soft spot for him.'

'Hmm,' said Daphne. 'Well, that Francesca's got a piece of my mind coming when I next see her. Talk about a wasted journey. We came all the way out here, and for what? Nothing.'

'Well, not quite,' said Sarah with quiet satisfaction. 'I think we've got a lot further on, actually.'

'What on earth do you mean?' Daphne said crossly. 'We arrived, got imprisoned, then just about escaped with our lives, thank goodness.'

'Yes... but I found something in the garage, when the lights came on.'

'You did? What is it?'

Sarah opened her hand, and showed Daphne the sparkling diamanté gem, winking up at them. 'The last time I saw something like that, glittering out of the corner of my eye, was in the room where Daffyd Jones died. And who do we know who wears diamanté every time we see her?'

'Ooh, ooh, I know, it's Matilda! No, it's Francesca – except her jewels are real. Oh, I give up, Sarah, who is it?'

'Well, you're just about to find out,' said Sarah, putting the car in gear. Then, with a crunch of gravel, they were off.

* * *

A few minutes later, Sarah parked neatly on the esplanade right outside Daffyd Jones's majestic seafront property, and Daphne, who'd been fruitlessly guessing who the gem might belonged to, slapped herself on the forehead.

'Oh my goodness! Of course. Deirdre always wears that great carbuncle of a brooch, I don't know why I didn't think of that!'

'Well done, Daph. It's definitely worth checking. Let's see what she has to say for herself about it,' said Sarah.

They clambered out of the Volvo, Hamish in tow, and made their way up the slight hill to Daffyd Jones's house. In the distance, Sarah spotted a woman with a purple coat marching along the esplanade. Marlene, surely, from the fish and chip shop. She only ever seemed to wear that colour. She must be in a rush to get back to her customers.

Sarah turned to face the view. The amazing panorama was slightly marred today by the sight of Ewan Smith's white van, advertising his plastering skills, parked two doors down. Sarah had the same sea view herself, but much as she loved the pretty lattice panes of her cottage, they just didn't offer quite the same sweeping effect as floor-to-ceiling Georgian windows.

Sarah stepped forward to ring the bell, and they both waited as the chimes died away. Nothing happened. They listened for footsteps in the hall, but all was quiet, except for the far-off screeching of the gulls wheeling in the sky far above them.

'That's very odd,' said Sarah. 'I wonder where they can be?'

'Maybe they've had to go and see to the, you know, arrangements,' Daphne said with a moue of distaste.

'Oh, you mean the funeral?' Sarah was surprised. 'I wouldn't have thought that would be happening for a while,' she said carefully, avoiding mentioning all the complications a violent death brought in terms of post-mortems, inquests and even legal proceedings. They tended to slow things down somewhat. 'Funny there isn't a police officer here, though. Matthew said one would be sitting with them. Oh well, I suppose we'll just have to try later.'

'Wait a minute,' Daphne said, looking swiftly from left to right to check the esplanade was deserted, then shoving one of the big flowerpots beside the front door to one side. 'Ah, thought so.' She bent down, then straightened up with a spare key in her hand.

'I don't know why people do that, it's such a burglary risk,' Sarah tutted.

'Well, you should thank your lucky stars in this case, otherwise we'd be shivering out here all day,' said Daphne, stepping forward and unlocking the door. 'Coo-ee! Anyone here?' she yelled as she walked into the hall, with Hamish and Sarah bringing up the rear.

The hallway was still and silent. 'You're right, Matthew and Deirdre must have gone to see the undertakers after all,' said Sarah. Well, they'd no doubt be back very soon. This could be her only opportunity to have a look round without being subjected to the watchful gaze of the widow. Daphne, arrested by her reflection in the large mirror in the hallway, stopped to adjust her scarf, and Sarah slipped past her, opening the door to the sitting room.

A second later, she really wished she'd stayed outside. Because there was Deirdre, sitting in one of the blocky leather armchairs, gazing out to sea – stone dead.

TWENTY-FOUR

At first, Sarah wasn't quite sure it could be true. Perhaps Deirdre would blink, then the impression of fatal stillness would evaporate and life could continue as normal. But the woman didn't move a muscle, and her ghastly pallor was unmistakable. She sat there, rigid, staring on through sightless eyes, straight into eternity.

'Daphne, don't come in,' Sarah called, then she shut the door on Daphne's protests for good measure. She walked very slowly towards the chair. There was something distinctly disconcerting about the woman, upright in the chair, only the sagging of her jaw and, now that Sarah was closer, a fogging in her eyes, telling their grim story.

As she approached, she noticed something was clasped tight in Deirdre's right hand. The woman's knuckles were white, as though she had clutched the object for dear life. It was a biro, and Sarah could just make out the logo, Merstairs Mortar. Hmm, that had certainly cropped up before, but shock was playing havoc with her memory. She needed to concentrate on what she could see right here, right now. There was a glass, half-full of a dark liquid that looked like sherry in front of her, and on the edge of the table a smear of what looked like a pink substance. How peculiar. But everything about this situation was odd.

For once, she broke the police taboo and touched the body, reaching out for the woman's left wrist just to check there was no pulse. But the unyielding flesh told its own story. This woman was long gone.

Sarah almost stumbled to the door and then collapsed onto Daphne, who was waiting right outside. They both stopped Hamish from going in, then looked at each other, wide-eyed, in the hall.

'Is it Deirdre? Is she...? She can't be! She is, though, isn't she?' Daphne said in a hoarse whisper.

'Come on, let's go outside,' Sarah said weakly.

'And ring Mariella?' Daphne said, a tremor in her voice.

'You guessed it,' Sarah said with a tiny shake of the head.

* * *

Outside, with the waves now crashing against the beach, the two women waited for the police. Mariella had promised to get there as soon as she possibly could.

'And Deirdre's really dead? You're sure? But how?' Daphne said with the beginnings of a wail.

'Shh, now. I don't know, but I'd say it looked... peaceful,' Sarah said, putting an arm round her friend and hoping that was true. At the moment it was just a very strange sudden death. No signs of violence, it was true. But people didn't usually just drop dead for no reason.

'I wonder where on earth Matthew is?' she said, partly to give Daphne something new to think about.

'My goodness, this is going to be so awful for him! So soon after losing his father. He's going to be devastated,' Daphne said.

'The poor man.' Sarah shook her head. 'They didn't seem like the greatest parents, but to lose them both in quick succession like this, it's so awful.'

'Do you think... you don't think, do you?' Daphne's expressive face was a picture of woe.

'What, Daph?'

'Well, that it might be another, oh, you know I hate saying it...'

'A murder, you mean? I wish I could cheer you up by saying no. But I'm not sure. I couldn't see any signs of anything sinister, but the chances of Deirdre just dying out of the blue, straight after her husband, have to be pretty slim.' Sarah's brow was knotted.

'I suppose you're right,' Daphne said glumly. 'Ugh, people can be so awful. Thank goodness for pure souls like Hamish.' She reached down to pat the little dog, who looked up at her with loving eyes.

Sarah knew exactly what she meant, but didn't want her friend to lose that boundless faith in humanity that was one of her most endearing characteristics. 'Well, let's not pre-judge things. Look, here comes the cavalry,' she said reassuringly, as a police vehicle and Mariella's car drove up simultaneously. There was only one parking space, however, and there was a bit of a tussle for who was going to get it. Sarah was glad to see Mariella persisting and shoe-horning her car into the spot, leaving the two constables to double-park further down the esplanade.

Mariella leapt out of the car and had soon reached her mother and Sarah, standing a little forlornly outside the Jones's house. Sarah was ready for the usual telling off, but this time Mariella just embraced her mother quickly, patted Sarah on the arm, and went up the steps to the front door. She pushed at it, but it remained closed.

'How did you get in?' She lifted her eyebrow.

Sarah showed her the key under the pot, and Mariella shook her head. 'Oh for goodness' sake. Come with me, Aunty Sarah,' she said as she crossed the threshold.

'Could you look after Hamish, Daph?' Sarah asked her friend. With an important job to do, the time would weigh on her less heavily. Daphne nodded somewhat bleakly and sat down on the top step. Hamish immediately hopped onto her lap, licking her nose, and Daphne couldn't help but let out a weak giggle. What a good boy he was.

Once back inside, Sarah straightened her shoulders. 'She's in here.'

'It's really bad, I take it?' Mariella looked frankly at Sarah.

'Well... no. It's not gruesome, it's just eerie and a bit chilling,' Sarah admitted. She shouldn't let herself get spooked, as a medical professional (albeit retired) and a woman of science. But there was something about Deirdre's faraway – very, very faraway – gaze that had really got to her.

Opening the door and seeing it all afresh was not as bad as she'd feared, however. She and Mariella stepped into the room, the detective wearing gloves and shoe protectors. There was no sign of a disturbance, nothing to suggest violence. Everything was tidily in its place, right down to the remote controls and racing newspaper on the empty chair, the one that had been Daffyd's. And in the other seat Deirdre sat on silently, seeing nothing, feeling nothing, hearing nothing.

The strange atmosphere of the room settled on them and Sarah found herself watching Mariella's reactions. The detective stepped forward carefully, observing everything quietly, displaying great respect towards the dead woman but also a keen interest in gathering all the facts she could from what was in front of her. Then, just as she was straightening up, the door behind them was flung open – and both women screamed.

TWENTY-FIVE

Mariella recovered first, facing the man in front of her as calmly as she could. 'We weren't expecting to see you here,' she said, only the faintest touch of colour in her cheeks betraying her heightened state of alert.

'W-why shouldn't I be here? I live here, don't I? And what's wrong with my mother?' said Matthew Jones, fidgeting with his sling, his own face reddening by the second.

Sarah, who'd now recovered a little, went up to him and put out a hand. He pushed her away with his sling, staring fixedly at his mother – almost as fixedly as she was staring herself. 'Mother! Mum, what's the matter?' He made as though to run to her but checked himself. 'What's this? What's going on?' he asked Sarah and Mariella, his chin jutting and his cheeks now brick red. 'What have you done to her? Why isn't she saying anything?'

'I'm so sorry, Matthew, this is an awful business,' Sarah said, trying to adopt the calming tones she'd used in the past when breaking bad news to relatives.

Mariella frowned at her and gently but firmly took over. 'There's no easy way to tell you this, Matthew, but as you may now be able to guess, I'm very sorry to tell you that your mother has passed away. Now I'm afraid we will have to leave the room. The pathologist is on the way.'

'What do you mean, she's dead? Her eyes are open, aren't they?' Matthew wailed, his face crumpling. 'Mum! Mum?' he said, shaking Mariella off and striding towards his mother's chair. 'Wake up, Mum,' he said, grabbing her arm, then recoiling as he felt the lifeless flesh. Deirdre's diamanté brooch twinkled briefly as it caught the light, a couple of its stones missing. Matthew lurched backward, he almost fell over trying to get as far as possible from his late mother, then he ran from the room.

'Well, this is a pickle,' said Mariella, turning to Sarah once they'd heard him pelt down the hall. 'I thought the house was empty.'

'So did I,' said Sarah, putting a hand to her chest. 'I suppose Daphne and I were so shocked, we didn't stop to think Matthew might be upstairs somewhere. We did call out, but maybe he didn't hear us? It's such a big house for three people. Well – one now.'

'OK. Anyway, I think it's time you left this to me, Aunty Sarah, and took Mum and Hamish home. She looks peaceful enough.'

'Oh, but there are a few anomalies,' Sarah started, but Mariella put a hand on her shoulder.

'I'll go over everything in the room, don't you worry,' said Mariella. 'It's just going to be a wait for the pathologist now. I'll get Twee— um, the boys, to take Matthew into the station for a brief chat while the SOCO team does its bit.'

'Of course. Sorry, Mariella, I feel we should have checked the premises. But honestly, finding Deirdre pushed everything out of my mind. At least it's not another gunshot we're dealing with,' Sarah said.

'It certainly wasn't your responsibility to check the house, and what you thought you were up to, letting yourselves in, is another matter,' said Mariella. 'Remind me to have a very stern word about that as soon as I have a free moment. Anyway, as far as the gun goes, at least we've managed to clear Charles. His cleaner, Molly Ferguson, actually sold the revolver when she was minding his shop a month ago.'

'Oh, she made a sale, really? Who bought it?' Sarah asked.

'That's the annoying thing,' said Mariella. 'There were actually two purchases at more or less the same time, and Mrs Ferguson got so flustered she didn't note either down properly. Both customers paid cash, too. We showed her a picture of Daffyd, but she wasn't at all sure. One man was wearing a woolly hat, the other was muffled up to the ears in a scarf. Well, it's been cold. She kept meaning to tell Charles, but Francesca has kept her so busy with the Christmas decorations that she said she hasn't had a second. Just our luck, really. OK, I need to get on now,' she said, ushering Sarah kindly but firmly out of the front door.

Sarah joined Daphne on the step. The two constables were finally huffing up the slope to the house.

'Time to make ourselves scarce, before they get here,' Sarah said, indicating the policemen.

'Oh, the undynamic duo! Right you are,' Daphne said, still clasping the little Scottie to her heart.

As they walked away quickly, Sarah's head was spinning. While she was relieved Charles was off the hook, there was still a gun rattling around somewhere in Merstairs. And now Deirdre was dead, too. However tranquil the scene might have looked, Sarah was convinced there must have been foul play involved. But what on earth had happened? There had been two stones missing from that brooch Deirdre always wore. Now that Sarah could think about it clearly, she realised that one of them had been at Daffyd's murder scene. The other had been in

Francesca's garage, leading them to visit Deirdre's house – and find her body.

Had Deirdre ever been to Francesca's place? Were the half-glass of liquid and the pen involved? And who, or what, could have left that pink blob? Mariella was too busy to hear her theories – so that meant Sarah was just going to have to do what she did best, and work it all out herself.

TWENTY-SIX

'Hmm,' said Daphne when Sarah mentioned the new clues she'd spotted in Deirdre's sitting room. 'Maybe I should commune with the spirits, see if Pongo can shed any light on things?'

'Your spirit guide, you mean? I'm not sure there's any need for that,' said Sarah quickly.

'I don't like your tone, Sarah,' she said, her scarf wobbling. 'Pongo's been an immense help to many of my clients.'

'I'm sure he has. Or is it she?'

'Such concepts carry no weight in the spiritual realm,' Daphne said reprovingly.

Keen to get off the topic, Sarah started musing aloud. 'Have you heard of this company, Merstairs Mortar? It keeps cropping up. And their pens keep appearing in the strangest places,' she said, thinking back to the green room and now the Jones's house.

'Sounds vaguely familiar,' Daphne said. 'Let's do a search,' she added, getting out her phone. 'Hmm, nothing's showing,' she said, holding out a page with no clear results. There had been premises, but they appeared to be closed, and the web address didn't work.

'That's really odd,' Sarah said with a frown. 'OK, well, I'll keep asking around. In the meantime, we also need to think about other sources of guns, since Charles's is now out of the running. Do you know of any Merstairs groups that use them? It seems mad even to suggest it, but you never know.'

'Oh, let me think...' said Daphne. 'There's my Tai Kwando, there's the knitting group, I haven't been back since Pat, well, you know,' Daphne said with a gulp. 'What else is there? The Mermaids, of course, the Merstairs Militia, the Men of Merstairs, the Merstairs Mudlarks, the—'

'Wait!' Sarah was electrified. 'What did you say then? The Militia? They'd have guns, wouldn't they? And why does Merstairs need a militia anyway, for goodness' sake?'

'Oh, they're a historical re-enactment society, they refight all the famous Kent battles, like the battle of Rochester and all that,' Daphne said airily. 'But I think the guns are all made of wood.'

'Even so, it's worth investigating,' Sarah said. 'Just in case. There's no one in the choir who's also in the Militia, is there?'

'What, you mean apart from Matilda?' Daphne said, looking out to sea.

Sarah dug in her heels. 'You mean Matilda is one of these re-enacting people? Seriously?'

'Well yes,' Daphne faltered. 'But that doesn't mean anything.'

'She might have access to guns, she's in the choir, she was publicly humiliated just before Daffyd died... and actually, she also wears sparkly jewellery. Maybe Deirdre suspected Matilda, so she had to be eliminated? Maybe she was trying to incriminate her, leaving bits of diamanté here and there,' Sarah said. 'We really need to talk to Matilda again. Where do you think she'd be right now?'

'Actually, I know exactly where she'll be,' said Daphne, marching on ahead with Hamish at her heels.

They didn't have far to go. Daphne ground to a halt on the high street, in front of a small townhouse with a set of steep steps leading up to the door. It looked like a private house. 'Is this right, Daphne?'

'Yes of course. It's the Red House wine bar. Matilda works here. I can't believe you haven't been before,' Daphne said.

Now that Sarah looked at the place more closely, she could see tables and chairs through the windows and the paint colour on the outside was a dark red not dissimilar to a good Bordeaux. 'But Daphne, it won't be open at this time of day, will it?'

Daphne just pointed to a sign by the door saying, *It's Six O'Clock Somewhere*, and strode in. The place was empty of customers, but much to Sarah's surprise there was Matilda, stationed behind the bar.

'Well, goodness me, ladies, look what the tide's brought in,' said Matilda. Even at this hour she was looking glamorous, poured into a slightly inadequate tube dress in what seemed to be her signature colour of baby blue, this time with pink accents. Sarah looked at her bare arms and wondered how on earth she got by without a cardigan. 'What can I get you?'

'I could do with a really stiff drink, after the time we've had,' said Daphne theatrically, but after a glare from Sarah, she mumbled meekly, 'um, just a Dubonnet, thanks Matilda,' said Daphne. 'And Sarah will have a tonic. Is Hamish OK in here?'

'Of course he is,' Matilda trilled, coming out to give Hamish a big pat and slip him a dog treat.

'We did come here to ask a few questions,' said Sarah, when Matilda had started getting their drinks.

'Oh yes?' she said, immediately sounding a bit cagey. She turned away and busied herself with rearranging the lemon slices on a plate by the till. 'Paying by card? Thank you.'

'Yes, one or two issues have cropped up,' Sarah said. For a

second, she hesitated whether to mention Deirdre, after Daphne's near slip, but decided to try and clear up the gun business first. It would be worth observing Matilda carefully anyway, just to see if she showed any signs of a guilty conscience. 'Daphne here was saying you're a leading light in the Merstairs Militia.'

Immediately Matilda seemed to relax a little and Sarah wondered what exactly she had been expecting – perhaps a question about where she'd been earlier? 'That's right. I do enjoy a re-enactment.'

'I can't imagine you liking all that battleground mud much.' Sarah lifted an eyebrow.

'Ah, appearances can be deceptive,' Matilda said. 'Everything I own is machine-washable, and I rather enjoy getting down and dirty with the boys,' she added with the suggestion of a wink.

Sarah couldn't help smiling back. Then she plunged in. 'The thing is, Matilda, and there's no really polite way of asking this—'

'Ooh! Shall I brace myself?' Matilda asked saucily.

Sarah took a breath. 'The thing is, we're still looking for a gun, the kind of gun that could have killed Daffyd.'

Matilda stiffened. 'I thought you'd already put your boyfriend in the frame for that.' Her tone was not unfriendly, but she looked at Sarah steadily and Sarah suddenly realised she'd be a formidable foe.

'It turns out Charles's gun isn't involved after all.' Sarah shrugged. 'So the search is still on.'

'Well, I doubt anything we have for the re-enactments is any use, to be honest. The weapons are so ancient they would crumble if you tried to fire them. I suppose that's a bit like Charles's gun, too, though, isn't it, Sarah?' Matilda gave a sideways smile.

Sarah didn't much care for the insinuation, but she

supposed she deserved it, having been rather accusatory. 'Do you know who looks after the armoury for the Militia?'

'I do, as it happens. It's my Ewan.'

Sarah let this sink in for a second, then she asked another question. 'And did Ewan know about you and Daffyd?' She was really pushing her luck now.

Matilda slapped a tea towel down on the bar. 'There was nothing to know. Daffyd and I were over long ago, he made that perfectly clear. Ewan and I are very happy together!' she insisted.

'But you do both have access to all the Merstairs Militia's armaments, don't you?' Sarah said.

Matilda laughed. 'If you'd seen the rusty old box of rubbish that is our "armaments" you'd know how ridiculous a suggestion that is. None of them could shoot a tin can off a wall if you were a foot away.'

'But there are some, aren't there, that used to fire real bullets?' Sarah persisted. 'From that old TV show, *Broomstick Battalion*?'

'To tell you the truth I don't even really know. I never look, even though the box is in my shed. They're just stage props.'

'How do you know?' Sarah persisted. 'Have you ever tried firing one?'

'Well... no,' Matilda admitted. 'But they get used every time the Militia meet. We'd know if they were functional.'

'Not if you didn't try them with ammunition.'

'This is ridiculous. They don't work and they're not out on the street, are they? They're secured. The shed is always locked. I keep the key here,' Matilda said, getting up and rummaging in the small blue suede bag she kept behind the till.

'Love your handbag,' said Daphne admiringly. 'Those tassels are so pretty. Maybe I should downsize mine,' she continued, looking thoughtfully at her vast purple velvet number.

'It might help you find things more quickly,' Sarah said, then looked towards Matilda, who was now pulling items out of her bag and lining them up on the bar.

'Well, I don't know about that,' Daphne said significantly, and indeed, it did look as though Matilda was getting increasingly frantic.

'Is there a problem?' Sarah asked gently, when everything was out of the bag and Matilda was turning it upside down and shaking it.

'No... Yes... I don't know what to tell you. But the shed key is missing. I don't understand it. It's usually on the ring with the others,' she said, jangling the small bunch of keys held together with a diamanté fob in the shape of a letter M – which was short of a few stones.

'I'd love one of those,' said Daphne, eyeing it up covetously.

'This is just so strange.' Matilda shook her head.

'Not really, Matilda. It looks like someone took the key off your chain. Can you think who that might be? Who has had access to your bag recently?' Sarah asked.

'Access? No one. I keep it here by the bar... Oh. I never thought it wouldn't be safe. There's not much crime in Merstairs – well, theft, anyway.'

'Looks like someone is bucking the trend,' said Sarah.

'But why would anyone steal it?' Matilda began, then rolled her eyes. 'Oh, of course. In your view, to get to the guns. But they'd be so disappointed, though don't tell a soul in the Merstairs Militia I said that.' She looked round to check no one was listening. 'I haven't got the faintest idea how you'd get one of those silly old guns to fire, anyway.'

'I imagine it would be difficult. But then, you do live with someone who's pretty handy with DIY, don't you?' Sarah pointed out. 'And, as we said before, both of you had a decent motive to shoot Daffyd.'

'Ugh, I've had enough of this,' Matilda said, ramming objects back into her handbag any old how. 'You two just don't give up.'

'To be fair, it's more Sarah. I'm quite happy to give up most of the time,' said Daphne.

'You're as bad as Deirdre, hanging onto something long after it's dead,' Matilda said dismissively. Both Sarah and Daphne stared at her. 'What? What have I said?'

Now seemed a good moment to test exactly how much Matilda knew. 'You haven't heard, then?' Sarah asked, studying her carefully.

'Heard what? Oh, just tell me whatever it is,' Matilda said crossly, picking up their empty glasses and taking them to the bar.

'Deirdre's dead, Matilda,' Daphne said in a tremulous voice.

Matilda promptly dropped both glasses, which shattered on the floor, while she sagged against the bar. 'I don't believe you,' she said shakily.

'Just go down to the seafront and have a look. The house has been cordoned off by the police,' Sarah said. 'That's if you haven't already seen for yourself, of course – at close quarters.'

Matilda, getting a dustpan and brush, clattered around clearing up the mess. When she finally looked up, shock seemed to have been replaced with trembling anger.

'You and your insinuations! Well, as far as I'm concerned, Happy Hour is most definitely over. I think you should both leave.'

Sarah and Daphne did as they were told, bundling up their coats and clattering down the stairs with Hamish. Outside on the pavement Daphne turned to her friend.

'You don't really think Matilda did it, do you?'

'She certainly had good reason. The way Daffyd treated her was horrible, but I'm not sure what she'd have to gain from the second killing, unless Deirdre knew she'd killed her husband

and confronted her, say. But that seems unlikely. No, after that little chat, I've got my eye on someone else.'

'Who is it?' Daphne said, a touch nervously.

'Come along, you'll soon see,' said Sarah, pulling her coat around her and walking swiftly down the street with Hamish at her heels.

TWENTY-SEVEN

'I don't know where you're dragging me to at top speed,' puffed Daphne. 'And look at little Hamish, he's totally out of breath,' she said, pointing to the dog who, on the contrary, looked extremely happy with life, his ears pointing upwards in triangles even Isosceles would have been proud of, with his stumpy tail as busy as a windscreen wiper on a wet day.

'That's simple,' Sarah said, who was now having to catch her own breath a little. 'Didn't you see the construction going on earlier on the esplanade, just a stone's throw from the Jones's house?'

'No, and even if I had, it's not going to vanish in a puff of smoke, is it? I don't see why we have to get there at the speed of light.'

'If Ewan's seen the activity at the Jones's house, with Deirdre being discovered, or even nipped over there to kill her himself, he won't hang around,' Sarah explained. 'And now we know that Matilda's key to the Militia guns is missing. Who would have had easier access than Ewan? And he could easily have killed Daffyd too.'

'Well, why didn't you say so? We need to clear his name,

because there's no way he did it,' said Daphne, breaking into a trot and rapidly outstripping Sarah. But by the time they'd both reached the house with the scaffolding outside, there was no sign of Ewan's van.

'Drat,' Sarah said, leaning on the railings outside the house and trying to catch her breath. 'It looks like we've missed him.'

'Missed who?' came a deep voice, and then Ewan emerged from the house, his overalls a little covered in dust, but still emphasising his biceps nicely.

Daphne, who'd subsided onto the step and now had Hamish on her lap, wheezed. 'Sarah made us pelt all the way over here to talk to you,' she said, very pink in the face.

'I'm flattered,' Ewan said in his deep voice, with that gravelly undertone of a Yorkshire accent. He brushed the hair off his forehead in a gesture that had no doubt caused many swoons amongst the womenfolk of Merstairs. 'What's this all about, ladies? Urgent bit of plastering, is it?' A lazy smile played on his handsome face.

Sarah tried to compose herself. 'Not exactly... but we do need to talk to you. About something really important.'

Much to Sarah's annoyance, the slightly self-satisfied expression on the man's face didn't change. He seemed to believe this was a ploy to get his attention, which showed how spoiled he had been over the years by the admiring ladies of the town. 'Aye, it always is,' he said. 'Well, I suppose you'd better come in.' He pointed towards the open door.

'But this isn't your house, is it?' Sarah asked.

'Course not,' he said with a wink. 'But the owners won't mind. They're DFLs, anyway, and probably in one of their other places right now. I've just moved my van round the corner but I had to come back for some stuff. Come through.'

Sarah and Daphne looked at each other, then Sarah shrugged. She was sure the freeholder wouldn't be thrilled at Ewan inviting strangers into their house, but on the other hand, it really was nippy outside, even after their bracing walk. They trooped in, Ewan leading the way, his head down, his feet scuffing the floor slightly as he went. Sarah immediately noticed the strong smell of damp in the hall, with Hamish giving it a good sniff in passing.

A large sitting room opened off the hall, and it was clearly here that Ewan had been working. There was fresh pink plaster on the walls, waiting to dry off before being painted. Sarah had to admit he'd done a lovely job; it was smooth and flawless, like the icing on a strawberry cake. That wasn't what was making her stare at it, though.

'Have a seat, ladies, take a load off,' he said, pointing to a large sofa shrouded in a sheet, and sitting down on a smaller chair opposite, his head hunched forward and his shoulders up by his ears. Sarah looked at him. Was that posture defensive? Or was something else at play?

'Now, what's all this about?' he asked with another megawatt smile. 'Worried about me not being able to fit you in? I'd always have time for either of you two lovely ladies.'

'Um, it's not that,' said Sarah, as Hamish toddled over to the man and flung himself on his back, all four paws in the air. He was devoted to his mistress, and liked Daphne very much, but sometimes the company of other big, rough, tough males just like him was all he craved. Now he lapped up lots of tickles and tummy-rubs from the chap in the tight overalls. Ah, this was the life.

Sarah, watching with a somewhat jaundiced eye, wondered not for the first time about her dog's taste in men. But then, he hadn't spotted that tell-tale daubing at Deirdre's place. Gazing around the room, she was now convinced it had to be plaster.

'He's a great little chap,' Ewan said, when Hamish had finally righted himself and curled into a loved-up heap at his feet. *Little?* thought Hamish, head on one side.

'No barking, boy,' said Sarah, patting his head. There was

no doubting the plasterer's charm, but she couldn't let that stop her asking the all-important question. 'The thing is, Ewan,' she began, when suddenly Daphne burst into speech.

'Because of these deaths, Sarah's got some ideas into her head about you and she feels we need to straighten it all out,' Daphne said earnestly. 'But I can tell your aura is pure, so I don't know why we're wasting the time, frankly.'

'Hang on there, deaths? What are you talking about? I know about Daffyd, but I swear on my mother's life I had nothing to do with that,' he said piously, putting one dusty hand against his broad chest.

'But I went to her funeral last year,' Daphne said, eyes wide.

'Well, yes, but the point stands.' Ewan was unabashed. 'All right, I had a row with the stupid man right before he died, but that was just coincidence. I couldn't let him insult my Matilda like that, could I?'

'So you really haven't heard about the second death?' Sarah asked.

Ewan looked from one woman to the other. 'What? Not a thing. I've been in here all day, working away. I had the radio on but there was nothing on the news.'

'You mean you didn't see all the comings and goings just along the esplanade?' Even Daphne sounded a little disbelieving. The wide window in front of them was almost as beautiful as the one in the Jones's house, affording a sweeping view of the sea, the esplanade, and all the business of the town – including several police vehicles parked this way and that, some with their blue lights still flashing.

'No. Had my back to the window, didn't I? You can see from the work I've done,' he said, gesturing to the wall.

Sarah looked at it carefully, then looked harder still. 'Hmm,' she said. Then she turned round to face him. 'Don't you want to know who's died? You don't seem at all curious.'

Ewan's face took on a shuttered look. 'I keep myself to myself, don't I?' he said.

'Do you? You made quite a scene at the choir rehearsal.'

'Matilda wanted it like that,' Ewan mumbled.

'You mean... she asked you to intervene?' Sarah said.

'Not exactly, I was genuinely angry. But we agreed I'd come in and shout a bit, scare Jones off. But I didn't hang around. He was fine when I left. Listen, I've got to get on,' he said, eyeing up the walls. 'Got a lot more to do.'

'We won't keep you much longer. But you still haven't asked who's just died.'

'Not my business...' He shrugged. 'But go on, tell me. I can see you want to,' he said with that lazy smile.

'It was Deirdre Jones,' Sarah said, observing him narrowly. 'Daffyd Jones's wife.'

Ewan looked taken aback. 'That's weird,' he said. 'Right after her husband. Someone doesn't like that family much. Well, I didn't hear another gunshot and I didn't see anyone running off or anything. So it's nothing to do with me.'

'I'm sorry, Ewan,' Sarah said, standing up. 'But you're already involved.'

'How do you make that out?' he said, also getting to his feet and now towering over her. 'I've told you, over and over, I've got no part in it.'

'But you were at the house earlier today,' she said, fixing Ewan with a steely gaze.

'You're suffering from delusions,' Ewan said dismissively. 'Daphne, you need to get her home, she's losing it.'

Before Daphne could react, Sarah spoke up again. 'If I'm deluded, how do you explain the smear of plaster at the scene, on Deirdre's table? Right by the chair she died in? I expect if the forensics people do their job properly, they could even get your fingerprints off it.'

There was a long silence, during which Ewan tried to avoid

Sarah's eyes, and Daphne shifted restlessly, seeming reluctant to change her view of her favourite plasterer, yet shocked by this development. Then Ewan seemed to give up. 'All right, then. You're more of a terrier than that dog of yours, aren't you?' he said. 'I suppose I'll have to tell you.'

Ewan shook his head, then sighed, then finally started to speak. 'Yes, OK, I admit it. I was over there at the Jones's house, but only for five minutes. Matthew asked me to go over, quote for some work on the cornices. He said he needed it done in a hurry. I sat at that little table, I suppose it's possible I had some plaster on my hand. But Deirdre came in, told me where to go, and I obliged. She was fine when I left.'

'She didn't want the work done?' Sarah asked.

'No. It was all a right mix-up, Daffyd's idea or something, and she didn't want to go ahead any more.'

'Right,' said Sarah, a little crestfallen. 'I suppose that clears it up.' Then she remembered another line of attack. 'You're in the Militia, aren't you?'

'Yeah, that's just playing, like,' Ewan scoffed.

'Right,' said Sarah. 'And what about Matilda's key to the munitions box?'

'That thing in the shed? What about it?' Ewan looked baffled.

'It's missing, Ewan. As I'm sure you know.' Sarah regarded him sternly. 'And Merstairs Mortar, what do you know about that?'

Ewan threw his hands up in the air. 'This is all news to me. I've not touched the box and I've never heard of that company.'

'Well, I'm sure you can tell the police the same story. When they come to interview you. Let's go now, Daphne,' Sarah said, pulling at a slightly reluctant Hamish, whose glance at Ewan seemed almost to apologise for his mistress's wrong-headed notions. When they got to the hall again, Sarah sniffed the damp air. 'Doesn't this smell bother you?' she asked him.

'What smell? Look, I need to get on,' he said, stooping forward with one hand on the door.

Daphne bustled out after Sarah and the door slammed behind them. They were soon on the esplanade again, the wind playing merry hell with Sarah's neat bob, Daphne's scarf and Hamish's tousled coat.

'You were quite rude to him, Sarah, the poor chap,' said Daphne crossly. 'I don't know where you think we'll get our plastering done after that.'

'Lucky we don't need any, isn't it?' Sarah said unrepentantly.

'It's not like you got anywhere grilling him,' Daphne continued. 'He explained visiting the house and said quite clearly he'd had his back to the view the whole time later on, so he can't have seen a thing.'

'Well yes, that's what he said, Daph. But didn't you notice something about that?' Sarah said, turning to her friend. 'He was lying. And I can tell you why.'

TWENTY-EIGHT

Daphne stood with her hands on her hips, her scarf blowing around her head, confronting Sarah and little Hamish. 'Well go on, then. If you're so clever.'

'OK. You saw the plaster in that room, didn't you, Daph?'

'Of course,' said Daphne crossly. 'He did a magnificent job. It was smooth as silk. Smoother, probably.'

'Yes, *very* smooth. Just like him. But, if you noticed, the plaster on the wall by the door, the bit he said he'd been doing today while Deirdre was, well, breathing her last, was a very pale pink. The plaster at the other end, around and above the big picture window, though – that was quite a dark pink colour.'

'So what? He obviously likes to cover the whole spectrum of pinks,' Daphne said, rewrapping her scarf before the wind could steal it away from her.

'Yes, but plaster is dark pink when it's wet, Daph. When it dries out it goes very pale. So despite what he told us, it's quite clear that Ewan was plastering all round the window today, when Deirdre Jones was dying. So he could have seen something. In fact, he surely must have seen something, unless he was plastering with his eyes shut. And, because he's lied about that, maybe he's lied about not being involved as well. Maybe he did kill her after all, maybe he was furious when she cancelled those repairs, and then he popped back and finished his work.'

'Oooh, I can't believe anyone could be so cold-blooded! Not with that smile. And that's really rather clever, Sarah, about the plaster colours, you're getting so cunning in your old age,' Daphne said.

'Less of the old,' Sarah said, but she did preen a bit. Afternoon telly always seemed like a bit of a guilty pleasure for someone who'd had such a busy career – but she'd never have known so much about plaster without watching all those DIY home improvement shows.

'But I thought you said there was no obvious cause of death with Deirdre?' Daphne said, digesting the rest of what Sarah had said.

'There isn't. But there were some suspicious circumstances – the blob, and the glass. Ewan's explained the blob but that liquid in the glass could contain a poison. There's that pen with Merstairs Mortar written on it as well. If it's a building company, then Ewan must know it, surely, whatever he says. Even if there's no obvious cause of death for poor Deirdre, that doesn't mean she wasn't murdered, or that Ewan didn't see it, or do it himself, or even see who *did* do it. And I think we need to say all that to Mariella, before Ewan's plasterwork round that window dries.'

'Right you are. I'll just give her a ring.' Daphne started to rummage in her bag, and Sarah bit her lip. If she added up all the time she'd spent waiting for her friend to find items in that portable void, why then—

'Got it!' Daphne cried triumphantly. A minute later, she had a rather cross-sounding Mariella on speakerphone.

'I can hardly hear you two for the wind,' she snapped. 'Can you get into some shelter?'

Immediately Daphne's eyes lit up. 'Let's go to the Oyster Shell,' she said, mentioning the newest café on the seafront.

'All right,' said Mariella. 'I'm not far off. I'll come and join you in five minutes.'

Sarah and Daphne were soon inside the café, attractively done out in pale greens and blues, with little oyster shells on the tables containing the salt and pepper. There were sea-themed Christmas decorations everywhere, featuring fish and mermaids in Santa hats. The café had a lovely view of the coast, but it was safely behind glass which was ideal on a chilly day. Sarah picked a table away from the other customers. Privacy was a scarce resource in Merstairs, where the slightest bit of gossip gave you a brief edge over almost everybody, and flapping ears were an epidemic disease the likes of which she had rarely seen.

'We don't need to wait for Mari to get our cups of tea, do we? I'm feeling a bit hoarse,' Daphne said, rubbing her chest. 'And maybe a snack would help me keep my strength up. I lost my appetite after, um, Deirdre's house, but I think I could manage a little something now.'

Sarah went off to do the honours, returning with a tray groaning with scones, extra-thick cream and tangy blackberry jam, as well as a teapot and three cups.

'I don't know what you're getting excited for, Hamish, none of this is for you,' Sarah said, giving him a loving pat. He settled down happily enough at her feet, and was gazing up at her as if to mesmerise her into dropping her scone when Mariella flung open the door and sat down in a flurry, hair flying.

'I don't have long. I shouldn't be here, really, so I hope this is good,' she said, looking sternly at both women before picking up her cup of tea and taking a grateful sip. 'No sign of that blasted phone, and interviewing everyone is taking forever. Lovely tea.'

'I think you'll find it interesting,' said Sarah, explaining about Ewan and the plaster – both on the wall and on Deirdre's table.

'Hmm, I see,' said Mariella, taking another sip of tea. 'Ooh, that is good. I've been racing around all day – well, you can imagine – and not least because of the PM on Deirdre,' she said to Sarah, keeping a weather eye on her mother. 'Dr Strutton is a marvel, she's managed to make a start... and I have to say, at the moment she's still pretty baffled.'

'PM? Deirdre will hardly be suffering from pre-menstrual tension any more, darling, anyone could tell you that,' said Daphne, luckily getting the wrong end of the stick while she munched her scone.

'Well, that's intriguing,' said Sarah. 'I imagine Dr Strutton's seen most things in her time. It looked like a simple heart attack... but I don't believe it was for a second.'

Daphne coughed, spraying a few crumbs to Hamish's great delight. 'Must you?' she mumbled.

'Sorry, Mum, but this could be important,' said Mariella. 'Go on, Aunty Sarah. Let's have your theory, then.'

'Well, she was a quiet, nervous woman. A natural-looking heart attack could have been induced, as she showed signs of hypervigilance – a sort of over-reaction to stimuli. She jumped a mile when you dropped that saucepan at her house, Daph.'

Daphne wiped the last traces of jam off her face with a napkin. 'Oh, poor thing. A bit like shell shock, I suppose.'

'Exactly,' said Sarah. 'She would have been very easy to trigger. Her system was on red alert the whole time.'

'Could that have had an effect on her health?' Mariella asked.

'Most definitely, I would say. But I still don't think that was the cause of her death.'

'What? I thought you were saying it was?' Daphne sounded indignant.

'I said it looked like it. But that's if you're ignoring what we saw at the scene.'

Mariella leant forward. 'Go on, then, Aunty Sarah. Don't leave me dangling.'

'Well,' said Sarah, rather embarrassed to be pointing this out to Mariella. After all, she had been at the scene too. 'If you remember, there was a glass half-full of some sticky-looking liquid on the table...'

'Of course there was!' Mariella slapped the table for emphasis and all their teacups jumped. 'I told Deeside to log it and send it for analysis. Trouble is, it's almost easier to do it myself than leave it to that lot. I've had so much to do, following up on all the alibis... But that's no excuse, I'll have to chase it up. Thanks for reminding me, Aunty Sarah.'

'Thank goodness. I can't believe it was lovely Ewan,' said Daphne – seeming to forget he'd been in the room with the suspicious glass.

'Actually, we caught up with a TikTok fan filming on the esplanade this morning,' Mariella said, a frown between her brows. 'She retook the footage umpteen times to get it right. She was opposite the Jones's house for an age, and one thing is quite clear from what's on her phone.'

'Oh? What's that?' Now it was Sarah's turn to sit forward.

'Just this,' said Mariella, tucking a banknote under her plate for the waitress. 'Ewan Smith only went into Deirdre's house for five minutes this morning. She was fine then. The windows are so big, you can see right into the room, and she was on her own in there after Ewan left. The layout is really unusual, there's only one way in or out of the house; through the front door. So what on earth happened to her after that?'

'That's the question, isn't it?' Sarah said bleakly. But the mention of the Jones family had jogged a memory. She said goodbye absently to Mariella, who was rushing off to check on the toxicology report, and turned to Daphne.

'I'm just going to drop in on Charles. I need to check something.'

'It's like that, is it?' Daphne nudged her.

'I don't know what you're getting at, it's purely to do with the investigation, and it's quite urgent. You're welcome to come too if you like,' Sarah said defensively.

'Don't mind if I do,' said Daphne.

'Well, excellent,' said Sarah, feeling she'd been had somehow, and hoping against hope that Charles would have the piece of information she was looking for. This could be the detail that would blow the whole case wide open.

TWENTY-NINE

It was good to be in Charles's loft-style flat above his shop once again. Sarah felt it contained interesting clues to his personality. The art books, for instance, which he obviously read with great enjoyment, the tomes devoted to antiques which she was less interested in, and even the air of a quietly self-sufficient, unadorned yet very comfortable bachelor domain, were all intriguing signposts. Today, however, she was anxious to get on with the matter in hand.

Charles, although rather surprised to find Sarah and Daphne on his doorstep, had shown his usual beautiful manners in ushering them upstairs. He'd found one of Tinkerbell's toys for Hamish to first worship, and then gnaw, and was currently making both ladies a cup of excellent coffee. The deliciously bitter aroma swirled around the high white walls of the place and Sarah felt quite intoxicated, gazing into his blue eyes.

'Ahem. I thought you were desperate to ask about something?' Daphne said to Sarah. Then she turned to Charles. 'We've come about the guns. I think.'

'Oh, not that again,' said Charles, passing a hand across his high forehead. 'I'm so tired of trying to explain my stupid lapses on that. I honestly couldn't feel worse if I tried.'

'I did want to cover that quickly but there was something else as well... Still, since Daph's brought it up, Charles, did you know it wasn't your gun that was involved, and it looks like it could have been one of the Militia's?' Sarah said.

'Thank you, yes, dear lady,' Charles sighed. 'Mari told me. But even so. The idea that it could so easily have happened... I can't think how I came to be so lax.'

'Oh well, we all know the answer to that one,' said Sarah, putting her cup down.

Daphne nodded. 'Francesca, as per usual. I wouldn't put it past her to have given people access to those keys just to make you look bad.'

'Come now, Daphne, Francesca would never do that, she would hate to see me accused of murder.'

Sarah and Daphne, who had both seen the glee on the woman's face when they'd talked at her house, remained silent.

'I suppose I ought to be grateful that someone else turns out to be just as careless,' Charles continued.

'Hmm,' Sarah said. 'But I've really come about something else. Matthew Jones.'

Daphne sat up a little straighter and Charles looked surprised. 'Oh?'

'It's just that he mentioned having worked for you – or rather, his mother did. And you let him go? Could he be disgruntled enough to be trying to get you into trouble, with all the guns business?'

Charles looked at Sarah for a moment and then burst out laughing. 'You have met Matthew, I take it? He's no evil genius. Yes, he worked for me when I had a City job, a while back. But there weren't any hard feelings when he left. It was a simple case of last in, first out. He wouldn't hurt a fly.'

'OK then,' said Sarah, 'I suppose that sets my mind at rest.'

She was silent for a moment, sipping her coffee. Now her mind wandered back to Matilda, and from her to Ewan, and the plastering again. 'I've just had another thought.'

'I'm not sure I like the way you've said that,' said Daphne. 'Is it terrible? Has someone else died?'

'Nothing like that, Daph. But we all assumed, didn't we, that because Ewan was plastering around the windows down on the esplanade, and he didn't see anyone going in or out of the Jones's house, that no one visited them – apart from him for five minutes.'

'That's right,' Daphne said. 'Any more coffee, Charles? And a biscuit might be nice, while you're up.'

Charles hesitated for a moment, then got to his feet. 'Not quite sure what I've got in that line, but I'll have a look,' he said. 'So, you still don't think Ewan himself has been ruled out?' He started rummaging in the kitchen cabinet over the sink.

'Well, quite possibly. All we know is that he was a bit cagey, to say the least, about what he was up to in the morning. Just because he says he didn't see a thing, doesn't mean he didn't slip over to the house again. *After* the TikTok person had stopped filming, of course.'

'Aha,' said Charles, unearthing a tin of biscuits like Tom Thumb pulling out a plum. 'Oh, that's no good, they were an early Christmas present, they're a bit fancy.' He made to stow them away again.

'Oh, bring them here, Charles, they'll do nicely,' Daphne insisted, looking thrilled as he deposited the glossy box on the table. 'Wow, these are really nice. Who did you say bought them for you?'

'I didn't,' said Charles weakly.

'Lovely colour,' said Sarah, noting the rich purple hues of the tin, and its winsome pattern of bunches of violets. There was only one woman in Merstairs who habitually dressed from head to toe in that shade, and she was one of Charles's many old flames.

'Er, yes,' said Charles, rapidly levering off the offending lid and putting it on the floor, out of sight. The sides of the tin were still a rich, almost papal shade of purple but Sarah decided to let the whole thing go. She'd never been a jealous woman before now – there had simply been no need with Peter, who'd had eyes for no one else – and she didn't intend to start at this late stage of life, whatever the provocation.

'I don't feel like ringing Mariella to tell her to check the CCTV cameras along the esplanade, I don't want to get another flea in my ear. There's no doubt she'll have already thought of doing it, anyway,' said Sarah, as Daphne started to rifle through the tin. 'I think there's a description of the contents on the back of this, Daph,' she said, scooping the lid off the floor, where Hamish was busily sniffing it, and handing it to her friend.

'Oh, thank goodness,' said Daphne. 'I live in dread of wasting calories on something I don't like. You know how strict I am, Sarah.'

'I do indeed,' said Sarah, trying not to meet Charles's eye, when suddenly there was a ring at the doorbell.

'Well, who on earth can that be?' Charles seemed stunned at the prospect of having yet more visitors to his previously tranquil flat.

'Only one way to find out.' Sarah smiled.

Charles clattered down the stairs to answer the door with the little Scottie at his heels. There was no mistaking the gravelly Yorkshire tones of the new arrival.

'Surely that's Ewan's voice?' said Daphne, in one of her incredibly loud whispers.

'Shhh,' said Sarah. 'I'm trying to hear.'

But she didn't have to strain for long, as Ewan followed Charles and Hamish back up the stairs and rather uneasily eyed the two women. 'Ah. Didn't realise you'd be here,' he said, a flush spreading up his cheeks.

'Take a seat,' said Sarah, then remembered it wasn't her place to welcome guests. 'If that's OK, Charles?'

'By all means. A coffee, old chap?' Charles asked hospitably.

'Maybe a tea. Had so many coffees today I've got the shakes again. I really need to cut down,' Ewan said, holding out his hands. Sure enough, there was a visible tremor there.

'Again, you said? Is this happening often?' Despite herself, Sarah had swung into doctor mode.

'Oh, only once in a while,' said Ewan, seeming unconcerned. He sat down a bit untidily at the bench, knocking the biscuit tin down the table. Daphne rescued it like a mother caring for a newborn baby, but then switched almost all her attention to the plasterer.

'You must get tired, on your feet all day with such a physical job. There's a lot of stretching with plastering, I suppose?' Daphne said. 'Not to mention flexing those muscles.'

'Funny you should say that,' he said, bending his bicep obligingly while Daphne munched on a biscuit, transfixed. 'Last few weeks I've had terrible aches and pains. Keeping me up at night, it is. I suppose that's why I've been relying on coffees to get me going in the morning.'

'That sounds like a nasty vicious circle. Have you thought of going to your GP?' Sarah asked, studying Ewan's face intently as he answered.

'Not easy to get an appointment these days, is it? No, I'll leave that to those who really have a problem,' he said lightly. 'Anyway, I suppose I should explain why I'm here.'

'Here's your tea, old man,' said Charles, passing a mug his way. Ewan reached out for it and jogged it slightly before picking it up. Charles wiped away the spill and soon they were all settled and looking at the newcomer expectantly.

'Well, it's not easy to say this. I know what it's like being accused,' Ewan said, looking briefly at Sarah and Daphne. 'It's not nice. Charles'll understand, after that gun business.' Charles nodded, and Ewan went on. 'That's why I came to you, mate. I wouldn't really wish to point the finger at anyone else. But the trouble is, unless the police find proof that it wasn't me who somehow did for Deirdre, I'm still looking a bit tasty for whatever happened to her, and old Daffyd too. I could have forced him to kill himself I suppose. I've got the muscle power, you could say,' he said with a wink at the ladies. 'I was around at both times, and there was no love lost with him, not after the way he treated my Matilda. Well, you saw what it was like the night he died. There were other things too... But all that to one side, hand on heart I didn't do it,' he said, looking solemn.

Daphne, by this stage, was gazing at the man almost as rapturously as she'd peered into the biscuit tin earlier. She gave a little sigh now. 'We really don't think it was you, Ewan,' she burst out.

Sarah gave her a quick quelling look. 'We're very interested in what you have to say about other suspects,' she said. 'And we certainly wouldn't think any the worse of you for making, erm, suggestions that could be helpful to the enquiry.'

'No, we wouldn't.' Daphne shook her head, mesmerised by Ewan's magnetic gaze.

'Absolutely, go ahead old chap. It's the right thing to do,' said Charles heartily.

Ewan seemed to gather himself. 'All right, then. Have you thought about the previous choir soloist? Daffyd was even meaner to her than he was to Matilda. She really had it rough for a while, it's a wonder she didn't strangle him with her bare hands.'

Daphne shuddered at this image, but Sarah perked up. 'What was her name?' she asked.

'That's easy, it was Griselda Grantham.'

At once, Charles dragged his chair back from the table with a clatter and rushed over to the sink, where he set about washing up his cafetiere. Sarah looked at him in surprise, then turned back to Ewan. 'Griselda Grantham? That name sounds vaguely familiar, though I don't think I've met her.'

'You might remember her from the old days. She was a bit of a star at one point. You know, musicals, films and such like.'

'Oh? Oh yes, it's coming back to me. In fact, I remember seeing her in something, it must be at least twenty years ago, what would that have been?'

'Oooh, ooh, it's on the tip of my tongue,' said Daphne. 'Oh damn, it's gone,' she said, replacing it with a biscuit.

Charles, eyeing the rapidly depleting tin sadly from over by the sink, spoke up. 'Perhaps I can help. She was in a rather dreadful film called *Those Merry Women*.'

'Of course,' said Sarah. 'Yes, I remember now. It was a sort of feminist retelling of the Robin Hood myth.'

'That's quite a deep evaluation of it, Sarah. It was just a romp with lots of ladies in short tunics and tights, as I remember it,' Charles said with a smile.

'That's right. And one of them, Robina Hood, had to shoot an apple off Big Jemima's head,' Daphne chipped in. 'She needed a steady hand, and a good aim... and a lot of practice with guns. It was all filmed with pistols, not bows and arrows, for some reason.'

'Who played Robina? Don't tell me it was...'

'Yes,' said Daphne, clapping her hands together. 'It was Griselda Grantham.'

THIRTY

Sarah left Charles's flat with a spring in her step, dragging a reluctant Daphne behind her.

'There was a really nice orange cream in that tin, Sarah. You could have waited until I'd had that.'

'Aren't you feeling a bit full, Daph? Besides, Charles probably wanted to hold onto that tin to regift it. It wasn't really his taste.'

'Oh, who'd give a half-empty tin as a present?' said Daphne, blithely overlooking the fact that it was she who had emptied it. 'And anyway, oranges are full of vitamin C. You don't want me to get a horrible deficiency, surely? So I dare say I could manage a little something if you wanted to stop for a break,' she added, ever hopeful.

'We've got no time, Daph, you know that. We really need to crack on and find this Griselda, and see what she's got to say for herself. Ewan's right, she's got a motive that's probably every bit as strong as Matilda's.'

'Well, we don't even know her proper address. All Ewan could tell us is that she lives in the biggest house in Reculver. I mean, Reculver is full of big houses.'

'He said it's right next to the beach, and we can't miss it. He also said she'd be walking her two dogs down there at this time of day. So it'll be perfect for Hamish. You'd like to stretch your legs, wouldn't you, boy?'

Once they had Hamish's hearty assent, Daphne seemed to realise further protest was useless and they trooped off to Sarah's car for the short drive to Reculver.

Sarah always loved this route out of Merstairs, bringing them ever nearer to the stunning landmark of the Reculver Towers. These were the remnants of a twelfth-century church, which was itself a reconstruction of a seventh-century chapel. Even this was not the oldest building on the site, an honour which went to a Roman fort started in 43 AD. The huddled ruins of all these endeavours were now facing their most ferocious battle yet, as the sea crept closer by the year and the ancient stones did their best to cling on to dry land.

'Isn't this beautiful?' said Sarah, as she parked the car near the English Heritage site.

'Stunning,' said Daphne a little glumly.

'Come on, Daph, a good brisk walk on the beach will sort you out,' said Sarah, who had no difficulty in attributing her friend's fit of the grumps to a huge drop in her blood sugar levels in the aftermath of her biscuit blow-out.

'Oh all right, just to please Hamish,' Daphne said, bundling out of the car and grabbing the little dog's lead as he chased his own tail with excitement at the prospect of a whole new beach to explore. Once they'd descended the steps down onto the sand and shingle below, Hamish's joy really abounded, as the beach spread in a huge crescent, hugging the coast but also calling to the sea, which flirted with it, flicking waves back and forth as though teasing a long-time lover.

'Any sign of this Griselda?' asked Sarah anxiously, craning her head in one direction and then the other. As far as she could see, they were walking in lonely splendour. Just as they reached the curve of the headland, though, a huge white dog with black spots, like a dalmatian but seemingly inflated to at least twice the size, bounded round the corner and almost knocked both ladies to the ground. Hamish, who had never met a four-legged friend on this scale before, tried to do his usual thorough sniffing greeting but was too short to get any further than the newcomer's fine ankles. Just when Sarah and Daphne had brushed themselves down, another massive spotty dog sprinted round the same corner and all was sandy confusion again.

Sarah was holding out a hand to Daphne when the dogs' owner appeared, a little out of breath and staggering slightly. She was a tall woman, lean, angular and elegant, with long black hair. Her face was thin and somewhat lined, but she had magnificent cheekbones and deep green, magnetic eyes.

'Oh, are my boys creating havoc again? I do apologise. Thor! Hammer! Best behaviour now,' she said to the dogs, who both immediately dropped to the ground and panted gently. 'That's the worst of Great Danes,' she said, putting a slender white hand up to flick her hair out of her eyes with long, trembling fingers. 'No one ever seems to be expecting them.'

'Well, um, yes,' said Sarah. She was a recent convert to the wonder of dogs but was finding these creatures a lot more than she bargained for. 'They're... truly beautiful,' she said, stepping back. Hamish had no reservations at all about his new friends, but curled up between them, evidently enjoying the fact that they made rather good windbreaks against the gusty breezes on the beach.

The woman smiled briefly and made to move on, again missing her footing slightly, when Sarah stopped her. 'Just a moment. You're Griselda Graham, aren't you?'

'Oh,' said Griselda, with a rapidly suppressed smirk. 'You don't look like the autograph-hunting type. And it's been a while. But I suppose you're the right age to have seen some of my work.' Her smile was wider now, though still a little haughty.

'It's not—' Daphne started, but Sarah broke in.

'We recognised you, of course. And we did want to talk about some of your, er work, though it's a bit later than the films.'

'I see,' Griselda said, her head on one side. 'You sound like quite serious fans. Well then, as a treat, why don't you come with me to the café over on the promenade? I usually have a quick cup of tea after my walk.'

'Oh, yes please!' said Daphne.

She sounded exactly like an exuberant fan, and not for the first time Sarah blessed her wonderful enthusiasm. 'Sounds lovely,' she said weakly. 'Now, where's Hamish?' She looked up and down the beach, and was starting to get alarmed, when she glanced back at the Great Danes and realised the little Scottie was very sensibly taking shelter right underneath one of them. Whether it was Thor or Hammer, she couldn't have said, but whichever it was, they seemed perfectly relaxed about the situation. She only hoped Griselda was going to be as happy when she realised what Sarah and Daphne were really up to.

THIRTY-ONE

A few minutes later, the group was ensconced in a cosy little café that had a very relaxed policy on dogs. Thor and Hammer were greeted enthusiastically, and there was even a special stroke for Hamish, who was very much enjoying being part of this enormous gang. Sarah had always suspected the Scottie saw himself as a much bigger boy than he actually was. She hoped hanging out with the Great Danes wasn't going to give him terrible delusions of grandeur.

With all three dogs under the table, there was scarcely room for Sarah, Daphne or Griselda's legs, and they had to sit as though riding side saddle. This was another slightly surreal element to the situation, added to Griselda's unshakeable belief that they were diehard fans of her work.

'So, when did you really start following my career?' she asked, picking up her tea. Her hands, so long and beautifully expressive, quivered slightly and made the cup jump around. She fiddled in her coat pocket and brought out a hip flask. 'Little nip, just to keep out the cold?' she said, offering it to them both. 'Suit yourselves,' she said quickly when she got no takers. She sloshed a generous measure of what smelt like brandy into her cup and raised it to her lips again. 'Ah, very warming,' she said. 'Now, what were we saying? Oh yes, I asked when you became such big fans?'

'Oh, well, for me, it was, um, really quite recently,' said Sarah, wishing she could just blurt out the truth, but desperate to find out a little more about Griselda's connection to the Jones family before coming clean.

Griselda turned to Daphne and raised her eyebrows. 'Me? Oh. Well I loved you in that Robin Hood thing,' Daphne said cleverly. Sarah beamed her approval.

'*Robina* Hood,' Griselda corrected her. 'Such an interesting part. I remember the director saying to me, so few women could have taken the role. It was quite an ask, subverting the patriarchy like that. If we'd gone too far, you see, the powers that be could easily have suppressed the release of the whole film.' She shook her head reminiscently.

'Do you really think that?' Sarah couldn't stop herself from asking.

'Of course.' Griselda widened her extraordinary emerald eyes.

Sarah decided they'd probably done enough shilly-shallying around. 'We're particularly interested in a much later phase of your, er, journey. Specifically, your work in the Merstairs Muses choir.'

'The choir? But that's just a local thing... and run by an awful person, who doesn't have a true artistic bone in his body. Whereas my film work, that has genuinely changed lives,' she said, trying but failing to look modest.

'Nevertheless, we'd love to just ask you a few questions about it,' Sarah said.

'Why on earth would you be interested in that?'

'Good question,' said Daphne, who was rubbing the enormous belly of one of the dogs.

Sarah squirmed somewhat in her seat – not easy when she

had nowhere to put her feet. 'The thing is, as you'll be aware, Daffyd Jones has just died...'

Griselda, who'd lifted her tea to her lips, almost dropped it in shock. This time, it wasn't her trembly hands at work. 'What? What on earth do you mean?'

'Didn't you know?' Sarah was astonished.

Griselda looked as though she'd had the stuffing knocked out of her. She took a quick swig of her tea, this time without incident. 'I hadn't heard a word. Gracious me.'

'And Deirdre, too,' added Daphne.

'Deirdre? Oh, yes, you mean that little mouse, Daffyd's wife. Both of them? How absolutely terrible.' Griselda now looked rather grey. Then she shook herself. 'I've been more or less incommunicado, wrapped up in my preparations for my next role...'

'Oh, what's that?' Daphne asked.

'I can't really say,' Griselda said, eyes wide. 'My agent would kill me if even a word got about. Oh, perhaps I shouldn't have said that.'

'Just to keep us on track. You're saying the news about what's happened to the Joneses hasn't reached you at all?' Sarah persisted.

'Why would it?' Griselda said simply. 'I left the choir quite a while ago, that Cookie Monster girl took over, the one who always dresses in blue fluff' – here it was Daphne's turn to choke on her tea – 'and that's the last time I thought about that lot, really. Apart from my collaboration with Gwendoline Randall for the Christmas carols, of course.'

Sarah was electrified. 'You know Gwendoline?'

'Yes, I said so. Aren't you listening? She and I got fed up with Daffyd, the silly man. So every Christmas we have our own carolling group, with much more artistic flair. There's a little sing-off and then we do our bit by the clock tower while the Christmas lights are turned on officially by Francesca. That's the mayor – she's a big fan too,' Griselda confided.

'I see,' said Sarah. 'So you're in direct competition with Daffyd's choir? Or you were.'

'Hardly. Oh, the choir members were lovely enough, you understand,' she said with the sort of on-off smile a star bestows on lesser mortals. 'But Daffyd, well. He simply couldn't cope with being upstaged. He was used to being the big cheese, really, and when I turned up, I mean!' She shrugged her shoulders, as if to indicate how badly Daffyd Jones had been eclipsed. 'I had no choice but to leave, he wasn't good at dealing with real talent. He had a heart attack, I assume? He was always red in the face, particularly when he was shouting at me. Or did they both die in an accident? Tut tut, life can be cruel.' She took another swig of her tea. 'Honestly, I've had a few difficult directors in my time, talented people, who try and get the best out of you by fair means or foul... but he was the end.'

'I'm afraid it wasn't a heart attack. Daffyd was shot and, well, the police are still doing tests to see what happened to Deirdre.'

'Goodness gracious,' said Griselda, looking stunned. 'That's extraordinary. I wonder who would do that? Deirdre was all right, totally in Daffyd's shadow, of course, but lots of people loathed *him*. He was the most god-awful, jumped up little squit. He'd somehow got the impression that a couple of moments of fame entitled him to behave like a diva for the rest of his days,' Griselda said. 'Waitress! My tea has gone cold. Fetch me another,' she snapped. Belatedly, she remembered her audience. 'Oh, would you two like another drink? Do order anything you like.'

'Um, no thanks.' Sarah shook her head.

'I might grab a snack...' Daphne started, but Griselda turned to her.

'I don't know how you can think about food at a time like this. I'm terribly sensitive to tragedy, you know. I probably won't eat again all day,' she said, not thanking the waitress when a fresh tea appeared, but quickly dosing it from her flask and then taking a hefty sip. Sarah was beginning to suspect that square meals weren't an overriding interest for Griselda.

'Were you anywhere near the rehearsal on Monday? Or were you on the esplanade in Merstairs earlier today?' Sarah persisted.

'Of course not! I live here in Reculver now and, well, for reasons I won't go into, I don't drive any more,' Griselda said crossly. Sarah immediately wondered whether she'd had her licence taken away. 'I haven't been to those choir rehearsals for ages, and after what Daffyd said to me, well, I certainly don't owe him a thing.'

'What did he say, just as a matter of interest?'

Griselda looked at Sarah again. By now, the quantity of enhanced tea she had drunk seemed to be somewhat blurring her thought processes. But she still looked rather quizzical. 'For s-superfans, you don't seem to be asking many questions about my main body of work. And you ssseem pretty obsessed with Daffyd's tinpot local choir,' she said, slurring a little. 'If I didn't know better I'd think you were trying to check my alibi,' she said, collapsing into giggles.

Sarah smiled politely. 'It's just lovely to hear more about, um, challenges you've faced,' she said.

'Hmm.' Griselda swayed a little, and under the table one of her dogs whined. 'Well, I suppose it doesn't matter now. He said some cruel things about my age, my looks… he even made some very peculiar accusations about me being dependent on certain sussbstances! Me!' She laughed again. 'But look how I'm showing him,' she finished off, putting her elbow down heavily on the table, only for it to slide off.

'Whoopsie,' said Sarah, propping the woman up. 'I wonder if we should see you home?'

'Ccertainly not! Anyway, don't you two want an autograph?

That's what your type is always after,' said Griselda, making a big effort and patting down her pockets for a pen. Just as Sarah was worried she'd got her hand stuck in her coat, Griselda triumphantly drew out a biro. The logo printed on it caught the light. It was quite unmistakable.

'Wait a minute! Can I see that?' Sarah said, pouncing.

THIRTY-TWO

'Your friend is quite strange. Do you think she's drunk?' said Griselda, going almost cross-eyed as she whispered loudly to Daphne.

'Um, no, she's just, er, checking your pen works,' Daphne said, looking askance at Sarah.

'Merstairs Mortar, it says on it.' Sarah brandished the pen in front of the sozzled woman. 'It's exactly the same as the one on the desk when Daffyd Jones died, and the one Deidre Jones was clutching when we found her. Where did you get this from?' she asked.

Griselda looked at Sarah in befuddled surprise. 'Well, keep your hair on. Daffyd Jones gave it to me. Last week, I think it was. He, Geraldine and I always meet on neutral territory once before the carol ssing-off. We went to that pub Geraldine loves, the Ship and Anchor. They do good measures, I'll give them that,' she said, rattling her hip flask which now sounded rather empty. 'About time for me to go. D'you want those autographs or not?'

Daphne and Sarah looked at each other. Daphne nodded

politely and pushed a napkin towards the woman. 'That would be so great,' she said with a cheesy smile.

Griselda took up the biro and scrawled something totally illegible, then shoved the napkin back to Daphne. 'There. That should make you a pretty penny if you sell it on eBay,' she added with an attempt at a wink. 'Now I must be going before the off-licence s-shuts... I mean, before it gets dark.'

'Would you like us to come with you?' Sarah asked, as the woman swayed to her feet.

'Do you think I was born yesssterday?' she said. 'Never let the fans know where you live. The dogs will take me. They're my guardian angels,' she said, trying to gather up their leads and dropping them.

'I really think we should see you home...' Sarah started, handing the leashes to her.

'I said no! Honestly, you just can't take no for an answer, can you? Old dears like you two are the worst,' Griselda snapped, bumping into the café door as she lurched out onto the street, where the brace of enormous dogs proceeded to tow her away.

'Poor lady,' said Daphne. 'She really did seem a bit tiddly.'

'Yes.' Sarah shook her head, smarting somewhat at the 'old dears' comment. 'I'd say she's her own worst enemy, that one. For a second, when I saw that pen, I really thought it might have been her that did for Daffyd. It's such a weird coincidence. But even if Griselda had been around on that awful night, her hands wouldn't be steady enough to shoot Daffyd. And I can't believe Deirdre would let her into her house, even if she'd managed to call a taxi to drop her in Merstairs. I'm sure the two deaths are connected somehow, though.'

'What makes her drink, do you think?' Daphne asked.

'Perhaps it's the fact that her glory days are behind her,' Sarah said. 'That must be so hard.'

'Ha, well, I suppose that's good news for us. Our glory days are all in front of us,' Daphne said, finishing her tea with a smile as they both got up.

They were about to shut the café door, when the waitress shot forward and tapped Sarah on the shoulder. 'That's four teas, please,' she said. Griselda, for all her apparent largesse, had left without paying. Her film star days might be over, but her deep sense of entitlement was still going strong.

* * *

They were just drawing up outside their cottages in Sarah's Volvo, with Hamish snoozing in his harness in the back after all the fun with his giant new friends, when Sarah's mobile rang. Fishing it out, she could see it was Pamela Strutton, the pathologist.

'Dr Strutton, how's it going?' she asked, trying not to sound too baffled that the woman was ringing her at all.

'I've finished with poor Deirdre Jones. Mariella asked me to ring, she's in the thick of making house-to-house enquiries, but she wanted you to know.'

'Know what?' said Sarah, on tenterhooks now.

'Well, exactly what Mrs Jones died of.'

THIRTY-THREE

Sarah looked at Daphne, who was sitting next to her in the car, her face a mixture of curiosity and alarm. Sarah knew just how she felt.

'So, what actually killed the poor lady in the end?' Sarah asked.

'It was natural causes, after all. I couldn't find a thing wrong with her, and believe me I tried – as far as I could on the budget DI Brice allocated. If she hadn't suddenly died, she really could have lived quite a while. Her heart was sound, lungs not bad for a smoker, kidneys fine – her liver had taken a bit of a hit, it looked like she was a drinker, or she was going that way. I was only permitted a limited toxicology panel, but she was definitely taking something for insomnia.'

'Oh really? Zolpidem, or daridorexant?' Sarah asked.

'Flunitrazepam, as it happens.'

'Flunitrazepam? That's basically Rohypnol, isn't it?' Sarah said thoughtfully.

'Exactly. Better known as the date rape drug. Still a perfectly legitimate sleeping treatment, though,' replied Dr Strutton. 'So all in all, it was very unexpected. As she was the wife of a very recently deceased man, I was on the lookout for foul play. Unless, of course...'

'Unless what?' Sarah asked, agog.

'Unless, perhaps, the stress and guilt of killing her husband put her system under so much strain that her heart couldn't take it. Whether Deirdre was strong enough to force Daffyd's hand and shoot him, or whether she could have tricked him somehow, is another question. Anyway, her heart stopped beating. In this case, I suppose, the challenge is going to be determining exactly what caused that. Inner turmoil, or an outer stressor of some description. Well, good luck.'

'Oh, er, thank you,' said Sarah quickly – but there was an efficient-sounding click. The pathologist had already gone.

'What was that? What did she say?' Daphne was desperate to hear the news.

'It's a bit mysterious,' Sarah admitted. 'There's no clear reason why Deirdre died.'

'You mean, it might not even be murder at all?' Daphne looked very cheered by this news.

'I'm sorry, Daphne, I just don't think she died of natural causes, whatever the official theory is. I wonder if Mariella's got the results back on that half-glass of liquid from the Jones's house? I think it's going to be up to us to prove Dr Strutton wrong this time, much as I like and respect the woman.'

'I thought doctors always stuck together?' Daphne said.

'Well, we do – but there are some things that are more important than professional etiquette, and murder is definitely one of them. She was very clear that DI Brice hadn't given her the funding to get all the answers she wanted, and she's passed the baton to us. Now we need to sort it out either way.

'It's my Mariella's job, not ours, and she is working her socks off,' said Daphne. 'Besides, if Deidre got Daffyd to pull the trigger, then died herself, then the case is over, isn't it? And thank goodness for that.'

'It's a neat solution, I admit that... Except I don't think Deirdre would have had the strength. She was tiny, Daffyd was huge – I just can't see it. No, we've got to keep going. Mariella is doing a brilliant job, but there's so much to get through... especially if you always have to do things by the book.'

'Hmm...' Daphne didn't sound convinced. 'But now you mention books, can you lend me the one we're discussing in the group next week? I didn't quite get round to ordering it from the library, what with all this nasty business.'

'Of course, Daph,' Sarah said, respecting her friend's evident desire to change the subject. She hadn't finished it herself, and the peaceful evening when she'd sat by the fire and flicked idly through the pages could have occurred in another lifetime, it felt so long ago. It didn't seem likely she'd have an opportunity to finish it for a while, so Daphne might as well have it. 'Come and get it now, if you like.'

As they approached the little cottage up the tidily weeded path, Sarah realised there was a light on deep within the house – probably in the kitchen, judging from the muted glow. Burglars? The hairs on the back of her neck rose, and she stepped in front of Daphne and shielded her with her body as she approached the front door. Just as she was trying to get the key in the lock, with a hand that trembled almost as much as Griselda Graham's, it swung open. She gasped.

THIRTY-FOUR

Before Sarah had time to scream, she was being pulled into a hug and a kiss with Charles, who was looking very fetching wearing her best apron, while holding a wooden spoon. As soon as she could speak, and her pulse returned to normal, she managed to squeak, 'Well, this is a surprise.'

'Harrumph, it certainly is,' said Daphne, squeezing past the couple with Hamish. 'Don't look, boy, I'm not sure that's PG enough for your eyes,' she said, marching into the kitchen.

Sarah followed a little sheepishly, and Charles brought up the rear with a big smile. Once in the kitchen, Sarah saw that Daphne was getting out cutlery.

'Charles, you've only set the table for two, but don't worry, I'll have that straightened out in a trice,' she said, bustling around adding a knife and fork and then looking out an extra plate and glass as well. Finally she plonked herself down at the head of the table. 'So. What are we having for supper?'

Charles, who now seemed to be suppressing a sigh, if not something more trenchant, shrugged his shoulders. 'It's my signature salmon en croute,' he said.

'Oh yes! Marlene said that's really good,' Daphne said blithely.

Sarah put a jug of water down on the table a little more forcefully than was perhaps required.

'Careful!' Daphne said, mopping up the spillage with one of Sarah's best napkins. 'You probably can't see properly, with these silly candles in the way.' She blew them out and turned on the bright overhead light, leaving them all blinking. 'Might as well get these flowers off the table too, they take up a lot of room,' she said, shoving a vase of beautiful red roses – a gift from Charles, Sarah assumed – onto the sideboard. 'Right. Ready when you are, Charles.'

The ruffles on Charles's apron now looked a little sorry for themselves, but he gallantly got out the oven gloves and was soon coaxing two perfectly puffed salmon en croutes from the oven. He looked at them sadly for a moment, then Sarah took over, taking a knife and expertly cutting the golden pastry into three portions.

Soon they were all tucking in. 'This really is delicious, Charles,' Sarah said, touched that he had gone to so much effort, even if it had been somewhat derailed by an unrepentant Daphne. Hamish, too, was very much enjoying the odd flake of pastry that floated his way. It was rather like that snow from a couple of days ago, he decided – but much tastier.

They ate in happy silence for a while, Sarah reaching for Charles's hand under the table, which seemed to cheer him up a lot.

'This is lovely. There's nothing like an excellent meal with friends,' Daphne said, toasting Charles and Sarah, and rather redeeming herself.

'Absolutely,' said Sarah. 'Although I suppose since we're all here, we ought to think about where we are with this Jones business. Three heads are better than one, after all. Sorry, four,' she added, patting Hamish.

'Now you've gone and ruined it,' Daphne said pettishly. 'There's nothing I want to talk about less at the dinner table than death and destruction.'

'Do you want to talk about it away from the dinner table?' Charles was at his most quizzical.

'Not much,' Daphne conceded. 'Oh all right, then. If you must.'

Sarah plunged right in. 'I think we should discount Deirdre killing Daffyd and then dying of remorse, I just don't believe that happened. So who do we have in the frame? Griselda must have been a great shot at one point, because of all the training she underwent for her film role – but these days she's like an aspen in a high wind, her shakes are so bad. She had a pen just like Daffyd's – but it turned out that he gave it to her himself. Where on earth did Daffyd get the pen, though? It had that company logo on it…'

'Oh? What was it?' asked Charles.

'Merstairs Mortar. A construction firm, I suppose. Have you heard of it?'

'Yes of course,' said Charles. 'But it's an estate agency – or was. They used to be based on the high street, but they went bust a few weeks ago. They sold all the fancier houses round here – Francesca got them in for our divorce valuation,' he said glumly.

'That's interesting,' said Sarah. 'And that explains why we couldn't find anything when we searched online earlier, Daphne. But I wonder why Daffyd had several of their pens?'

'Oh, he was a stingy chap. Loved a freebie. Probably found them lying around somewhere and held onto them,' Charles said. 'Where are we on suspects you've already talked to? Matilda, for instance?'

'Even though she may have had access to a weapon that would work, I believed her when she said she had no idea whether any of the guns were viable. And if Deirdre had died first, it might have made sense, as Matilda would have been getting rid of the competition. But this way round, no. And as for poor Ewan, he hasn't got a hope.'

'Sorry, why are you saying lovely Ewan doesn't get a look-in?' Daphne said, bristling.

'I'd have thought you'd be pleased he's out of the picture,' Sarah said with a slightly sad smile. 'But in fact I think there's a medical reason why it's very unlikely he killed Daffyd. Have you noticed anything about him?'

'Not at all,' said Daphne. 'He looks fit to me. *Well fit*, as Mariella might say,' she tacked on with a giggle.

Sarah shook her head. 'Actually, he's got a collection of symptoms I really don't like the look of. I wouldn't mention this if he were my patient, of course, but as he's not... Charles, when we were in your flat he said he keeps getting the shakes in the morning, remember? Then he often stands with that curious forward-leaning posture, as though he's looming over you...'

'I don't mind that,' said Daphne, fanning herself with her hand.

'Then he said he couldn't smell the damp in that house he was plastering, and it was really bad, you've got to admit that, Daph,' Sarah added.

'Well yes, it was a little whiffy. But he wanted to get rid of us at that point.'

'Even so,' said Sarah. 'I think he might have early onset Parkinson's. Although he doesn't have much of a hand tremor, it would make him an unreliable shot. He might also have trouble manhandling someone as large as Daffyd. To be honest I'm not sure he'll even be plastering for much longer. He could still have scared Deirdre to death, though.'

'Oh Sarah,' said Daphne, her eyes filling with tears. 'That's so awful! The poor boy. And I can't believe he'd have done that to Deirdre.'

'You're probably right. Don't worry about him too much,

Daph. There are drugs these days that can keep things at bay,' Sarah said, trying to be upbeat.

A silence fell as they all contemplated poor Ewan's fate. 'Look, there's nothing we can do on that front,' Sarah said with determined brightness. 'Let's go back to the case. That's where we might be able to make a difference. So, who else have we been looking at? We don't think Matthew was in that back room at the right moment, and anyway his arm is in a sling so how could he have forced his father's hand? Deirdre seemed too wet to have done it – and now she's been killed, or died, anyway,' Sarah said.

'Charles, you looked like a great prospect, with that silly gun of yours, but even you're in the clear,' said Daphne, reaching for the potatoes. Sarah was glad to see she was cheering up enough to tease her old friend.

'Well, thank goodness for that,' said Charles. 'I've had some anxious moments, I don't mind telling you. But the Merstairs Militia is seeming like our best bet for firearms now. Even if Matilda and Griselda are out, there are plenty of other enactment fans who had access to that box of weapons.'

'Yes,' said Sarah eagerly. 'And don't forget, Matilda's key to the gun crate is missing, and she said there were other *Broomstick Battalion* guns in there.'

'Good gracious,' said Charles. 'Well, I suppose that makes me feel a little better about my own slip-up on that front.'

'Exactly,' said Sarah, squeezing his hand under the table. 'We need another contact in the Militia, who might know who else has got their hands on guns recently, then we can see if any of those people also had a motive,' Sarah said. 'Sometimes it seems like the whole of Merstairs can be put into a Venn diagram, with interlocking circles showing which clubs everyone's in. Is there anyone who hasn't joined an organisation?'

'Well, me,' said Charles. 'Though I must admit the historical side of the Militia does have its appeal, you know.'

'Does it?' said Sarah, not feeling convinced.

'Oh yes. Splendid costumes, retracing famous battles, even the weaponry, though they won't have anything a patch on my blunderbusses, of course.'

'Of course not,' said Sarah. 'Come on, then, pudding time,' she said, getting up and clearing the plates. Charles had made a rather delicious looking (if slightly wonky) pavlova which was sitting on the sideboard, with two bowls and spoons. Sarah added one extra of each and put the pudding in the middle of the table, with a jug of cream. 'Any more history fans that you can think of?'

'Mmm,' said Daphne, pulling the pavlova towards her. 'Yum. What did you say?'

Charles, meanwhile, wrinkled his brow. 'There's a fair few people in the Militia. Quite a lot of women enjoy it... I mean, not that I only know the women,' he said hastily. 'There's also, oh, wait a second, someone you know too, Sarah. David Cartwright.'

'Dave Cartwright? From the Men of Merstairs? Oh, that's interesting. I bet he wouldn't mind telling me more about the weaponry. That's something we should definitely be looking into tomorrow.'

'Right. Well, as we'll be setting off from here, I might as well stay the night,' Daphne announced from deep in the jug of cream.

Sarah and Charles looked at each other, then Charles shrugged, and Sarah smiled ruefully. She wasn't entirely sure if Daphne was doing it on purpose, but she seemed to have developed a most inconvenient phobia about being alone in her own house. It was beginning to impinge on Sarah's – and Charles's – lives. There was going to have to be a conversation about this at some point. Soon. But maybe not quite now. It would hardly be right to evict her, with two recent unsolved murders in the area.

THIRTY-FIVE

The next morning, bright and early, Daphne was in the kitchen at Sarah's house, burning the toast. Sarah rushed downstairs, a particularly nice dream having been interrupted by the distinctive smell of scorched bread.

Daphne was at the table, absorbed in an old copy of a medical journal, totally unaware of the conflagration developing right next to her. Sarah expertly unplugged the toaster, got the oven gloves, removed the flaming bits of bread, and threw them into the sink to be extinguished by a deluge of water from both taps.

'Ah. Morning, Sarah. I wondered what was keeping you. You're usually up way earlier than this,' Daphne said finally, looking round a little disapprovingly.

'Am I?' Sarah said weakly. 'I don't suppose you've made any coffee, have you?'

'Coffee would be absolutely lovely, thank you,' Daphne said, holding out her mug and returning to her reading.

'What's that you've got there?' Sarah said curiously, filling the kettle and turning it on.

'Oh, you ought to read it. It's about sudden death syndrome,' Daphne said.

'Daph, that's it!' said Sarah, sitting down with a thump. 'That's probably what did for Deirdre. A stress-induced crisis resulting in multi-system failure. That's exactly the sort of thing Dr Strutton meant. Well done for finding that! I'm impressed. I'm a bit surprised you're studying that journal, though. It's not your usual fare.'

'Oh, have I made a breakthrough?' Daphne looked thrilled, then she came clean. 'To be honest, there was nothing else lying around to read and I can only understand about one word in ten. I thought they were talking about *feeling* like death. I can really sympathise with that. I'm often exhausted after a reading with a client. It takes such a lot out of me,' Daphne said with a virtuous air.

'Mm, yes,' said Sarah.

'Anyway, I made the toast, as you were taking such a time about things,' Daphne carried on, apparently oblivious to the fact that her attempt was now in the bin.

'That was good of you,' Sarah said, cutting more bread and putting a choice of jams on the table.

'Oooh, your raspberry. I wondered when you'd be getting that out,' Daphne said, holding the jar up to the light, where it glowed a glorious dark pink.

'Today's the day. I reckon we need something special before questioning Dave.'

'That twit Dave Cartwright? You're sure that's necessary?' Daphne said, digging a knife into the jam.

'Daph! The toast's not done yet,' Sarah pointed out.

'Ooops,' said Daphne, licking the loaded knife unrepentantly.

'Here you go,' said Sarah a moment later, as the toaster popped up. Luckily it seemed none the worse for its adventures.

She slid the butter and a nicely browned slice toward her friend. 'Let's decide on a strategy.'

'Oh, don't worry about that. You ask your questions. I'll be actually taking his psychic temperature, working out with my knowledge of the spiritual world whether his aura is misaligned by bad deeds. It's a pretty essential component of our investigations, I think you'll agree. Any more toast?'

Sarah patted her friend fondly on the shoulder as she passed by to cut some more bread.

* * *

Half an hour later, Sarah made a mental note to buy more bread, milk, butter... well, everything, really, as she locked up her cottage. She took Hamish's lead and she and Daphne strode out to try and run Dave Cartwright to ground.

For most of the summer months, the Men of Merstairs were a somewhat sorry fixture down by the crazy golf course, where they sat on the wall and passed comment on the world from the perspective of a group of largely middle-aged white men who considered themselves very hard done by for one reason or another. Much though Sarah had come to like Dave Cartwright, when their paths had intertwined over the past months, she wasn't sure this life of perpetual low-level grumbling was really doing him much good. He needed a proper occupation, which would give him a more cheerful outlook, and probably cause a lot of his resentments to disappear. Still, he was an adult, and free to make his own choices.

'Do you think the Men of Merstairs will still be down on the far side of the beach now? It's getting pretty chilly these days,' said Sarah, turning the collar of her coat up as the wind whistled round them.

'Oh no, they'll have decamped to the old bingo hall,' said

Daphne. 'It's in the same direction, though, and not much further on.'

As they passed the intersection with South Street, Sarah looked down it and was surprised to see Matthew Jones coming out of the bookies, BetStairs. She waved at him, but he didn't notice her. Then Daphne grabbed her arm. 'Look, we're nearly there.'

Sarah followed Daphne's pointing finger and saw an old building on the fringes of the beach. She'd never really noticed it before, but now she could just about make out the battered signage and started reading, '*old Farts*, oh my gosh, that's... that's quite a name,' she said, unable to resist a giggle.

'It used to say *Golden Farthings*, that was the name of the bingo hall, but it looks like some of the letters have dropped off,' said Daphne, hooting with laughter.

'Are you sure they weren't pushed?' Sarah said with an answering snort. 'Oh gosh. I'd better try and get my face straight before we go in there. The Men take themselves very seriously.'

A few minutes later, and with a bit more composure, Sarah pushed on the door and entered the old bingo hall, with Daphne and Hamish following. 'I'm sure this place should be locked up,' Sarah whispered. 'Won't they get vandals in here if they just leave it open?'

'Not if it's guarded by the old farts, oops, the Men of Merstairs,' said Daphne, putting her hand to her mouth.

Sarah shook her head and looked around. The entrance was large and echoey, with posters still on the wall advertising big prize nights. There were double doors at the end, which must lead to the large hall where the sessions had once been held. She stepped forward, only for Daphne to seize her arm.

'Be careful,' she said. 'What if it's not the Men of Merstairs here any more? What if it's a gang? What if it's the man who killed Daffyd and frightened Deirdre to death?'

Sarah patted Daphne's hand. 'Well, we'll never know who it

is if we just stand here dithering, will we? Would you and Hamish like to wait while I have a little look?'

'What? You'd abandon us here, exposed to anyone who might come along?' Daphne looked quite wild-eyed at the thought.

'You'll be fine, Daphne. You're near the exit, aren't you? If there's any trouble, you can run for help. And besides, you've got Hamish looking after you. He won't let anything bad happen, will you, boy?' She patted the little dog on his tufty head and he panted at her in a slightly non-committal way. It looked as though Daphne wasn't the only one having doubts about this whole thing.

Sarah shrugged. She'd dealt with the Men of Merstairs before, and they wouldn't say boo to a goose, even with extensive coaching beforehand and group therapy afterwards. She strode forward, took a deep breath, and pushed at the doors.

Inside, all was quiet and very dark. There was a pronounced smell of mildew, which seemed to be coming from the dusty-looking curtains all around the sides of the room. She could just about see a raised dais at the end, with a few cheap chairs arranged in a rough circle. Sarah got out her phone, fiddled for the torch function, and waved the beam around. The whole room seemed deserted. She couldn't help a wave of relief sweeping over her. This was a creepy place, and she was almost glad she'd come up with nothing. They'd just have to search for the Men of Merstairs elsewhere.

She was about to go back through the doors again when a hand slammed down on her shoulder, and a voice growled in her ear. 'Oh no you don't.'

THIRTY-SIX

Sarah wheeled round, her eyes wide, and found herself facing what looked like a typical Man of Merstairs – pinkish face, the physique of someone who spent a lot of time sitting on a wall, and a distinctly tetchy expression. Only this one was also very, very tall, and broad with it.

'What you doing here then, eh? Trespassing?' he growled.

'Um, I was just looking for Dave Cartwright,' Sarah said, cursing the fact that her voice had come out all wobbly. She cleared her throat and tried again. 'Anyway, unless you're the owner of this bingo hall, you're trespassing too.'

'Well, I am the owner, aren't I?' said the man, in even more menacing tones than before.

Darn it, thought Sarah. 'Oh. Oh, I see. In that case, I'm very sorry, sir. I came looking for a friend...'

The man peered down at Sarah angrily. 'Friend, is it? Don't see anyone here but us, darling.'

Daphne was around somewhere with Hamish, but Sarah wasn't going to get them in trouble too. 'Sorry. Well, I'll be going now,' she said, trying to sound as matter-of-fact as possible.

'I don't think so. Not after setting foot on my property,' the man said, louring at her.

Just then, there was a rattle as someone else came through the doors. 'Nigel, what are you up to, mate? I thought we said the meeting was going to be in the old café downstairs. This room's too big and echoey and a couple of the guys think it's creepy.'

Sarah knew that voice. 'Dave? Is that you?' she said, trying to peer over the tall man's shoulder.

'Dr Vane, fancy seeing you here,' Dave Cartwright said happily.

'Oh thank goodness, Dave,' Sarah said. 'Your friend, er, Nigel, seems to have mistaken me for some sort of burglar or spy or something…'

'Don't mind Big Nige, his bark's much worse than his bite, isn't it, Nige, old chum?' Dave slapped the man heartily on the back, and he winced.

'Just a bit of fun,' Nigel said, somewhat sheepishly.

Inside, Sarah was smouldering. Fun, indeed. In her view, those badgering elderly ladies – and for once she put herself voluntarily into this category – should face severe penalties. *Very* severe. But she had to overlook that and try and get as much information as she could out of Dave, now she'd found him.

'Come on downstairs, the gang's all there,' Dave continued.

'I'd better just collect Daphne and my little dog,' Sarah said hesitantly.

'No need, they're already down there. Daphne's a right caution, isn't she? She's doing some palm readings. I must say, she has a way about her.'

'She certainly does,' Sarah said, feeling a prickle of alarm. She'd managed to survive her encounter with the Men of Merstairs's horrible lookout, but now it sounded like Daphne was going to plunge them into fresh trouble with her crystal-gazing shenanigans.

* * *

When she got downstairs into the disused café, however, Sarah soon saw that Daphne and Hamish had the situation perfectly under control. Hamish was on his back, allowing himself to be worshipped by various members of the group, while the rest were clustered round Daphne. She was peering at the massive hand of one of the tallest, widest men Sarah had ever seen, a chap who made Nigel look like one of Daphne's garden gnomes.

'...And I foresee difficult days ahead,' Daphne was intoning in her special 'Beyond' voice. 'Yes, it's essential that you remember this: go with cerise, not scarlet. Let that be your watchword!'

The chap shambled away from the table, muttering 'Cerise, not scarlet,' under his breath, and his place was taken by another eager victim.

'Um, Daphne,' said Sarah, leaning across to get her friend's attention, and getting some exasperated tuts from the men for her pains. 'We really should stick to the matter in hand, don't you think?'

Daphne waved her new client's palm around. 'What's this, if it's not a hand?' she tittered, and the men joined in. But she got reluctantly to her feet, patting the man on the shoulder. 'Well, that's all, boys. But do come along to my shop on the esplanade if you'd like to have an individual consultation.' She delved in her handbag and brought out a fistful of rather dog-eared business cards which they fell upon eagerly.

'Honestly, Sarah, my best morning's work in ages, and you have to come along and break things up,' Daphne hissed as she went over to her friend.

'Well, I'm sorry, Daph, but we do have more pressing

matters to deal with. I'm sure that bloke will pay you for what he's heard so far.'

'Oh drat,' Daphne said, slapping her forehead. 'I knew there was something. I forgot to charge them.'

Sarah suppressed a smile. That perhaps explained why Daphne's readings had been so popular. Well, she hoped they'd all come along to Tarot and Tealeaves and make amends. 'OK, let's try and get back on track. Dave, could we have a quiet word, do you think?'

'Me?' Immediately, Dave Cartwright blushed to the roots of his hair. Sarah had forgotten how shy he was.

'If you wouldn't mind,' she said a little more gently. 'Um, we could sit round there?' She pointed to the far corner of the café, which looked even dustier than the rest of it.

'Oh. All right. I suppose it's about my Albie?' A shadow passed across his face.

'No, no,' Sarah hastened to reassure him. Dave's nephew was in prison, thanks to Sarah's detective work on another case. He was bound to resent it, she realised, no matter how richly the boy deserved all the jail time the courts had thrown at him. 'It's about something else completely.'

Seeming mollified, Dave followed the two women over to the table. Hamish was still doing sterling work occupying the rest of the gang, who were vying to stroke him behind the ears, just the way he liked it. 'What's all this about, then?' he asked, sitting down rather heavily on the rickety chair.

'It's about the Merstairs Militia,' Sarah said, cutting to the chase. 'And its connection with Daffyd Jones's death.'

'What do you mean? You're not saying the Militia done it, are you? We just re-enact battles, nothing weird about that,' Dave said in protest.

Sarah begged to differ, but now was not the time. 'It's more that the Militia has access to firearms.'

Now Dave Cartwright looked at Sarah sideways. 'I thought there was some talk about Charles Diggory's gun collection...'

'That wasn't the case,' Sarah said firmly.

'He should have been a lot more careful with those keys, though,' Daphne weighed in.

'Yes, but that's not the issue here,' Sarah said, as patiently as she could. 'The thing is that the Militia, as I understand it, has quite a variety of weapons...'

'Yeah,' said Dave. 'That's what makes it fun. But you couldn't kill someone with a plastic musket, could you?' He tilted his head towards her as if willing her to see sense.

'Agreed. But there are other guns, aren't there? Replicas, or real weapons that have been decommissioned, like the ones the Militia got from *Broomstick Battalion*.'

'Oh well, you'd have to talk to an organiser about that. I don't like any that might be loud,' Dave said uneasily.

'Sorry, did you say loud?' Sarah asked.

'That's right,' Dave was rapidly turning pink again. 'Don't like a bang, do I?'

'Oh I see, so you don't really get involved with the weaponry?' Sarah realised with a sinking heart that Dave wasn't going to be the fount of all knowledge she'd been hoping for.

'No, makes me feel ill, it does. Especially since... well, never mind about that.' He shifted in his seat. 'And I'm not mad keen on all the fake blood, neither,' he rushed on. 'Fair turns my stomach. I just sort out the costumes, really. Or take them home for the wife to deal with,' Dave said with a small laugh.

Not for the first time, Sarah felt a little sorry for Edna Cartwright. 'Who would be more into the armoury side of things?'

'Well, there's a few of them that deals with logistics. Nigel there, he's a great man for a fight.'

Now why doesn't that surprise me, Sarah thought to herself. 'And the guns?'

'The guns are more for the really hardy types, the founding fathers of the group, if you like.'

'Who exactly would they be, then?' Daphne piped up.

'Well, Francesca Diggory's been involved since the get-go, Daffyd Jones used to be one of the bigwigs of course, with his boy, then there's, let me see, maybe Ewan.'

'I see. So they supervise the weapons, do they?' Sarah asked.

'Well… more or less,' Dave said. Again, he seemed uncomfortable.

Sarah suddenly realised something. Dave knew more than he wanted to about those guns. 'You were talking about bangs earlier,' she said.

'Um, was I?' Dave scanned the horizon, as though looking for help. None came.

'Why would one of those guns be loud, unless… Dave, I think you know that one of those guns had been reactivated. Am I right?'

Dave Cartwright stared at her, like a deer in the headlights.

THIRTY-SEVEN

'I can't talk here,' said Dave nervously. 'The walls have ears, you know,' he said, looking around wildly.

'I don't know about ears, but I'd say they probably have mushrooms, the whole place smells terrible,' said Daphne.

'I take your point, Dave,' Sarah said, standing up. 'Probably better to discuss this outside, somewhere a bit more discreet.'

Dave nodded, and quickly took his leave of his fellow Men. Sarah, worried Dave might try and sidle off once they were outside, tucked her arm into his on one side, and Daphne followed suit on the other.

'I've got a great idea for where we should go. I don't think any of your chums will show up,' said Daphne, leading them off to Marlene's Plaice.

Sarah wasn't a massive fan of the overwhelmingly purple interior – or, actually, of the proprietress, for that matter – but they did a great cuppa and it was out of the wind. Marlene had, of course, gone in for mauve Christmas decorations, but they looked surprisingly tasteful, dangling from a pretty frosted artificial tree by the counter, while silvery tinsel was twisted around all the window and door frames. Better still, there was no sign of Marlene herself. A girl in an uncomfortably tight-looking purple waistcoat and miniskirt, teamed with thick woolly tights that looked a bit more weather-appropriate, was doing the honours.

Once there was a steaming mug in front of Dave, he started to look a bit more cheerful. Sarah ordered from the little-used non-deep-fried section of the menu and they were soon enjoying rather delicious cheese and ham toasties. Hamish was more than happy to deal with any overspill. They were bundled up warmly, with a view of the sea relentlessly pounding the shore, while a few hardy seagulls drifted through the air. The birds looked so cold that Sarah almost felt like knitting them hats and scarves.

'Now then. I think we should talk about that reactivated gun,' Sarah began gently.

'I was afraid you'd say that,' said Dave, stirring sugar into his tea as though his life depended on it. 'I mean, I just spotted it with the rest – it stood out because it was proper metal, heavy like. I had a go one day when I was waiting for the rest of the Men to join the re-enactment. I was a bit bored, to be honest. I picked it up, and woah!'

'Did you shoot it?' Sarah's eyes widened in surprise.

'No, but I cocked it, and it clicked proper-like, like they do on Westerns. I looked down the barrel and it was clear. Well, after that, I threw it back in the box and tried to forget about it.'

'Why on earth didn't you say something?' Sarah was really struggling to understand Dave's actions.

Dave shuffled his feet under the table. 'You know what Daffyd was like. He would have had a go. Matilda was always busy... Ewan would have laughed at me. Matthew wasn't around that much. They were the ones in charge. I felt it was better to keep a low profile,' Dave said, brushing cheese crumbs off the lavender tablecloth, to Hamish's excitement.

And look how that turned out, Sarah thought to herself. But it was clear he was woebegone enough about his foolish silence.

'Any ideas about who might have taken it?' asked Sarah. Dave shook his head sadly. 'All right,' she said. 'Let's move on. I'm surprised Daffyd was one of the leading lights of the Militia. It doesn't sound like him. He was all about music – and self-aggrandisement. I can't see how historical re-enactments fit in with either of those passions.'

Dave, seeming relieved to get off the subject of the gun, thought hard. 'Yeah, I know what you mean. Daffyd was always blowing his own trumpet. But there's quite a lot of music in the Militia. Drumming, a bit of a fife occasionally. He wanted to expand that. Said there was a fine tradition of battle hymns that was dying out.'

'Dying out because we haven't been to war for a while, touch wood,' said Daphne, patting her elaborate headscarf.

Sarah, who wasn't sure that exactly counted as wood, but also tried not to be superstitious as she was a woman of science, cleared her throat. 'Well, anyway,' she said. 'How did the tunes go down with the Militia?'

'Not well. Not well at all,' admitted Dave. 'I quite liked the idea of a rousing battle song, but a lot of the guys, they thought it was just a distraction. And then, Daffyd really wanted to sing them himself. He was very critical of any attempts to join in.'

'I bet he was,' said Sarah, remembering again just how nitpicking Daffyd had been about his poor old choir. 'That can't have improved people's moods much.'

'No,' said Dave slowly. 'And I suppose the final straw was that incident at the Battle of Maidstone last year.'

'That was last year, was it? I thought it was a while ago,' said Daphne, patting Hamish.

'What? Oh, the battle was in 1648. But we re-enacted it in the summer. Daffyd was keen to include a song, he said Oliver Cromwell's New Model Army would have found it appropriate but there were lots of objections. I mean, would the Roundheads really be big on singing? A lot of them were Puritans,' Dave said.

'Sounds like you all take it very seriously,' Sarah said approvingly. 'There seems to be a good sense of historical accuracy.'

'Oh, yeah,' Dave said, cheering up a bit at this praise, like a flower warming itself in the sun. 'We try and get the details right. Take the Battle of Deal, for instance.'

'That was earlier, wasn't it? Fifteenth century?' Sarah screwed up her forehead in the effort of remembering long-ago history lessons.

'1495, that's right. It's going to be a corker, we're doing that this year.'

'How on earth do you remember these things, Sarah?' Daphne asked rather crossly.

'Oh, I always had a soft spot for the Princes in the Tower,' Sarah said. 'Perkin Warbeck pretended to be one of them, and said he was reclaiming his rightful title from Henry VII.'

'But he didn't succeed?' Daphne asked.

'He ended up being executed,' said Dave. 'Should be a great show though. You'll come, won't you?' he pleaded.

'I think I'm washing my hair that day,' said Daphne. 'And fighting isn't at all good for my chakras.'

'Um, I'm sure we'll do our best,' said Sarah diplomatically. 'Who's going to be playing the part of Perkin Warbeck?' she asked.

'Oh, oh, that's going to be Daffyd's lad,' said Dave, 'and Marlene's going to be Lady Catherine Gordon, his wife.'

'Really?' Sarah seemed electrified. 'Right then, Daphne, I think we should be off. I'll leave this for Marlene,' she said, tucking some money under her empty teacup. 'Come on now, Hamish, let's be having you. Thanks so much, Dave. You've been very helpful.'

'Have I?' the man mumbled, not seeming over-pleased at the idea.

Sarah smiled encouragingly at him and then led Daphne out.

'What was that all about?' Daphne said as soon as they were outside. 'First of all you insist on dragging him to the café, then you decide to rush off. I was just about to order a cake, if you must know.'

'We can go back and have a cake in a minute, Daph. But there's something I've got to check on first. You heard what Dave said.'

'Yes, a lot about Roundheads and battles and whatnot. Nothing that helps us at all.'

'That's where you're wrong, Daph. I think Dave Cartwright might just have given the game away.'

THIRTY-EIGHT

Daphne was just turning to Sarah, her mouth forming a question, when a gust of wind whipped the scarf off her head. There followed a merry dance, with both Hamish and Daphne on the trail of the bright fuchsia fabric as it skittered along the sands. The colour was so vivid against the leaden sky and dun-coloured water that Sarah stopped to enjoy the spectacle, completely unable to stop herself from laughing behind her hand.

'They look like they're having a time of it,' came a voice over her left shoulder. Sarah wheeled round, to see a tall, well-built man in a shiny suit and equally shiny overcoat, sniggering along at the antics unfolding on the beach.

'Oh hello, I know you from somewhere, don't tell me,' said Sarah, racking her brains. The man's rather blinding teeth were a clue – whitening was not much of a trend in Merstairs – and as for the suit... Suddenly it came to her. 'Oh, you're the estate agent who sold Daphne the beach hut with the body in it! Michael, isn't it?'

'Shhh,' he looked around a little furtively, but the only witnesses were a couple of seagulls who looked at them impassively, apparently disappointed they weren't mounds of chips, and Daphne and Hamish, who had run themselves ragged but now finally had the scarf triumphantly under control. 'That's right, Mike Benchley at your service. But the less said about that whole episode the better.'

Sarah rather agreed. It hadn't really been Mike's fault. Daphne had not checked out the hut at all before buying it, with unfortunate consequences. 'Where are you off to now?' she asked, happy enough to change the subject. To her surprise, Mike continued to look furtive. He even took a pair of sunglasses out of his pocket and perched them on his nose, looking absurd in the cold, not to mention the growing twilight.

'Are you hiding from someone?' Sarah asked, raising her eyebrows.

'Sensitive eyes. The glare, you know,' he mumbled, gesturing at the beach, which was getting darker by the minute. Sarah frowned. The only glare for miles around was coming from Mike's own teeth.

'You didn't say which house you were going to look at?' Sarah was now getting extremely interested in Mike's next steps.

'Oh, er, it's one of those along here,' he said, waving vaguely to the magnificent row of houses looking out to sea, their bow windows billowing out to meet the coastline. 'Well, mustn't keep you,' he said, making to scurry off.

'Wait a second,' Sarah said urgently. 'I was just wondering... do you know the Jones family?'

Mike jumped. 'Oh, well, only a little bit, just to say hello to...' His eyes slithered away from hers. 'If you'll excuse me, I have an appointment. They're thin on the ground at the moment, so I'd better make tracks.'

'Is business not good?' Sarah asked.

'Well, the winter's never great, but this year has been tough. Bit of a shocker, really. Worst I remember for a while. Don't quote me on that, though,' he said, with another flash of white and a jot more of his trademark joviality. 'Things could pick up any time. Bound to. In a month or so. Six to eight, tops. If not, next year, for sure.'

'That's interesting... I heard about another estate agency that folded recently, Merstairs Mortar. Do you know anything about them?'

'Of course,' said Mike. 'A competitor. Now if that's all—'

'Sorry,' said Sarah. 'But do you know why the business failed?'

'I heard they had a big contract that fell through. Final straw,' said Mike, looking pensive.

'Right. Back to the Joneses again. You know about the tragedies, of course,' Sarah went on. 'I just wondered what sort of a family they were. Daffyd Jones was... difficult, people say.'

As she'd hoped, Mike's desire to show off his local knowledge triumphed over his keenness to escape. 'That's an understatement. He was a friend – sort of – but the shouting could get you down.'

'Yes, his poor wife,' Sarah said sympathetically.

'I felt worse for Matthew. Growing up with a dad like that... cutting you down at every opportunity. He always had to be top dog, did Daffyd. Even if it meant making his own son feel two inches tall. I don't know why the lad didn't get out of Merstairs. He can sing too, you know.'

'I had no idea,' said Sarah. 'He certainly didn't get a look in at the rehearsal I went to.'

'He wouldn't,' Mike said. 'Daffyd couldn't risk being upstaged. You'd think he'd be proud and want Matthew to carry on his legacy. But no, he was all about shutting the boy up, just to maintain his own status. And sometimes he could act out of character... like in our last phone conversation, just before... But I've said too much,' Mike said. 'Best be off, now,' he said, scurrying away with another two-second flash of that magnificent smile.

Sarah turned and watched him go, wondering what the lost commission was at Merstairs Mortar, and also what Daffyd had said to Mike on the phone, when Daphne and Hamish panted up to her. Daphne was holding the scarf aloft. It was a little wet and sandy in places, but still in one piece. 'Well done, you two,' Sarah said warmly, and both looked highly gratified at the praise.

'Right, that's enough of freezing our toes off here,' said Daphne. 'Let's get home and you can make us all one of your lovely hot chocs,' she added, turning to go.

'Wait a minute, not just yet,' said Sarah urgently, nodding her head in the direction of Mike, who was now climbing the slope to the row of Georgian houses. 'We need to stay here for a bit, look as though you're telling me something important.'

'I *am*,' Daphne said rather crossly. 'Hamish and I are jolly cold and we want to go home. If that's not crucial information, I don't know what is.'

'Shhh, there he goes... yes, just as I thought,' said Sarah. 'He's going into the Jones house.' It had suddenly struck her – those roughly ripped-up papers she'd seen spilling out of Daffyd's briefcase at the scene of his murder. There had been dimensions noted down – they must have been for estate agent particulars. 'Daffyd and Deirdre both had those Merstairs Mortar pens – they must have been planning to put the house on the market, when the company went bust. Now Mike must be trying his luck.'

'Well, he'll get short shrift,' said Daphne. 'The Joneses have been in that house forever. I can't imagine Daffyd selling for a minute, he loved having such a swanky place, and Matthew only wants to follow in his dad's footsteps. Anyway, can we please go?' said Daphne, now moving restlessly from foot to foot. 'If I stand here a moment longer I'm going to turn into a lemon popsicle, and then you'll be sorry. You don't even like that flavour.'

'Yes, of course,' Sarah said thoughtfully, taking Hamish's lead and marching off.

'Hey, wait for me! It's hard to walk fast with frostbite, you know,' Daphne said, bringing up the rear. 'I hope you're going to tell me about Dave Cartwright, too.'

'As soon as you've got that hot chocolate in front of you,' said Sarah over her shoulder.

* * *

Sure enough, Daphne was a lot happier when she had a huge mug in her hands, brimming over with marshmallows and swirly cream. Hamish was settled in his basket crunching a biscuit for a good boy, and Sarah was sipping her own tea. The kitchen was wonderfully warm and welcoming, the red and white checked cloth glowing in the cheery light, while outside, the night darkened rapidly and the sea disappeared into velvet blackness.

'So, you think Daffyd had actually put the house up for sale?' Daphne asked absently.

'You thought he wouldn't do that. So now I'm wondering about Mike instead,' Sarah said. 'There's something about that man. I don't trust him an inch. It makes me wonder, actually…'

'What do you mean?' Daphne wrinkled her nose.

'It's just occurred to me. Do you think an estate agent would actually consider… speeding someone's death along, in order to get their house on the books?'

'That would be totally evil,' Daphne said with a shiver.

'Yes,' Sarah replied slowly. 'But it would be possible, wouldn't it?'

'It must be worth a pretty penny, the Jones house,' Daphne conceded. 'That terrace never usually comes up for sale. And it's one of the few that hasn't been divided into flats. Must be worth millions.'

'Hmm,' Sarah said. 'That's a hefty commission. Mike more or less said business hasn't been good for a while, and we know the other estate agent closed down. It's clearly a hard time for them. I'm really beginning to feel he might be a suspect. I wonder if it's time we caught up with Mariella about all this? Plus, well, Dave did mention Marlene in the re-enactment...'

'Oh come on, Sarah. Is that what you were on about before? You're not serious,' Daphne said over the rim of her cup.

'All right, it was just a thought,' Sarah said, abashed but no less determined to check her hunch out when she got a chance. 'Mariella must have some other leads by now.'

'If she does, we'll be the last people she'd tell,' Daphne said, taking a leisurely slurp of her drink.

'All the same. Could you give her a ring? I really want to get a bit further on, see what her thinking is.'

'OK then.' Daphne sighed and fished out her phone. 'But she's going to be cross, you know.'

A couple of minutes later, Mariella's voice was blasting out of the speaker, sounding frantic as usual. 'What's up, Mum? I haven't really got time to talk.'

'Sarah was just wondering where you've got to in the Jones investigation,' Daphne said, dropping her friend in it with a smile.

'Honestly, you two, you just need to accept the evidence. Poor Deirdre died of sorrow, and as for Daffyd – well, we're working on that and it's confidential.'

'All right,' said Sarah, though she disagreed entirely about Deirdre. 'I take your point. There's someone else you should be considering though, Mike Benchley, the estate agent. He's valuing the Jones house, as we speak. And he's told me business has been bad lately... have you asked him where he was when Daffyd died? I'm convinced someone helped Daffyd pull that trigger, and Mike is a big man, definitely strong enough to twist his arm.'

'Oh for goodness sake, Aunty Sarah! We already knew Daffyd and Deidre had decided to put their house on the market, so you can forget about Mike having anything to do with it. He's lived here all his life. All right, he's a bit shifty-looking, but he keeps his deals above board. He's never even dropped an ice cream cone on the esplanade, as far as I know. I don't think a downturn in the housing market is going to make him into a killer, however convenient it would be for you. Now look, much as I love to be second-guessed by my mum and her chum, I do have to get on.'

'Well, that's you told,' said Daphne with a wince. Sarah nodded glumly. She'd been sure she was on the right path at last.

'Is that all, then, ladies? I've got a lot of forms to fill in,' said Mariella.

'You're not still thinking of a transfer to Canterbury, are you darling?' said Daphne, sounding emotional.

'Mum, you know Canterbury is only down the road. I wouldn't even have to move. But I might get a bit more...' now she whispered into the phone, 'I might get a bit more *respect* there. You know what I mean.'

It was Daphne's turn to sigh. 'All right. I understand. But think of how much worse it's all going to be, crime in the big city.'

'It's hardly London, Mum. And don't make me tot up how many murders we've had in Merstairs lately. I'm just counting my lucky stars there won't be any more to go on that list.'

But by the next morning, Mariella seemed to have run out of luck.

THIRTY-NINE

The first sign that there was something amiss was when Sarah was woken up by a siren wailing at 6 a.m. As she'd only just trained Hamish to realise this wasn't the ideal time to leap out of bed, it was galling to be woken by something that wasn't small and Scottie-shaped. When she pottered over to the window to peep through her pretty floral curtains, she spotted a police car drawn up outside the clock tower, a little further down the esplanade. And wasn't that Mariella's car whooshing past, coming to a haphazard stop right behind the other vehicle? Something had happened. There was only one way to find out what it was.

Sarah was dressed in a trice and urged a surprised Hamish to get going before they'd even had breakfast. She filled her pockets with his favourite dog biscuits just in case they weren't home for a while. Her next stop was to tap on the spare room door.

'What on earth?' said Daphne, opening the door a crack and revealing a lime green kaftan. 'What's going on? Have you had a nightmare you want me to interpret?'

'This whole case has been a bit of a nightmare, but no, it's not that. Do you know why Mariella is parked by the clock tower right now, with the Terrible Twosome in tow?'

'Along the esplanade?' said Daphne, brushing copious amounts of red hair out of her face. 'No idea. Give me two seconds to get dressed,' she said. As good as her word, she re-emerged a few moments later wearing an assortment of woollies over her kimono. Downstairs, both shoved on boots and threw on their coats. 'That girl is working way too hard at the moment. Up all night with those blasted transfer forms, then at work with the lark. She really needs to sort out her work-life balance,' Daphne muttered as they hurried out of the cottage.

They were soon bustling along the seafront towards the clutch of police vehicles, their flashing lights and hectic colours clashing with the gaily decorated shops and cafés gearing up for Christmas. As they watched, one of the marked cars' door was shoved open and a very tired-looking PC Deeside more or less fell out onto the pavement. Then the same happened on the other side, with PC Dumbarton.

'Goodness, they really don't look at their best at this hour,' said Daphne, as the breeze caught her coat and revealed her lime kimono in all its glory.

'Well, it is early,' said Sarah, feeding Hamish a biscuit. He didn't look any the worse for missing his official breakfast. On the contrary, his ears were pricked and his tail was wagging as they got closer to the small knot of people who'd congregated on the beach.

'Oh dear, I think Hamish has mistaken DI Brice, Tweedledum and his friend, and Mariella, for people who want to play a lovely game of throw-the-stick at the crack of dawn,' said Sarah, as the dog pulled on his lead.

'Well, at least Mari will think we're innocently walking him, not trying to poke our noses into her investigation,' said Daphne, slowing down a bit as they neared the huddle of activity. 'Uh-oh, seems they've found something. I don't think I'm going to like this.'

Sarah looked shrewdly at the scene. It did indeed look rather ominous in contrast to the jolly Christmas decorations on the other side of the road. Tweedledee was now looping crime scene tape around a couple of the benches on the esplanade and trying, without much success, to make a large square by digging the other corners into the sand. The wind didn't think much of that idea. Worst of all, there was a mass in the middle of the square about the size and shape of a dead body, covered by a blanket.

'Daph, could you take Hamish over to the Beach Café and get him a bowl of water? Here's a bit of money, order yourself a nice breakfast,' Sarah said quickly, pressing some notes into her friend's hand.

Daphne went rather pale, swallowed once, and averted her eyes from the blanket. 'Oh, right, yes, OK then,' she said, taking Hamish's lead and trudging away. 'Not another one,' she muttered as she went.

At that moment, Mariella' s head went up. She saw her mother but made no move to hail her as Daphne walked gingerly past on her way to the café. Then she spotted Sarah. After a moment's indecision, she gestured for her to approach.

'I suppose you just happened to be going for an early morning walk, did you?'

'That's right. Hamish was keen to get out and about,' said Sarah evenly. 'Now that I'm here, anything I can do?'

'Well, I don't want any I-told-you-sos,' Mariella said, then looked significantly towards DI Brice. 'You'd better ask him.'

Sarah took a breath. She and the detective had never really seen eye to eye, but Mariella undoubtedly had a good reason for suggesting she approach him. She walked boldly over. 'DI Brice. Good morning. I just happened to be walking my dog, and I saw all the commotion. Is there anything I could possibly assist you with?'

Brice looked her up and down in a rather insulting manner, then suddenly seemed to place her. For a detective, it really took him some time to remember faces. 'Ah. You're the doctor lady.'

'Retired, but yes, that's right.'

A cunning look came over the man's ruddy features. 'As a matter of fact, it's rather handy you're here. Dr Strutton is on her way, but her car got a flat tyre over Ramsgate way so we're looking at up to an hour... it's going to be a bit of a race with the tide. Might as well get you to have a look just in case.'

'Oh, I see, you might need to move the body before the pathologist gets here? Right,' said Sarah, frowning. That wouldn't be good for any forensic traces. 'Are you taking photographs of the scene, may I ask?'

'Of course,' Brice said crossly. 'And I don't need you to tell me how to run things,' he started – then remembered he was actually asking her for a favour. 'That is, it would be useful if you could follow me.'

Sarah suppressed a small smile. The poor man would clearly rather not involve her, but he had no choice. The tide waited for no one, not even Dr Strutton.

'Right, I'll follow you,' she said, in a neutral professional tone.

The sand was wet and after a few steps, she could feel water starting to seep into her shoes. In her rush to get out this morning, she had pulled on canvas trainers, which she now realised was a major blunder. The beach was at the stage where every footprint rapidly filled up with water, and a leaky shoe was no different. Her toes were soon feeling very damp and chilly.

Not nearly as damp and chilly as this poor body, she realised, as they reached the hump on the beach. DI Brice, with very little ceremony, pulled off the blanket and revealed the dead, cold corpse, lying flat with its hands tidily by its sides and its legs stretched out. The face was bleached of colour, the eyes staring sightlessly at the clouds flitting across the bay. The mouth sagged open. Sarah would have recognised those teeth anywhere. Only one person in Merstairs had a set like that. They were whiter than the clouds, and brighter even than a seagull's wing.

FORTY

Whenever Sarah was confronted with a dead body, her overriding emotion was pity. For the person who had passed away, for the loved ones who would shortly have their lives upended, and even for the human condition that condemned everyone in the world to an exit at some point. But for Mike Benchley, the situation seemed especially poignant. Just yesterday, he had been full of life and suppressed excitement, about to get his hands on a tidy commission and no doubt busily planning for the future. Now only the irrepressible gleam of his teeth hinted at that exuberant personality.

What was more, last night Sarah had earmarked him as a promising suspect in Daffyd and Deirdre's murders. His financial woes would have created the sort of pressure that often made people turn to desperate remedies. The fact that he'd now turned up dead on the beach didn't rule Mike out – but she had to admit it made the whole thing much less likely, especially taken with Mariella's news that Daffyd and Deirdre had decided to sell up before their deaths. Yesterday the estate agent had shown no signs of remorse, only a questionable haste to turn his fortunes around with a large sale. Today it seemed that he'd had nothing to feel guilty about. There was still, Sarah strongly believed, a murderer on the loose in Merstairs. And that someone would be more dangerous than ever now, after pulling off their third killing.

Her first action was to walk around the body, assessing it carefully from every angle. Although its position looked neat and poised, there was nothing to show it had been placed there deliberately. There were no marks in the sand suggesting it had been dragged from the esplanade, or even pulled out of the sea. It looked as though he had floated there on the tide. She went round again, this time looking very carefully for injuries. There had been nothing obvious in her first pass, but on the second sweep, she did see something. At the top of the man's head, there was an area where the hair wasn't lying smoothly, as it should have been, but looked strangely lumpy. She hesitated to touch anything, but she did squat down and invite DI Brice to do the same.

'Can you see here, Inspector, this area of the skull has been damaged? It shouldn't look like that. I'd say it has been shattered by a heavy blow, probably from a large blunt instrument like a piece of wood, metal, something strong and hard.'

'Would that be the cause of death, then?' said Brice, leaning down as far as he could and studying the area she was pointing out.

'As far as I can tell, yes. But that's without moving the body. There could be more damage to the back of the cranium.'

'There's no blood, though,' Brice said accusingly.

'Well, a lot of the bleeding could have happened internally, that can be the case with head injuries. And he's been cleaned pretty thoroughly by the sea. Probably been in there for a number of hours, I'd say.'

'And then washed up here? I see. So when are we talking about, exactly?'

'For the time of death? That's hard for me to say, without

taking the temperature of the corpse, plus there's the fact that he's been in extremely cold water for a period of time. But he was fine when I was talking to him here yesterday.'

Brice did a double-take. 'Oho, like that is it? You were the last person to see him alive, were you? Didn't mention that. Chatted to him, got in an argument, something of that sort, I'll bet?'

'Um, no. We had a perfectly civilised discussion,' said Sarah, rattled despite herself. 'And I'm sure I won't have been the last person he spoke to, either. It wasn't particularly late.'

'Got any witnesses to back you up there?' Brice looked increasingly cheerful at the prospect of wrapping up the case in under an hour.

'Daphne... but actually she was, well, chasing a scarf on the beach. I don't think she saw much... Oh, this is ridiculous, Inspector. I left Mike fit and well more than twelve hours ago. I think he's probably been dead only around eight to ten hours.'

'A minute ago you couldn't tell,' Brice sneered. 'Now suddenly you know a time of death that conveniently exonerates you. Which is it, Doctor? Do you know when he died because you've got first-hand knowledge... or are you just making it all up?'

Sarah sighed and got to her feet, not without difficulty. She really needed to do some yoga or something for her joints. 'Look, I was doing you a favour by giving you my views. But if you're going to use them against me, then I'll be off.' She spoke as politely as she could, but inwardly she would have given a lot to have a good yell at the infuriating man. No wonder Mariella was filling in those Canterbury forms.

'Right, I see,' said Brice, looking her up and down and clearly finding her wanting. 'Don't go making any trips now will you, Doctor? You'd do well to remember – I know where you live.'

'No need to thank me for my input,' Sarah said pertly. Then she brushed herself down and took off across the sand.

Her feet were thoroughly sodden now, and she'd more or less been accused of murder. That was what you got for interfering, she supposed. She kept her head down when passing Mariella and didn't really look up until she got to the Beach Café.

When she arrived, she found Daphne sitting at a table with a rather suspiciously contented-looking Hamish. There was a large empty plate in front of her, while in Sarah's space there was another, with the remnants of a cooked English breakfast.

Sarah took a careful look. Hmm, the bacon was gone, so the mystery of Hamish's sheepish expression was solved. As for the scrambled egg and mushrooms, she was pretty sure that Daphne would have made short work of them. She'd been left with a soggy-looking bit of toast, one lonely sausage and some cold baked beans. She pushed the lot aside, and instead took a sip of tea. It was a bit stewed, but still helped to warm her up.

'That DI Brice.' She shook her head. 'I don't know how your Mari has any patience with him.'

'She's a saint,' Daphne said. 'I'll get this out of your way,' she said, carefully removing the sausage from Sarah's plate and chomping at it. 'What's he been up to now?'

'He more or less accused me of murdering Mike the estate agent,' said Sarah.

Daphne went red in the face, and for a second Sarah wondered whether she was choking on the sausage. Then she swallowed with difficulty. 'Mike? Mike from the agency in the high street? Where I bought my beach hut?' Her wide eyes filled with tears.

'Yes, I'm afraid that was him on the beach. I'm sorry, Daph, I should have broken that more gently. I didn't realise you'd be quite so upset. After all, he did sell you a hut containing... well, we don't want to go over all that again,' Sarah said. 'How about I get you a fresh cup of tea?'

Daphne nodded. 'It's just a shock. He was a good man.' She sniffed into a napkin and reconsidered. 'Well, he definitely had good teeth.'

Sarah couldn't help smiling at that as she got up, and Daphne grinned too, in a rather watery sort of way. Hamish put his little muzzle on her knee and she stroked his ears. By the time Sarah was back with a fresh pot, Daphne was looking more herself again.

'Sarah, this is all getting ridiculous,' she said. 'We need to get to grips with this before anyone else dies. I really think it's high time I did what I do best and get the spirits on our side.'

'OK,' said Sarah a little nervously. 'What would that involve, exactly?'

'Well, one can't be too precise about these things.' Daphne threw out a hand and nearly knocked the hot teapot off the table. Sarah grabbed it by the handle. 'Obviously a séance, then I could do some candle charms, throw runes, a reading or two… you know the drill.'

'That sounds… amazing,' Sarah said. 'Maybe, before we do that, we should go along to one of the Merstairs Militia meetings. We've ruled out a couple of people, but that's still the likeliest source of firearms. These deaths have to be linked somehow, whoever shot Daffyd must have moved on to Deirdre and now Mike. It'll be a good chance to watch people's behaviour. Someone's got a lot on their conscience, so something might strike us.'

'As long as it's not a medieval battleaxe,' said Daphne, forking up the last of the baked beans from Sarah's plate. 'Are you sure you aren't going to get peckish?'

Sarah thought back to the bleak scene on the beach. Throughout her medical training, and then her long career as a GP, the sights she'd seen had not dampened her appetite one whit. Perhaps it was because she was now retired that the thought of food held very little appeal. 'I'm fine for the moment,' she said. 'Who would know when the Militia are next meeting?'

'That's simple,' said Daphne. 'They get together every Saturday morning, come rain or shine, in the big field at the end of the beach, past the crazy golf. I know that because it was a bit annoying when I was in the Tai Chi group. We had to change our times because there was such a big cross-over.'

'Right,' said Sarah. 'Well, we'd better get our skates on.'

'What do you mean?' said Daphne, wiping a fragment of toast around the rim of Sarah's plate.

'Well, today is Saturday. So we need to get there as soon as possible.' Sarah said, picking up her bag and Hamish's lead. She sounded confident, but inwardly she was quaking. The scene on the beach had shaken her, and the knowledge that there was still a very bold murderer walking around Merstairs didn't help matters. It could easily be a member of the Militia, and it looked as though at least one of their guns was still a lethal weapon. Exactly what would they be walking into?

FORTY-ONE

The Men of Merstairs weren't in position on the wall by the crazy golf when Sarah and Daphne sped by. They must be inside the old bingo hall, Sarah decided, and she couldn't really blame them – it was freezing out on the wide expanses near the beach, especially with her soaking wet feet. But she didn't let that, or Daphne's stream of complaints, get in her way. They were soon at the field on the way out of Merstairs, by the road leading gently up to Reculver on the hill above the Merstairs bay. It was quite a scrubby patch of land, used by schools as a makeshift playing field, if the football markings on the ground were anything to go by.

The outlandish costumes worn by the knot of people in the centre of the space were a clue that their interest was definitely not football. Some were wearing Viking helmets, others were dressed as Roundheads in severe black and white, there was someone who looked as though he could have been in the American War of Independence, and there were a couple of Cavaliers with flowing wigs, large gauntlets and bright, puffy breeches. There were some drums and a lot of flags, but nothing that Sarah could see by way of weaponry.

As they got nearer to the little group, one of its members peeled off and came towards them. Underneath the huge plumed Cavalier hat, Sarah was astonished to make out the features of Charles Diggory. When he got a bit closer, he swept off the hat and performed an elaborate bow. Daphne started to giggle and did her best curtsey in return. Sarah just stared in surprise, unlike Hamish who looked genuinely pleased to see him.

'Charles, I had no idea you were part of, um, all this,' said Sarah, when she felt she could trust her voice. 'In fact, you were saying proudly, what seems like a minute ago, that you were about the only person in town who didn't belong to a club.'

'I'm not a member, as such. It's a new thing, I'm just trying it out today,' Charles said a mite shiftily. 'This costume came into the shop, shame to waste it. Besides, I found I was spending a lot of time on my own. Thought this could be fun, you know.'

Sarah felt her cheeks flush. Was this a not-so-oblique attempt to lay the blame for his odd move at her own door, or rather at Daphne's? The implication seemed to be that if Daphne hadn't more or less moved into Sarah's cottage, then Charles would be with her, not a group of eighteen or so motley re-enactors in silly costumes.

'I see. Well I hope you'll really enjoy it,' she said, sweeping past him to join the rest of the group.

Behind her, Daphne raised her eyebrows and Charles jammed his hat back on his head with a much less courtly gesture. Meanwhile, Marlene from the fish and chip shop, dressed in a huge crinoline and a sash matching the colour of Charles's hat plume, caught his eye and twinkled at him over the edge of her fan.

FORTY-TWO

When Sarah had recovered from the shock of seeing Charles dressed up to the nines, she told herself sensibly that what he did in his spare time was really nothing to do with her. After all, she didn't seek his permission every time she went off to do a bit of sleuthing, did she?

She had always tried to keep him up to date on her thoughts, however. This time around, though, had there been a difference? Things had been moving at pace, certainly – who could have predicted the death of Mike the estate agent? – and Charles hadn't been round for a couple of days. It was rather worrying, she had to admit. It suggested that if she didn't pay him a lot of attention he'd just wander off and get entangled elsewhere. Even now, hard though she was trying to concentrate on any Militia members holding likely looking firearms, she couldn't help noticing out of the corner of her eye that Marlene had cosied up to Charles and was getting him to inspect the heel of her boot, while she hung on his arm 'for balance'. Huh, as though a child wouldn't have been able to see through that little ruse.

Hamish, meanwhile, was straining on the end of his lead,

obviously dying to go over and join Charles and Marlene. Sarah tried not to feel betrayed. 'Come on, Hamish, settle down. How about a biscuit?' she added, fishing one out of her pocket.

'Harrumph. Don't take any notice of that,' Daphne said, materialising at Sarah's elbow and jerking her head in the direction of Charles and Marlene. 'It's nothing. Really.'

'Shouldn't Charles be telling me that?' Sarah sniffed, deliberately turning away from the provoking sight. It was absurd. Here they all were, in their sixties (though Marlene looked quite a bit younger if Sarah was honest) and they were still acting as though they were in the playground. Well, if Charles had found a new playmate, then good luck to him.

'Sarah, look over there,' Daphne said, now pulling at Sarah's sleeve.

With a wrench, Sarah tried to redirect her attention. What was it that Daphne wanted her to see? A group of men had clustered around a large metal box. It looked like a child's drawing of a treasure chest. There was even a massive padlock swinging from its lock. As she watched, one of the men drew out a large black key and turned it. Was that Matilda's stolen key? The casket was thrown open, to reveal an assortment of guns, knives and what even looked like hand grenades.

'Is that really legal?' Sarah said, then started to run towards the knot of re-enactors. 'Excuse me, should you be using those? In light of what's been happening recently?'

Sarah wasn't usually a loud person, but her anxiety caused her to yell out the words, and the rest of the Militia turned to look at her as she thundered up the slight incline towards the box. She arrived, puffed, at the scene, took one look at the weapons, and flipped the box shut, narrowly avoiding the fingers of one of the re-enactors who had been delving inside. 'Daphne, call Mariella right this minute,' she ordered.

'Now hang on a second,' said one of the Militia. With a slight start she realised it was Dave Cartwright, looking entirely unlike his usual self in full chain mail, including a hood which covered his weak chin and usually peaceable features. 'I've got a lot of time for you normally, Dr Vane, but right now you're bang out of order.'

There was an approving murmur from the rest of the group, and several of the men glared at her. She took a step back. 'I just mean, in view of the shooting of Daffyd Jones, who I think you all knew, is it really wise to be playing with guns like this? And did someone steal this key from Matilda? I understand she is the one who usually has it.'

'Well, we aren't "playing", for a start,' said Dave, still sounding truculent. 'For your information, Ewan gave me the key earlier in the week.'

'Really?' said Sarah. 'Matilda had no idea where it was, when I saw her.'

Dave tutted. 'He didn't tell her. She's got her hands full at the moment, she had to take Ewan to the doctor, wouldn't say what it was about.'

'I see,' said Sarah. She hoped the appointment would go well – for once wishing she might be entirely wrong in her suspicions. Then she peered at the weapons in the box, rather regretting that she still hadn't made that appointment at the opticians. She reached out a hand. 'May I?' There was a grunt of approval from the crowd and she picked one of the guns up. It weighed almost nothing. Perhaps not surprising, as it was entirely made of plastic.

Sarah rummaged in the box, but there was no sign of anything that looked like a revolver. She looked at Dave, but he shook his head slightly. The reactivated gun from the ill-fated show *Broomstick Battalion* wasn't there now.

'Happy?' Dave said, not waiting for Sarah's glum answer. 'Today we're just having a free-for-all, that's why everyone's come in their favourite costumes.'

Sarah supposed that explained why some of the women had

simply picked attractive fancy dress rather than military costume – like Marlene, for instance. Although Sarah was resolutely standing with her back to Marlene and Charles, she could still hear her trills of laughter. And, as Sarah had just made quite a big fool of herself, it wasn't hard to imagine that those giggles were directed at her.

'Come on, Sarah, let's go home,' said Daphne at her side. A little whine from Hamish seemed to second the motion.

'Just a minute,' said Sarah. She was determined not to leave without making some progress. 'Who's in charge of the group?'

'Oh, well, we think of ourselves as a bit of a collective,' said Dave defensively. 'A bit like the New Model Army.'

'I think Oliver Cromwell probably considered that he was at the helm there,' Sarah said firmly. 'Who is your, um, commander, then, if you prefer that term?'

Dave shuffled his feet a bit and the men around him seemed equally sheepish. 'Well, for a long while it was Daffyd Jones. You know what he was like,' he said.

'I do indeed.' Sarah nodded.

'Since he's no longer with us, I suppose we've come to rely a bit on Matthew. His son, you know.'

Sarah raised her eyebrows. Matthew seemed so meek and colourless. 'I see. Is he here today?' She scanned the crowd but could see no sign of the diffident Matthew.

Just then, someone in full armour, including a gleaming metal helmet, stepped forward, brandishing a sword. Even though she now knew it was probably made of plywood, Sarah found herself ducking, much to the amusement of the onlookers. He was also carrying a shield, with a pattern of crossed muskets and musical notes.

As she watched, he pushed up his visor, and there were the unremarkable features of Matthew Jones, this time arrayed in a quite a cheery smile, considering the circumstances. 'Hi there. It's doing me g-good to get out and about, I must say. I'm really grateful to the Militia for taking my mind off, well, all the awful things that have been happening lately.'

Sarah couldn't help feeling her heart melt towards the poor young man. He had certainly been through the mill in recent days. Who wouldn't feel sympathy for someone who'd lost both mother and father in quick succession – no matter how weak that mother or overbearing the father. She smiled encouragingly. 'Sounds like just the thing to get you out of yourself.'

'That's exactly right,' he said. 'I knew you'd understand.'

'Absolutely. Listen, I hope you don't mind me bringing this up, but Matilda said the Militia had some old Second World War weapons from a local TV show. I couldn't find them just now in your armoury box?'

'Oh, do you mean *Broomstick Battalion*? Mum loved that,' he said, looking sad. 'But that show finished decades ago. Matilda must be mistaken.' He shook his head. 'We wouldn't be using anything like that today anyway, this is a get-together rather than a serious re-enactment. B-but it's great to meet up and share our enthusiasm, you know?'

'I can imagine,' said Sarah, wondering despite herself if Charles, too, was only sharing his enthusiasm. As another of Marlene's giggles floated over to her, it rather looked as though he might be doing a lot more than that. 'But a couple of other people have mentioned those guns to me. Do you know where they are?'

Matthew looked blank, then a strange expression came over his face. 'Oh my God,' he said. 'I can't believe this. I've suddenly realised what must have happened.'

Sarah turned to Matthew, who was now deathly pale. 'What do you mean?'

FORTY-THREE

'I think my father must have planned all this months ago,' said Matthew slowly. 'He must have sneaked the gun out of the box... then planned to use it... and for some reason did it in the choir rehearsal.'

Sarah put her hand on his shoulder automatically. She felt she should comfort him – even if she didn't believe his theory. He was right that someone must have taken the gun, though. Just not his father.

'Did anyone else have access to the box, do you know? Apart from Matilda, Ewan and your dad?'

'Well, the Militia's got a fair few members, as you can see. Let's go higher so you get the full measure of it,' he said, heading up the hill. Despite his sling, he solicitously helped her over the larger tussocks of grass, a job which she felt sure ought to be fulfilled by her supposed boyfriend. But never mind that.

'How's that arm doing?' she asked him.

'Oh, nearly there now, the GP says.' He smiled. 'Here we are. Quite the view, isn't it?'

They were now on the crest of the hill, looking down on the Militia members below, in their various bizarre costumes. It really was the oddest hobby Sarah thought, not for the first time but now with an additional fervour.

'Look, there's Dave Cartwright and the Roundheads,' said Matthew, pointing to a group in drab costumes. 'And there are the Cavaliers.' He waved towards a much more cheerful-looking bunch in satin doublets. Marlene's dress was a splash of violet against the green grass.

'While we're up here, I was surprised to hear your parents put your lovely house up for sale,' Sarah said, in as casual a tone as she could manage.

It seemed to have quite an effect on Matthew. He dropped his sword, narrowly missing his toes. 'I think you're mistaken,' he said. 'There was some talk, but Dad decided against it. Mum loved the house so much, you see,' he said with a sigh. 'I suppose it will have to go now, to settle their affairs. I'm not sure how all that probate stuff works,' he said in a woebegone way.

'Oh, OK,' said Sarah, thinking that probably explained why the pages of dimensions had been ripped through. Daffyd must have changed his mind. 'Plenty of time for all that,' Sarah said consolingly, rather sorry she had brought the matter up.

Just then, Daphne puffed up to join them, Hamish in tow. 'I must say, Charles does look great in that get-up. That feather in his hat really sets off his eyes,' she said dreamily.

'Yes, well. What are you playing? You're not from the same battle, are you?' Sarah eyed Matthew's armour.

'No, I'm Perkin Warbeck – pretender to the English throne,' he said, seeming to cheer up at the thought. 'I probably wouldn't have been wearing armour, to be honest, but I couldn't resist.'

'Did you win this battle, whatever it was?' Daphne piped up.

'Er, no, not exactly. In fact it was a bit of a fiasco, I fled. But James IV of Scotland let me marry a noblewoman, Lady Catherine Gordon – look, she's played by Marlene down there in the lovely mauve gown.'

The mention of that particular shade had Sarah peering down the hill again. She could still see the lavish skirts of Marlene's dress, but Charles's bobbing plume was nowhere to be seen. Probably gone off to see one of the other ladies, she thought crossly.

There was the sound of panting from the opposite side of the hill, and Charles stumbled towards them. 'Oh Charles, didn't see you climbing up from that angle. We were saying how much that colour suits you, weren't we?' Daphne said.

'Were we?' Sarah couldn't help narrowing her eyes, as Charles edged somewhat carefully towards her.

'I hope you haven't misconstrued anything you've seen down there,' he said breathlessly, putting a hand on Sarah's arm.

'I'm more interested in the investigation,' Sarah said, turning away so Charles's hand fell uselessly back to his side. 'Matthew was just telling us about Perkin Warbeck.'

At this, Charles bridled. 'Well, I don't really see why events in the fifteenth century would have any bearings on Daffyd or Deirdre Jones's deaths. Do excuse me, though, Matthew, old boy, my heartfelt condolences.'

'P-perhaps I should get down there and make sure everyone's making the best use of our time,' he said, clearly eager to escape the storm clouds gathering on the hill.

'Oh yes, good idea,' said Daphne. 'I don't want to get stuck in a domestic either. I'll take Hamish, shall I, Sarah?'

Hamish, who'd been looking from one of his favourite humans to the other, perked up at this. But Sarah had other ideas.

'I'll hang on to Hamish, thanks, and come with you,' she said. 'There's nothing up here that warrants discussion, as far as I'm concerned.' With that, she started stalking down the hill. If she hadn't missed her footing, and if Charles hadn't been right there to catch her, then she might have managed her exit with perfect grace and dignity. As it was, she merely said, 'Oh, all right, then,' handed Hamish's lead to Daphne, and turned to face Charles.

Daphne and Matthew Jones made themselves scarce, scampering down the rocky path like mountain goats – if those goats were very eager to avoid a difficult conversation, that is.

Sarah and Charles stood alone together on the top of the hill, neither one much inclined to start the discussion. Finally, Charles plucked up the courage. 'Look, it wasn't what it looked like.'

'Right. So what do you think it looked like, exactly? And why wasn't it that?' Sarah folded her arms.

'The thing is,' said Charles, looking rather absurd with his feather hanging down over his face. He blew it out of the way and it inexorably flopped back into position. 'I've been on my own for a long time.'

'That's fine,' said Sarah, preparing to go again. 'You can stay on your own.'

'But I don't want to,' Charles said, grabbing her with one long arm and pulling her closer to him. 'That's not what I want at all. I actually want to be part of this, part of your investigation... part of your life. Please let me. I came to this Militia meeting to see if I could find out anything for you, to make a few enquiries, if you like.'

'Did you?' Sarah looked up at him. 'You seem to have been spending a lot of time with... Oh, it doesn't matter,' she said, determined to be the better person. 'Did you find anything out?'

'Well, no,' said Charles, his face falling.

'Never mind,' said Sarah. 'I suppose it's the thought that counts.'

'The thought – and the feeling,' said Charles, scooping her to him.

The kiss they shared then, Sarah thought later, was a bit like something out of *Wuthering Heights*. The wind whistled around them, and her head started to swim, as it always did in his embrace. She broke away, still not quite won over, but the pleading look in those eyes was hard to resist.

'The trouble is, not everyone has got the message about, um, our relationship status, I think that's what people call it nowadays,' Charles said. 'If you come down the hill with me, hand in hand, I think that will help get it across loud and clear.'

Sarah looked at Charles long and hard. 'You could just tell people firmly,' she said.

'Not everyone's as good as you at that sort of thing,' Charles said softly.

'Oh, all right, then,' Sarah said, fairly certain she was being cajoled into something, but rather enjoying it at the same time. It was definitely better than the wintry feeling she'd had looking down on the Cavaliers a little earlier.

They started to descend the hill, hands clasped, and Charles was right – soon all eyes were upon them. She hoped he was serious about this, because there was going to be no getting out of it now. As she watched, she saw Marlene swish her skirts as she rushed down the road, clambered into her car, and roared away in the direction of Whitstable. Oh dear.

'It's a shame I haven't got us any further,' Charles was saying. 'I was talking to Matthew about it all earlier. He's having a hard time, poor chap.'

'I bet he is,' Sarah said, shaking her head. 'This time a few days ago, he had both parents. He must feel quite bereft.'

'That, and the responsibility for the Militia. And for the choir, as well.'

'The choir? Surely that's going to be disbanded now,' Sarah said.

'Oh, not at all,' Charles said, squeezing her hand. 'If you and Daphne still want to take part, now's your chance.'

'Really?' Sarah was astonished. 'Matthew wants to keep on with it? I'm really surprised.'

'Oh yes. He said Matilda is keen to sing. And of course

there's the Kent Choral Cup coming up, not to mention the carols on the esplanade. I'm sure he'd like to win that, in his father's memory, you know.'

'Hmm, yes,' said Sarah, but she was miles away. Matilda was raring to sing again, was she? Well, that was news. And the fact that the soloist was willing to give the choir another go was making those little wheels turn very fast indeed in Sarah's brain.

FORTY-FOUR

'If you were serious about helping me investigate, now's your chance,' said Sarah, turning to face Charles just as Daphne and Hamish came up to them.

'All sorted out now, is it, you two?' said Daphne with a heavy wink. 'No more of that star-crossed lover stuff, I hope. We were all rooting for you, Charles, me and the Militia boys,' she continued.

Sarah tutted inwardly, while Charles turned a little pink. 'Daph, I was just saying to Charles, I think we need to check out a few things with Matilda. Are you on for that?'

'Of course,' Daphne said, looking down at Hamish who panted happily at her. 'We're keen, aren't we, boy? Over to the wine bar, then? Probably about time for a spot of lunch now I come to think of it.'

Sarah glanced at her watch in surprise. 'I suppose you're right. Well, that's settled, then. Let's go, team.'

'Oh, ah, I'll have to join you there,' said Charles, looking shifty again.

What now? thought Sarah. He couldn't be getting cold feet already, could he? 'Oh, why's that?' she asked.

'Well, I'll have to get changed,' Charles said, sweeping off his hat and giving her another of those spectacular bows.

'Fair enough,' said Sarah, though she'd be a little sorry to see the costume go. Those breeches really did suit him.

As Charles strode off, Sarah and Daphne turned in the other direction and walked through the town to the Red House wine bar. As they clattered up the steps, they could hear the buzz of conversation and, sure enough, when they went through the door, almost all the seats were taken.

'Gosh, it's busy today, isn't it?' Sarah said, gazing around.

'I suppose it's the weekend,' Daphne shrugged, 'though that doesn't mean much now we're all retired. Look, there's a table at the back. Quick, I'll bagsy it and you get the drinks.'

At the bar, Matilda was wearing dangly blue earrings and a brave smile. Ewan, by her side, was doing his best to cut a lemon into thin slices. Judging by the mangled results, it wouldn't be long before he'd be making another appointment with his doctor. She felt heartily sorry for them both. But that didn't mean she could take it easy on Matilda.

'A Dubonnet and a tonic water, please. I hear you're rejoining the choir, is that right?'

Matilda, who'd been about to reach down for a tall glass for Daphne's drink, froze in the act and swung round. 'Who's been telling you that?'

'It's just something I heard at the Militia meeting earlier,' Sarah said, trying for nonchalance.

Matilda got the drinks together and pushed them towards Sarah. 'Card payment, is it?'

'Yes. I just wondered if you'd be getting a slice of the prize money, now Daffyd's out of the way? He must have been charging a pretty penny for private tuition, and all those entry fees. That'll all change now, won't it?'

At the mention of lessons, Matilda glanced over her shoulder at Ewan, but he was frowning ferociously at the squashed lemon and didn't seem to be listening. She turned back to Sarah with a grim expression on her face. 'I don't know who you've been gossiping with, but it's not true. I'm not interested in singing any more. Not with this bar to run,' she finished, just as Ewan cried out. The entire plate of lemon had hit the floor. 'Now if you'll excuse me, I'm busy.'

Sarah took the drinks over to the table thoughtfully. 'What's up with Matilda?' asked Daphne as she sat down. 'She looks like she's swallowed a wasp.'

'I don't think she enjoyed our chat,' Sarah said. Daphne winced. 'Well, I had to ask about her rejoining the choir. If she now stands to make some money out of the prize for the Choral Cup, that gives her a reason. And even if she wants to sing for Gwendoline and Griselda's carollers and beat Daffyd's lot, that's still important. She has a list of motives a mile long.'

'Who does?' said an unamused voice. It was Matilda, a bar cloth over her shoulder, pausing at their table while picking up empties.

'Oh, er, um, Matilda, didn't see you there,' said Sarah, taking what she hoped was a casual sip of her drink and going very pink.

Matilda looked from Sarah to Daphne and back again and leant forward. 'Oh, I see. You mean me. Well, yes, I did have reasons aplenty for wishing that snake Daffyd ill, but I'd never have acted on them. I'm a peaceful person at heart,' she said, taking the towel off her shoulder and wringing it out with her hands in such a forceful way that it made Sarah's eyes water. If Daffyd had been strangled, there wouldn't have been much doubt in her mind at this point. Then Matilda burst into speech. 'Anyway, ladies, I'm glad you're here because—'

At that moment, Ewan shouted to her from the bar. 'Matilda, I could do with an extra pair of hands,' he said, pointing to a spill on the bar and a crowd of customers all waiting to be served.

'I don't know what's up with him these days, all fingers and thumbs. He never used to be,' Matilda said under her breath. 'The GP said he was fine. I'll talk to you later, OK?'

Sarah and Daphne nodded, then as soon as Matilda swung away to bail Ewan out at the bar, they turned to look at each other.

'Well, that was awkward,' Daphne said with a grimace. 'Shall we go?'

'I don't think so,' Sarah said. 'If I'm not mistaken, Matilda came over to tell us something, but either decided she couldn't as this place is so full of ears, or she needed to get back to help Ewan. Whichever it was, I think we should hang around here for a bit, until she's got time to pass whatever it is on.'

'Really?' said Daphne a little peevishly. 'I've finished my drink, you know. And I'm sure Hamish wants to go.'

As Hamish was now deeply unconscious, the weight of his head pressing Sarah's foot into the floor, she didn't think much of that excuse. She cast around for a good way of getting Daphne to stay. 'We promised Charles we'd be here. He was just getting changed before coming along,' she said.

'Hmm,' said Daphne. 'He's taking his time. Well, we can just text him and say we've left,' she continued.

Sarah was out of ideas – until her eyes lit on the menu on the table. Of course. 'How about we have a little snack here, to pass the time?' she suggested.

'Honestly, Sarah, you think the mere mention of food is going to stop me wanting to leave. I'm a bit more complicated than that, I'll have you know,' Daphne said, reaching out for the card. 'Ooh, look, they do nachos. That sounds nice.'

'Why don't you go and order those for us?' Sarah said. 'I can't move because Hamish is snoozing on my toes.'

'The little pickle! Just like my Mephisto.' Daphne sighed. 'Makes my legs go to sleep when he does that.'

Sarah was only surprised it didn't cut off her friend's circulation entirely. But she smiled encouragingly, and Daphne trotted through the crowds to put their order in.

* * *

By the time the nachos arrived, slowed up by the fact that Ewan dropped the first batch on the floor and the second was scorched in the kitchen while all the clearing up was going on, the crowds had considerably thinned out in the Red House wine bar. Even Sarah was starving when Ewan finally set the big platter down on their table, and she and Daphne dug in with gusto. Hamish was woken from his slumbers by the smell of grilled cheese, but a couple of dog biscuits from Sarah's pocket perked him up once he'd been told, much to his astonishment, that nachos were human food and not meant for small Scotties. Sarah and Daphne were tussling in a good-natured way over the last corn chip, though there was little doubt who was going to win, when Charles peered round the door.

Seeing their waves, he made his way towards them and Sarah realised at once why he'd looked a little unsure when poking his head in. There was a large red mark on his cheek, consistent, she imagined, with a stinging slap from a very cross hand. This perhaps explained why he'd taken so long to get here.

'You've got something on your face, Charles,' Daphne said, chasing the last of the sour cream with the tip of the disputed nacho. 'You should get a doctor to look at that,' she added, burying her chuckles in her Dubonnet.

'No need. I can see it's not going to be fatal,' said Sarah as kindly as she could, as Charles lowered his eyes and sat down, looking crestfallen. 'Would you like a drink?'

'I'll get them.' Charles shot up again, looking pleased to have something concrete to do – and perhaps eager to forestall too many queries about his face. 'Usual, ladies?'

They both nodded assent, and before he was out of earshot, Daphne said loudly, 'Well, I didn't know Marlene had it in her. She must have been furious with him. No more fish suppers at her chip shop for a bit, then.'

'*Restaurant*, please, Daph. She'd hate it being described as a chippy,' said Sarah, finding it hard not to smile. It looked as though Charles had finally made things very plain to Marlene – or she had made them plain to him.

While Ewan served Charles at the bar, Matilda took the opportunity to pour a large measure of red wine and slip over to Sarah and Daphne's table. Much to their surprise, she sat herself down and confronted them.

'All right, then,' she said, taking a big slurp from her glass. 'You two have worn me down. I suppose I'd better come clean at last.'

FORTY-FIVE

Sarah and Daphne both looked at Matilda, agog, as the glamorous younger woman shook out her blonde hair and squared her shoulders. 'I told you a bit of a fib, earlier,' she said.

'Dangerous, during a murder investigation,' Sarah said mildly, but it seemed to rile Matilda.

'And there was I, thinking Daphne's daughter was the one supposed to be in charge. There are so many detectives in Merstairs nowadays it's amazing I ever get away with double parking on the seafront,' she said with a humourless laugh.

'Three deaths in a few days – I'd say that's a bit more serious than a traffic offence,' said Sarah, folding her lips.

'OK, OK, I was just trying to lighten the tone a bit,' said Matilda, taking another swig of her wine. 'It's been quite a day.' There was the tinkle of glass in the back room, as Ewan dropped something. Matilda sighed. 'Go home and get some rest, Ewan love,' she called.

'Sorry,' Ewan said gruffly, poking his head out of the store-room. 'I don't know what's up with me at the moment.'

'Don't worry about it. I'll see you later, darling,' Matilda said with a tired smile. As soon as he'd ducked back inside again, she rubbed a hand over her face. 'I'm not sure how much longer I can keep him on for, he's destroying our custom at the moment.'

'Maybe get the doctor to give him a really *thorough* check-up,' Sarah said. 'But getting back to what's been going in Merstairs lately – I know you might not particularly want to talk to us about it, but, well, it might save you time when Mariella gets round to questioning you.'

'Are you kidding?' Matilda said, knocking back another slug of her wine. 'I've been in and out of the police station like a blinking yoyo, talking to those two great oafs of hers – no offence, Daphne.'

'None taken. That's a good description of Tweedledum and Tweedledee.' Daphne smiled.

Sarah pricked up her ears at hearing that Mariella, too, had her suspicions about Matilda, but the woman hadn't finished speaking. 'Look, I know that I'm Miss Peacock in the conservatory with the lead piping, as far as you sleuths are concerned. But I honestly haven't had a thing to do with all this. Yes, I lost my key to the Militia box, or I thought I had, but it turned out Dave Cartwright had it all along. And I know I had a brief moment of madness with Daffyd – goodness knows what I was thinking – but haven't any of you ever made mistakes?'

Charles flushed, as Matilda's eyes raked his face, still a little pink after its contact with an angry female palm. Sarah raised her eyebrows, and Daphne nodded sagely. 'I once swapped my tried-and-tested crystal ball for a shiny new one. Such a disaster! My readings were wonky for weeks,' she said.

'Well... exactly,' said Matilda, leaning back as though the case was closed. 'I'll just help out with the Kent Choral Cup, and then that will be that.'

'Wait a minute,' said Daphne. 'You told us you weren't interested in that!'

'Little white lie,' said Matilda. 'That's what I came over to say. I didn't want to discuss it when the bar was full.'

'So you've signed up for the reboot of the choir? And you're planning on being a soloist again?' Sarah said.

'So what if I am? When did turning out to support the choir I've been a member of for years become a major crime?' Matilda said crossly.

'But don't you think it's a bit unseemly? Daffyd and Deirdre have only just died, in suspicious circumstances, and you're carrying on as usual?'

'Look, Sarah,' said Matilda, trying for a patient tone but unable to hide the annoyance in her words. 'I happen to have a talent for singing. Plus I enjoy it. If I can bring the Kent Choral Cup back to Merstairs, then I will. And if it's offensive in some way for anyone to be singing after the deaths, well, how about Matthew? They were his parents, and if he's not bothered I'm not sure why I should be.'

'Will you be benefitting financially if you do win the Choral Cup?' Sarah persisted.

'What if I am? I need all the money I can get at the moment, to pay for the endless breakages we've had around here,' Matilda said ruefully.

'But don't you see?' Sarah said. 'That makes your motive all the stronger. Daffyd wasn't about to share any of the prize money with you, was he? But now that he's out of the way, you'll be able to get your hands on it.'

'I don't know who's been spinning you a line about the prize money, but let me assure you, it's not likely to make anyone rich. I think it's a couple of thousand, and if Matthew splits it with the choir – which he ought to do – then we'll be grateful, but I don't think anyone's going to be swanking along the esplanade in a fur coat and diamonds, let's put it that way.'

Sarah sat up straighter. The mention of diamonds reminded her of those two flashing rhinestones, one backstage at the choir and one in Francesca's garage. Though poor Deirdre and her brooch were out of the running, she still needed to check with

Mariella what, if anything, the police had found out about them. Perhaps they had come from Matilda's keyfob after all?

'You already have the fur coat anyway, dear lady,' said Charles gallantly.

'My fun fur? Yes, I suppose I do. Well anyway, if that's enough grilling, I think I'm going to start closing up. Unless anyone wants another drink?' Matilda looked around the group. Hamish gave a little yip of excitement, but she shook her head. 'I don't think you're allowed any Dubonnet, but you've been a very good boy all this time. Used to your mum giving people the third degree, are you?'

Hamish wagged his tail in happy assent, while Sarah bit her lip and took stock of Matilda's answers. The woman was right, unless they were her bits of diamanté, there was nothing concrete to tie her to the deaths. And the fact that Mariella had questioned her more than once and apparently found nothing did rather suggest they were barking up the wrong tree.

'Oh well, thank you so much, we really enjoyed the nachos,' Sarah said as brightly as she could.

'You're very welcome,' Matilda said heavily.

Once they were out on the pavement again and walking away from the wine bar towards the twinkling strings of Christmas lights on the seafront, Charles piped up. 'Matilda was very patient with us, you know.'

'Yes, she was,' sighed Sarah. 'She's a nice woman, for all her prima donna airs every now and then.'

'I hope Ewan gets things sorted out. Don't you think you should tell them what you suspect?' said Daphne.

Sarah thought for a moment. 'I've considered it,' she admitted. 'But there's still the possibility I might be wrong. And the oath I took was to do no harm. Sometimes that can mean not getting involved – and that can be harder than anything else.'

Charles put an arm round Sarah, and she leant into his shoulder, while Daphne took her other arm. It was comforting having friends around her. She would do her utmost to make sure that Ewan had all the support she could offer, when and if the time came – and that went for Matilda, too.

'So where does this all leave us, as far as the investigation goes?' Charles asked.

If he'd been hoping to distract Sarah, it worked. Immediately her mind was buzzing again. 'Good question,' she said thoughtfully.

'Deirdre was always the most likely person,' Daphne chipped in.

'Well, except that it can't have been her. She's dead too, and Mike was killed after she'd died,' Sarah said.

They'd almost made it back to the cottages now. Sarah turned automatically to go up her path, her hand on the quaint old sunburst gate, when Daphne stopped her. 'It's time I hosted everyone for a change,' she said, leading the way past the massed ranks of her garden gnome collection up to her purple front door.

Sarah and Charles looked at each other. She wondered whether it had occurred to him, too, that Daphne might stay at her own house if they settled her in there. 'Great idea!' said Charles enthusiastically, bounding up the path. Sarah suppressed a smile and followed suit.

Once inside, and after Mephisto had flung himself out of the cat flap in high dudgeon at having his nap interrupted by Hamish, Daphne filled up the kettle, swept a mass of papers off the kitchen table, and told her guests to make themselves comfy.

Sarah sat in one of Daphne's well-upholstered armchairs with a sigh of satisfaction. Though she loved her own neat home, there was something wonderfully life-affirming about her friend's cosy place.

'I've got some bickies somewhere,' said Daphne, rattling through the cupboards and flinging open drawers. 'Or would you prefer soup? I have some amazing borscht on the go.'

Sarah rather drew the line at Daphne's beetroot concoctions. 'There are some biscuits here,' she said, unearthing a tempting looking selection box from under the latest copy of *Total Tarot* magazine.

'What? Oh yes, Sarah, I'm not surprised you're reading that, it's great, isn't it?' Daphne said, pouring boiling water into an enormous brown earthenware teapot. 'Though I mainly get it for the free Tarot cards every month. Useful, in case Mephisto eats any of my usual pack.'

'Of course,' said Sarah, slightly arrested by the cover of the magazine. It was a lurid purple, almost the same shade that Marlene had been wearing at the Militia meeting. It all came back to her. That sumptuous gown, the silken skirts, the way she'd been hanging on Charles's arm... but perhaps, more than anything, the fact that she'd been a part of the group at all.

Sarah turned to Charles, just as he took his first sip of the wonderfully strong tea Daphne had just poured. 'Has Marlene always been a member of the Merstairs Militia?'

FORTY-SIX

'Excuse me, dear lady, I'm sorry, I've made the most dreadful mess,' said Charles, trying to mop up his spilled tea with a cloth from the table.

'Not that, Charles! Honestly, that's my special cover for the crystal ball at Tarot and Tealeaves, as if you didn't know,' Daphne said, swiping the piece of fabric and folding it tenderly. 'Now, Sarah, you're not going to keep going on about Marlene, are you? I thought you two had sorted all that out,' Daphne added briskly.

Sarah, feeling a little shamefaced, just nodded and said, 'Of course.' Daphne was right. It really wasn't the moment to be chewing over all that, especially when she and Charles were now on such a good footing. But that didn't mean that she'd forgotten her suspicions for one instant.

* * *

By the time they finally left Daphne's later that evening, after the tea had made way for a very good red wine and the biscuits had been swapped for cheese and crackers, Sarah and Charles more or less floated next door to bed and a very satisfactory night, though Hamish, firmly left in the kitchen for once, might have disagreed.

By the next morning, however, after Charles had snatched a hasty breakfast and rushed off to make sure his antiques emporium was open bright and early to catch all the tourists who definitely wouldn't be passing on a drizzly Sunday, Sarah got to thinking again.

It wasn't jealousy, she told herself. It was just the simple fact that Marlene had popped up a lot in this investigation. Sarah had had a similar experience recently, when someone who couldn't possibly be a criminal had kept appearing on the fringes of her enquiries, and in the end, unlikely though it had seemed, they had been revealed to be the guilty party. Sarah wasn't going to be caught napping like that again.

Marlene was a member of the Militia, which gave her access to weapons. One of them was still operational, according to Dave Cartwright. She had also been a member of the choir. Daphne had said that being a soloist was a highly prized position in the town; it would be typical of Marlene to hold a grudge if Daffyd didn't give her a turn. Sarah could just see her getting slapped down by the awful choirmaster, and bitterly resenting it. She probably owned some sparkly jewellery; it was just her sort of thing. She had even been sauntering along the esplanade on the day of Deirdre's death. Had Deirdre, too, been suspicious, and had Marlene needed to silence her? Like the rest of Merstairs, she certainly would have known poor Mike the estate agent, and maybe had some ancient grudge against him over the purchase of her house or shop. It couldn't all be coincidence, could it, the way her name kept cropping up?

The trouble was that, if Sarah did start looking into the woman properly, both Daphne and Charles would think it was the green-eyed monster at work, and not a seriously thought-out deductive process at all. So, she could try and persuade them she had the best interests of the enquiry at heart, and it was nothing personal.

Or she could just go off and look into Marlene on her own.

There was no question which would be easier. Her recent conversation with Charles about the matter had been toe-curlingly embarrassing, and if she so much as mentioned Marlene's name again, either he or Daphne would be bound to jump down her throat.

No, there was no real choice, Sarah thought, as she finished her toast and washed it down with the dregs of her tea. She was simply going to be on her own with this one.

A small snuffle from the vicinity of the tartan basket by the cooker begged to differ, and she immediately went over to Hamish and gave him some lavish strokes on his tufty head, just the way he liked. 'Thank goodness for you, eh, Hamish boy? Otherwise I'd be off to investigate a murderer all on my tod. And we wouldn't want that, would we?'

We certainly wouldn't, Hamish decided, and gave a bark to emphasise his point. He'd take a nice walk over hanging off a clifftop with a murderer any day, he'd had quite enough of that kind of behaviour with the awful vet chap a while back.

'All right then, boy, let's go, shall we? I wonder if I should just put a note through Daphne's door, give her a head's up? No. I'll only get a long lecture when I'm back, if I'm wrong. And this time, I really don't think I am.'

With that, she clipped on Hamish's lead, and they ventured out into the rain.

FORTY-SEVEN

The walk along the esplanade was like any other, Sarah kept telling herself. True, the weather was absolutely terrible, which was rare in Merstairs, thank goodness. But the glinting Christmas lights were very cheerful, and what could be more natural than a lady of a certain age, out with her little dog, taking the air, getting some exercise, keeping fit, making sure her mind was active – and, most importantly, keeping an eye on the fish and chip shop on the seafront.

But, when she drew parallel with the eye-catching purple sign proclaiming she'd reached Marlene's Plaice, she was disappointed. The chippy was closed, firmly shuttered, locked, and, to add insult to injury, there was even a sign on the door saying 'We're Shut' in curly purple writing which looked very much as though Marlene had penned it herself. Drat.

Sarah couldn't quite believe she had been so silly. One of the wonderful things about Merstairs was that you could get chips at almost any hour of the day – except, of course, for 8 a.m. on a Sunday. It looked as though her interrogation of Marlene was going to have to wait.

Just as she was turning away in annoyance, someone came

up and tapped her on the shoulder. She jumped, then swung round to face a familiar figure. Nondescript hair, fawn jumper, shapeless coat covering his sling – it was none other than Matthew Jones.

'Sorry, didn't mean to startle you. I just saw you and your little dog – Angus, is it? Out for a walk, I suppose.'

'It's Hamish,' Sarah corrected automatically. 'Yes, erm, that's right. We thought we'd have a little wander.' Then she decided to come clean. Why not? Matthew Jones had more of a right to know what was in her mind than most people. After all, he was the one who'd been left an orphan by recent events. 'Actually, I was hoping to have a word with Marlene. But as you can see, she hasn't opened up yet.'

'Oh, she doesn't normally fire up the d-deep fryer until about eleven.' Matthew smiled. 'Likes to get her beauty sleep, I suppose. Marlene, hmm, that's interesting. Don't tell me you suspect her?'

Sarah laughed in a slightly unconvincing way. 'I've had a few different thoughts, since the mur... since what happened to your parents. Most of them have come to nothing. But I think I might be getting close now,' she said.

Matthew blinked. 'You've certainly been making lots of enquiries – like thinking the house was on the m-market,' he said. 'Very impressive. Why don't you come to my place for a coffee? We can discuss it all there. You can tell me all your other clever theories,' he said, looking at her admiringly.

'Well, it is pretty chilly out here,' said Sarah. 'Would you like to go inside for a bit, Hamish?'

The little dog wagged his tail happily. The beach would still be out there when they left, after all.

* * *

The view from the sitting room at the Jones house was as amazing as ever, capturing the wide curve of the Kent coastline and framing it perfectly, making the restless sea look like a Turner masterpiece in motion, if not quite as blurry. Matthew was downstairs, making the coffee with much less noise and kerfuffle than Daphne had managed the other day.

Sarah moved away from the window and felt the familiar disappointment at seeing the blocky furniture and large fake plants which Deirdre and Daffyd Jones had selected and lived with. The Christmas tree lights were now off, and the room looked less festive than ever. It was odd to think that Deirdre had sat on that sofa so recently, wringing her hands, as she had contemplated the armchair left vacant by Daffyd. Someone had moved the old newspaper and remote controls which had been there the other day – Matthew, presumably, unless they had a cleaner. In their place was a sheaf of papers.

Sarah knew she really shouldn't, but honestly, how could she possibly resist drifting over to the chair, and accidentally-on-purpose knocking the papers to the floor. Whoopsie! She picked them up quickly, disappointed they were blank – but then out dropped something. It lay on the floor, glinting. It was Deirdre's brooch. Sarah took it in her hand, looking at the gaps where the two bits of diamanté were missing.

What could this mean? Her mind raced. The first shiny little stone had been in the murder room, where Daffyd had breathed his last. Then second was at Francesca's garage. But it hadn't been Charles's gun that had done the deed, so even if Deirdre had found the strength to kill Daffyd, she must have got the gun from the Militia box instead, and there had been no rhinestones there. Or not that Sarah had seen, anyway. Oh, it was all so complicated.

She was just putting the bundle back in place on the arm of the chair when there was a noise outside the door. Phew, she'd been just in time. She moved towards the window. It wasn't hard to pretend to be glued to that view.

Matthew got the door open and walked in cradling a tray very carefully. Sarah quickly took it from him before the cafetiere, cups and a packet of biscuits could slide off.

'This is kind of you, Matthew. You didn't need to go to all this trouble.'

'Oh, not at all,' he said, fiddling with the plunger on the cafetiere. 'Life goes on, doesn't it? No reason why I shouldn't still drink coffee, even if I'm in mourning. Damn, I can't get this to work. I must admit, Mum usually made the coffee.'

'Here, let me,' said Sarah, moving over to Matthew's side. He seemed to be getting in quite a state.

'No! No, I'm fine, really. Just this blasted sling,' he said, sticking out his other hand to ward her off. 'I can manage. I've got to get used to doing it on my own. Mum's not around to help me any more.'

Sarah went back to the armchair thoughtfully. 'I suppose that's right,' she said after a beat. 'What a very sad thought. You must be distraught, Matthew.'

He turned back to the coffee tray. 'Oh, you know what men are like with their emotions,' he said. 'We like to keep things buttoned up.'

'Yes, why is that, would you say?' Sarah put her head on one side.

Matthew faced her and sat down. 'Heavens. I really don't know,' he said eventually. 'Oh, let me pass you your coffee.'

Sarah got up to take it from him. 'Mm, smells lovely,' she said, then she studied the cup closely.

'Anything wrong?' Matthew asked her solicitously.

'Not at all,' Sarah said quickly. 'This is your grandmother's set, isn't it?'

'Mm, what? Yes, I think so. Sugar? And do add your own

milk, I never know how much people want,' Matthew offered. 'Help yourself to a biscuit.'

Sarah did as she was bid and took the cup and biscuit back to the armchair, sitting rather carefully in it, remembering Daffyd Jones as she did so. He'd been such a huge bear of a man, a physical presence to be reckoned with. Such a transformation, from angelic choirboy to bully. And then here was his son, so inconsequential by comparison, slight and what Sarah's daughters might call 'weedy'. He looked nervous this morning, and the fawn jumper he seemed to wear relentlessly did nothing at all for his wan complexion. He certainly had the look of someone who spent far too much time indoors. There was a pile of copies of the *Racing Post* next to the chair, some with scribbles next to the horses' names. She hadn't noticed them before. On the top was one mentioning that day's Cheltenham meet.

'Do drink up, before it goes cold,' he said.

'Why, are you in a hurry to get rid of me?' Sarah said with a twinkle.

Matthew laughed and sipped his coffee.

'You should probably think about a mindfulness course or something, just to tide you over this difficult period,' she said sympathetically, raising her cup to her lips. 'You really are dealing with a lot.'

Matthew looked away and sighed. 'I s-suppose you're right.'

'And then you were saying you will eventually have to part with this place? The thought must be stressful.'

'Well, it's much too big for one person,' he said, stirring his cup.

'Is that what Mike Benchley said, when he came along the other day?' Sarah said mildly.

'You saw him, did you? Oh, you know what estate agents are like. He was always trying to get a foot in the door. I didn't have the heart to say no to him,' he said dismissively.

Sarah decided to get the conversation back on track. 'So, I was wondering about Marlene, as you know...'

'Oh yes, you said. How's your coffee?' Matthew said with a small smile.

'Lovely,' said Sarah. 'That reminds me, you kindly made your dad a cup at the choir rehearsal, didn't you?'

'Yes.' Matthew smiled sadly. 'He was very particular about it. I knew exactly what to give him. But you were telling me about Marlene?'

'Of course. Well, she just seems to pop up everywhere. It can't be coincidence. The Militia, the esplanade, the choir – oh, I understand the choir is still going after all?'

'Oh yes, that's right. There was some enthusiasm from the members... I didn't want to let them down.'

'There's the carol sing-off soon, isn't there? Not to mention the Choral Cup. The prize money is up for grabs, I suppose.'

'Well, that's not the point, of course,' said Matthew. 'It would be more as a tribute to my father, if we won.'

'Does that mean you'd let the choir keep the winnings, for a change?' Sarah asked.

'You do ask a lot of questions,' Matthew said, putting his cup down.

'I like to try and build up a picture of what's going on. It could help us sort out what happened to your parents.'

'We know what happened to my parents,' Matthew said sadly. 'There's nothing more to be said about it.'

'There's the little matter of who might have had a hand in it,' Sarah said.

'Ah yes. You want things to be complicated, it can't be Dad killing himself and Mum dying of the shock. It has to be Marlene from the fish and chip shop,' Matthew said. 'Well, go on, then, let's have your theories,' he said with a patient smile.

'I know you're sceptical, but just hear me out,' Sarah said, raising her cup again. 'Mm, really good coffee. Well, Marlene was at the rehearsal. So she could have slipped into the office on the fateful night, given Daffyd the gun to look at, and then yanked his arm up at the right moment... as she's in the Militia, she could have got hold of Matilda's armaments box key somehow. One of those *Broomsticks* weapons wasn't decommissioned. Could she also have scared your mother to death? Threatened her in some way? It's all such a tangle... And as for Mike...'

'Oh yes, Mike. I was forgetting about him. Do you think Marlene had a motive for killing Mike?' Matthew said, sitting forward in his chair now, hanging on Sarah's every word.

It was rather flattering, she thought distantly. Did Marlene have a motive? She'd thought of something only a moment ago. What was it? Oh, it was so hard to say...

'Sarah? Sarah, are you all right?' Matthew got up and leant over her.

Sarah let the cup slip from her hand. It crashed to the floor with a clatter. Hamish barked as her eyes closed, slowly, slowly. The last thing she noticed before they shut was Matthew's half smile, as he craned over her in that blasted fawn jumper.

FORTY-EIGHT

Soon, the only sound in the room was the faint whining of Hamish, as he nuzzled around his mistress's inert feet – and the cackling of Matthew Jones.

'Thought you were so clever, didn't you, retired so-called "doctor" Vane,' he said, looming over the woman slumped like a rag doll in the chair. He pulled off his sling and threw it on the sofa. 'I don't need that any more. It fooled you, though, so it just goes to show how stupid you really are – you're just a dotty old pensioner like the rest of them. Lucky I kept Mum's old insomnia medicine around, to dose her up when she got annoying. She was pathetic, really. Under Dad's thumb.

'Dad went mental when he found out I'd pretended to be him and put the house on the market with Merstairs Mortar. He went round there, shouting the odds, nicking all those pens. He ripped up the details. He was threatening to get me sent to prison. Everyone was going to find out. Then the firm went bust. But Dad wouldn't leave it there, it wasn't safe to have him blabbing. I rang Mike – and he rang Dad. That was the call he was taking in the rehearsal room. I had no choice – I had to stop him then. It was lucky I had the Militia gun ready in the locker, and I hid in there when that muscle-bound klutz Ewan waltzed up with Dad.'

'Then, when it was all done, Mum had the nerve to try and stand up to me. Well, I couldn't have that, could I? I wasn't to know the sleeping pills don't react well with alcohol. She'd been knocking it back recently. It weakened her heart, I suppose. I feel a bit guilty about that – *sorry, Mum* – but it's just as well, as she didn't want to sell either. And I like to get my way. As you've found out.'

Matthew was walking around the room now, getting into his stride. 'And as for your stupid little dog, well unless he keeps his trap shut, he'll go the same way. I'll drug him then throw him off the pier with you this evening. That's where Mike went into the water. Poor stupid Mike, asking one too many questions… he had to go. I'll just get an estate agent in from Whitstable instead. They'll never prove it was me who killed him. Blow on the head with a stone from the beach, into the water, over in a second. Much less fuss than Dad. I should never have tried to get fancy with a gun.

'I gave Dad his usual coffee at the choir rehearsal, but this time laced with some of Mum's sleeping stuff. Then, after he'd got rid of Ewan, and while he was nice and woozy, I used his own hand to shoot him, I thought it was inspired. But I made mistakes, I admit it. I should have just left the gun in the rehearsal room after firing it, of course. Instead I panicked when I came out, I could hear someone else coming – probably you, nosey old dear – so I ran to hide in the ladies' loo. I stuck the gun in my sling, with the phone. I probably should have put the gun back in the box, but instead I chucked it in the sea with the phone. It seemed cleaner.

'I did drop a bit of diamanté from Mum's ugly great brooch at the scene, and even in Francesca Diggory's garage, when I was there to discuss the Kent Cup with her, but no one picked up on that little clue. And I blobbed some plaster on the table, once I found Mum dead, to point to Ewan. Again, not one of you cottoned on. You believed I was shocked when I burst into the room. I've always been wasted on Merstairs,' he said bitterly, sitting himself down on the arm of Sarah's chair and prodding her none too gently in the shoulder. She didn't react, and he nodded happily before carrying on.

'If there's one thing I'm sorry about, it's Mike. But it was none of his business. So what if I've got a few debts? I don't have a gambling problem, I just need a winner or two. Dad could easily have helped me out, with all the money he stashed away from those stupid choral competitions. Then Mum could have agreed to divvy things up quickly after he was gone. But no. She wanted to keep tabs on me, said I couldn't be trusted with that sort of money. They were selfish, so selfish, both of them. God, living with them, you have no idea, Sarah Vane. They were the worst parents in the world. I had every reason to do what I did. You would have done the same.' He sighed and stared out to sea, the very image of the hard-done-by child.

'No, I wouldn't,' said Sarah, opening her eyes all at once and seeing with satisfaction the horror on Matthew Jones's face as he wheeled round to gape at her. 'I would never have done what you did, not in a million years. And if you think you're going to drug my dog, you've got another think coming.'

'You, you, damned old woman, you, you...' Matthew's lips were speckled with saliva, and his drab brown eyes were filled with a mad light as he rushed across the room and lunged at her, hands out to grab her by the throat and choke the life out of her. But he'd reckoned without Hamish, who gave a bloodcurdling growl and sank his teeth into Matthew's ankle.

'Ow, dratted little mutt, I'll wring your neck,' he said, kicking out with his leg, trying his best to get the determined dog away and keep his balance at the same time. But Hamish was having none of it, and in the breathing space he gave her, Sarah took up the largest remote control from the armrest of the chair and brought it down sharply on Matthew's head. It wasn't nearly enough to knock the man out, but it gave her the opportunity to get to her feet and start throwing everything she could at him – the coffee cup, the milk jug, the cafetiere, the tray, sofa cushions… she was fast running out of options when she heard a voice outside shouting, 'Oi!' She didn't want to turn to see who it was, as Matthew could come at her with full force, but she did see his eyes widen as he saw what was going on through the window behind her. In an instant, he'd abandoned his attack on her, and was sprinting out of the sitting room door.

Now Sarah turned towards the big picture window to see who had been yelling. To her astonishment, she caught the eye of the red-faced police constable, Dumbarton, who promptly bumbled up the steps to the house and could be heard hammering at the entrance. She ran into the hall, worried that Matthew might be lying in wait there to attack her again, but fearing she had no choice but to get help if she wanted to survive.

There was no sign of Matthew as she got the front door open with trembling hands. Dumbarton rushed in, almost falling on her. 'Where is he? Where's that blighter?' he said, his little piggy eyes darting here and there.

'Good question,' said Sarah. 'As far as I know, there's only one way in or out, and this is it,' she said, gesturing to the imposing Georgian entrance with its beautiful fan light above.

Just then, there was a curious whistling sound from above. Something flashed past them, and there was a sickeningly heavy thud. An object had fallen from one of the upper storeys of the house, hitting the ground hard. Sarah peered over the constable's shoulder. There was a crumpled beige and black heap lying on the lawn, in front of the magnificent window. It would have looked like a mound of old clothes, bizarrely chucked out of a window – had it not been for the familiar fawn colour of that jumper, and a man's foot, sticking out at an angle she knew to be anatomically impossible.

FORTY-NINE

'Do you think Matthew meant to do it? Throw himself out of the window, I mean?' asked Daphne, shivering a bit as she sat with her arm around Sarah.

They were in the covered section of the Beach Café, looking out towards a stormy sea, and blowing on comforting hot chocolates. On the wall beside them was a large poster for the Kent Choral Cup, with the word 'cancelled' scrawled across it in thick black pen. They could just see Charles, striding across the sands with Hamish and Tinkerbell, throwing sticks for the Scottie and picking Tinkerbell up when she felt like a rest, which seemed to be about every three steps.

'In one way, he had no other exit route, and once PC Dumbarton was inside, what chance did he have of escaping? The man was totally blocking the hall. But I'm sure he didn't want to die.'

'I like the way you're not calling that PC Tweedledum any more,' Daphne said, her eyes alight.

'Well, he saved my life, and Hamish's. I really owe him one. If he hadn't shown up, I dread to think what would have happened. I'd thrown everything I could get my hands on at Matthew and he was still coming at me. The only things left in the room were those chairs and the sofa, and I couldn't lift them. I'd really had it,' Sarah said. It was her turn to shiver at the memory.

'Imagine, that feeble twit Matthew being the killer all along. We thought he was so wet. Who'd have thought he'd have the get up and go?' mused Daphne. 'And as for that sling, well, it was so clever. You'd never have thought for a second he could have shot anyone with that on.'

'Well, I suppose he took his hand out, then put it back in again. Simple as that. I honestly never questioned it for a moment, I feel so silly for underestimating him. He didn't want me to examine him, but even that didn't make me suspect that his arm was fine all along. He must have been seething for years, being treated like that by his father,' said Sarah. 'I should have realised there was a lot going on under the surface.'

'I don't understand why he chose to put himself in that position, though. He was a grown man. He could have got out from his father's shadow, had a proper independent life,' said Daphne, absent-mindedly chewing a marshmallow from her hot chocolate.

'I wonder if it was the gambling debts that kept him there. Apparently he owed a fortune to some really awful people. I saw him come out of BetStairs one day, but according to Dumbarton he'd made a lot of big bets that were much less legal. And maybe staying with a bully like Daffyd made him feel safe. After all, it was what he knew, and something he'd grown up with.'

'You're making me feel sorry for him, Sarah, and I don't want to – he nearly killed my best friend, and my best friend's lovely dog, too. Imagine how upset Mephisto would have been, if Hamish wasn't next door any more?'

'Well, yes,' said Sarah, who thought Mephisto would probably organise a massive knees-up with all his moggy friends at the very thought. But she was touched by Daphne's words. 'It does feel like a close one this time. I'd like to ask your Mari if this detecting lark ever gets any easier.'

'Well, now's your chance,' said Daphne. 'Here she comes.'

Sarah looked round and saw Mariella trudging up the beach, hair flying. She couldn't quite read her expression. It wasn't as tetchy as it sometimes was – but then, she didn't look entirely thrilled with life, either.

A few moments later, Mariella sat down heavily at their table. 'I suppose I ought to thank you, Aunty Sarah, for putting your life in danger and somehow coming up with the goods,' she said, fixing Sarah with those frank eyes. 'But it goes without saying, you should have just rung us and we could have taken care of it. Then you wouldn't have had to chuck all the evidence in the sitting room at the head of our culprit.'

'Oh, I'm sorry, Mari. I hope I haven't destroyed anything vital,' Sarah said, mortified.

'That's fine,' said Mariella, her dimples appearing at last. 'There's coffee grounds and bits of glass everywhere, but at least you're still in one piece.'

'That's thanks to Dumbarton, not my aim with a missile,' Sarah admitted. 'If it hadn't been for him, well, I don't know what would have happened.'

'Shame he terrified Matthew Jones into throwing himself out of the window, though,' said Mariella thoughtfully.

'Oh, I'm not sure he should get the blame for that. Matthew was very unlucky, he hit the wall badly on the way down,' Sarah said while Daphne winced.

'Nasty,' said Mariella succinctly. 'Well, he'd gone down some really shady routes to carry on with his gambling habit. It turns out he'd fallen in with some loan sharks from round Margate way. People like that don't take no for an answer when it's payback time. I've already spoken to Dr Strutton, she says it would be perfectly possible for Matthew to manoeuvre his father's hand to shoot himself, once he'd dosed him with a little of the insomnia medicine. And she'll be running tests to see if it's still detectable in Daffyd's blood. Brice had forced her not to do a full toxicology panel originally, he's always trying to cut corners. Same goes for the PM on Deirdre. She now agrees the insomnia medicine, plus the booze, could have helped carry the poor woman off, just like Matthew said.'

'Yes,' said Sarah, with a relieved sigh. 'I'm glad. It's exactly as I thought, then. Flunitrazepam doesn't react at all well with alcohol.'

'You were right about the liquid in that glass, by the way. It was brandy, quite a strong one. No trace of the drug, but he could have given that to her earlier.'

'Right,' said Sarah. 'That reminds me of the choir rehearsal. Matthew passed his father a cup of coffee as soon as he arrived, remember, Daph? And Daffyd must have gone into the office about twenty minutes later. He stumbled on his way there, too. That could have been because he was sleepy. If it hadn't been for the call Deirdre wanted him to take, no doubt Matthew would have dreamed up another excuse to get him into that room and do the deed.'

They were all silent for a second, Sarah contemplating the depths of evil in Matthew's plan.

'And I bet that was the drug in your coffee, too,' said Mariella. 'Listen, I've got to ask you, how did you know not to drink it?'

'Well, it was mostly instinct. I went into the house thinking, um, someone else might have been the killer,' Sarah said quickly, not keen now to dwell on her suspicions about Marlene. 'Then when I sat down, I saw the pile of racing papers. Before, I'd assumed it was Daffyd who liked a flutter. But the top paper was today's, about races in Cheltenham, and it had been well thumbed. Once I realised *Matthew* was the gambler, everything made sense. He was looking pretty down in the mouth, when I saw him outside BetStairs a few days ago. Then impersonating his father on the phone to Mike to put the house on the market, dosing up Deirdre when she didn't want to sell after Daffyd's death, getting rid of Mike when he realised what was going on and, of course, shooting Daffyd in the first place – it was all about Matthew's burning need for money. And then there was the way he kept trying to get me to hurry up with the coffee. I pretended to be looking at the pattern, but in fact I saw a speck of powder on the outside of the cup... that got me thinking. I'd already put my phone on record, just in case I picked up anything interesting, but when he started to nag at me to drink up, I just threw the coffee into the fake plant by the side of the chair when he wasn't looking.'

'That's great, I'll get the forensics guys to see if they can get a sample out of the plant pot to test for corroboration. Not that there's much doubt about what Matthew did at this point,' Mariella said.

'Poor Matthew. I can't help feeling he had an awful life,' said Sarah. 'Those parents would have blighted anyone's chances.'

'Well I have no sympathy for him,' said Daphne. 'I was saying to Sarah, Mari, he really should have done what he could to get away from Daffyd and Deirdre, don't you think?' Daphne took one of Sarah's discarded marshmallows out of her saucer and started chewing it thoughtfully.

At this, Mariella looked rather uncomfortable. 'Speaking of which... my transfer papers have just come up. They've been approved. I'm going to be working in Canterbury from now on.'

Daphne spluttered. 'You're kidding? Already? You're going to abandon me!'

'Hardly, Mum, it's a fifteen-minute drive. I can be there and back any time you need me,' Mariella said. '*Not* that I want you to be ringing me the whole time,' she added quickly.

'Point taken,' said Daphne, reaching out to squeeze her daughter's hand. 'I'm happy for you, darling, I really am.'

Charles, Tinkerbell and Hamish panted up to the table, the two dogs flinging themselves down on the ground. Hamish promptly cosied up to Tinkerbell, and the little dog was either too tired to wriggle away, or she was finally softening towards him, because she perched her tiny snout on his leg and fell asleep. Hamish grinned at Sarah, the happiest Scottie in the world. Charles fell into his chair with a sigh.

'Well, those pooches should sleep well tonight,' said Charles, shining with virtue.

'Thank you so much, Charles,' Sarah said, feeling gratitude was expected, but also well deserved. Giving Hamish the long walk that was his daily due would have been a tall order for her today.

'How are you feeling now, my dear?' Charles said solicitously, leaning in to give her the full benefit of his blue eyes, heightened now by all that fresh air.

Immediately, the usual throng of butterflies started playing up in her stomach. 'I'm... fine, really,' she blushed. 'Though obviously it wasn't ideal,' she added.

'At bay, with a murderer! I'll say.' Charles shook his head. 'I've been thinking while taking the dogs for their yomp. Maybe there's a solution to all this. Something that would keep you a bit safer.' He cocked an eyebrow at her. 'Perhaps you can guess what I'm going to say?'

'Sounds like this is our cue to leave,' said Mariella. 'I've got a ton of paperwork to do in any case. Thank goodness for your phone recording of Matthew, Sarah. Otherwise we'd be stuck, as we can hardly interview him now his head's in several pieces. Come along then, Mum,' Mariella prompted Daphne.

'What? Oh yes, I'd better be getting to Tarot and Tealeaves,' said Daphne. 'I've got a client coming in later. I need to get the Major Arcana ready.'

Sarah smiled at Daphne, hoping that wasn't something Mephisto liked sitting on, or her friend would have a tug of war on her hands.

Mother and daughter pottered off together, no doubt discussing Mariella's looming move to Canterbury CID. Sarah looked at Charles rather nervously, hoping he wasn't going to say anything too drastic... but crossing her fingers this wasn't going to be another casual invitation to lunch either.

Charles gave a tentative smile and coughed before speaking. 'Let's take a little walk, shall we, while we chat?' He took her arm and they started to stroll towards the clock tower on the esplanade. 'Sarah, I've known you a while now... and, erm, I think it's fair to say things are going well.'

Sarah remained silent, remembering those flashes of purple that had turned up throughout the case, and the way they had made her feel. That was without even considering Francesca Diggory, who was usually the problem with Charles. But she gave an encouraging smile.

'The thing is, as you know, I do have my concerns,' Charles went on.

Here we go, thought Sarah.

'I worry about these investigations. Today, for example, I was sitting in my flat having a coffee while that man was trying to kill you. How do you think that makes me feel?'

'A bit perkier than you would have done without the caffeine?' Sarah ventured, trying to lighten the mood.

In the distance, along the esplanade, she could hear the sound of Christmas carols. It must be the sing-off she'd heard so much about. Yes, sure enough, she could see two groups of singers, one led by Gwendoline and Griselda, who was swaying more than the music would dictate, and the other with Matilda at the helm.

'I wish you would confide in me about these things, then we could tackle them together,' Charles was saying, reaching for her hand.

Sarah linked her fingers with his. 'I understand. But sometimes things happen too fast,' she said, dismissing the idea that the main reason she hadn't confided in Charles today was because she knew he'd object to her suspicions about Marlene – which had indeed turned out to be groundless, she was more than willing to admit that now.

'I just think that if I was on the spot all the time, I'd have more opportunity to get really involved,' Charles said, smiling at her.

'What do you mean, exactly, Charles?' Sarah asked, still unsure where this was going, and half-listening to the lovely sound of the choirs uniting to sing 'O Little Town of Bethlehem'.

'Well... I think, perhaps, I should move in with you... and Hamish, of course,' he added, getting a snuffle and a bark from the little dog for his pains.

'Into my cottage?' Sarah said, her head spinning. It was scarcely big enough for her and Hamish. Could she really find space for Charles and all his art books? And, more importantly, did she want to?

She thought for a moment – and then a smile spread over her face. Perhaps this was what she had been yearning for after all, the missing piece of the jigsaw. Perhaps also, when Charles was with her all the time, she would stop searching for things to solve, as everything would have reached its proper resolution already.

Over by the clock tower, the choirs finished singing the beloved carol's final words, about the casting out of sin and the rebirth of innocence, while the huge crowd erupted in cheers. The three women stepped forward to turn on the lights together. The esplanade was suddenly ablaze with gorgeous glowing colours, but all Sarah could see was Charles Diggory's blue eyes.

She smiled slowly, then his arms came around her and she relaxed into one of the very best kisses of her life. Well, she could definitely get used to this part of living together, she decided dreamily.

A LETTER FROM ALICE

Welcome back to Merstairs!

Thank you so much for reading *Murder in the Choir*, my fourth book featuring retired GP Sarah Vane, her Scottie dog Hamish and her friend Daphne. I love the breezy Kent coast and it's a joy to set Sarah and Daphne's adventures in such a beautiful spot. If you'd like to find out what Sarah and the gang are up to next, please sign up at the email link below. Your email address will never be shared and you can unsubscribe at any time.

www.bookouture.com/alice-castle

If you enjoyed this book, I would be so grateful if you could post a review on Amazon or Goodreads, so that other people can discover Merstairs too.

I'm also on social media, so do join me there. Happy reading, and I hope to see you soon for Sarah Vane's next outing.

Alice Castle

alicecastleauthor.com

facebook.com/Alicecastleauthor
x.com/AliceMCastle

ACKNOWLEDGEMENTS

Thank you so much to my fantastic agent, Justin Nash of KNLA, my wonderful editor Nina Winters, and all the team at Bookouture, for making Merstairs real.

PUBLISHING TEAM

Turning a manuscript into a book requires the efforts of many people. The publishing team at Bookouture would like to acknowledge everyone who contributed to this publication.

Commercial
Lauren Morrissette
Hannah Richmond
Imogen Allport

Cover design
Tash Webber

Data and analysis
Mark Alder
Mohamed Bussuri

Editorial
Nina Winters
Sinead O'Connor

Copyeditor
Deborah Blake

Proofreader
Anne O'Brien

Marketing
Alex Crow
Melanie Price
Occy Carr
Cíara Rosney
Martyna Młynarska

Operations and distribution
Marina Valles
Stephanie Straub
Joe Morris

Production
Hannah Snetsinger
Mandy Kullar
Ria Clare
Nadia Michael

Publicity
Kim Nash
Noelle Holten
Jess Readett
Sarah Hardy

Rights and contracts
Peta Nightingale
Richard King
Saidah Graham

RAISING READERS
Books Build Bright Futures

Dear Reader,

We'd love your attention for one more page to tell you about the crisis in children's reading, and what we can all do.

Studies have shown that reading for fun is the **single biggest predictor of a child's future life chances** – more than family circumstance, parents' educational background or income. It improves academic results, mental health, wealth, communication skills, ambition and happiness.

The number of children reading for fun is in rapid decline. Young people have a lot of competition for their time, and a worryingly high number do not have a single book at home.

Hachette works extensively with schools, libraries and literacy charities, but here are some ways we can all raise more readers:

- Reading to children for just 10 minutes a day makes a difference
- Don't give up if children aren't regular readers – there will be books for them!

- Visit bookshops and libraries to get recommendations
- Encourage them to listen to audiobooks
- Support school libraries
- Give books as gifts

There's a lot more information about how to encourage children to read on our websites: **www.RaisingReaders.co.uk** and **www.JoinRaisingReaders.com**.

Thank you for reading.

www.ingramcontent.com/pod-product-compliance
Ingram Content Group UK Ltd.
Pitfield, Milton Keynes, MK11 3LW, UK
UKHW041857020925
7695UKWH00002B/170

9 781805 502104